BIRD
ON A
WIRE

TAGAN SHEPARD

BELLA
B O O K S
2018

Bella Books, Inc.
P.O. Box 10543
Tallahassee, FL 32302

Printed in the United States of America on acid-free paper.

First Bella Books Edition 2018

Editor: Cath Walker
Cover Designer: Judith Fellows

ISBN: 978-1-59493-595-4

Other Bella Books by Tagan Shepard

Visiting Hours

Acknowledgments

Most people are lucky to have two good parents in this life. I have been blessed with four loving, kind, remarkable parents and for that I am more grateful than I could ever express. My mother, Dorothy, was taken from us all far too soon, but she is no less loved for her absence. My stepmother, Lucia, has been, since the moment she came into my life, as caring as any mother could be. My father, Louis, and my stepfather, Mike, are and always will be the best men I know. I could not love them more.

Not long after my mother passed, my dear friend, Jaren, lost her own mother. We spent many a night helping each other through our grief with shared tears and shared beers. I owe much of the inspiration for this book to her.

My continued gratitude to Jessica Hill at Bella Books for believing in me and my work. Also to Cath Walker who helped make this book much better than it was when it arrived in her hands, the mark of an excellent editor.

As always, thank you Cris for being my inspiration, my North Star, and my better half. I love you more every day.

About the Author

Tagan Shepard lives in Richmond, Virginia with her wife and her two feline children. She lost her mother on July 20th, 2008 after a five-year battle with metastatic breast cancer. She hikes to Mary's Rock in the Shenandoah National Park every year on that day to remember an amazing woman who died far too young. This is her second novel with Bella Books.

Dedication

For Dorothy, Jane, and Lindy
If a daughter's love was enough to sustain life,
you would all have been immortal.

PROLOGUE

"Birdie! Wait for me!"

The rustle of plump green leaves and the trickle of water over a rocky creek bed mixed with the pounding of tiny feet on unkempt grass. The two little girls giggled as they crested the hill and started down the other side, their footsteps sure on a steep grade as only those of children can be. They ran toward the sound of the water. If they had been asked, they could say exactly how many steps it would take them to arrive at their destination. They wouldn't have to think about it. They would just know, the way they knew their names and the way ice-cold lemonade tasted on a warm day.

The girl in front held her faded cowboy hat tightly as the breeze picked up. Her feet slipped inside the boots she had worn every day that summer. Sweat pooled between her toes and underneath her flannel shirt. The stitches on her matted suede vest were wide and they strained to hold at the point where her lean shoulders were beginning to round out and widen.

She turned to track the progress of her pursuer just before the grass gave way to pine needles. "Better hurry up, Princess! I'm gonna beat you to the tree aggggaaaain!"

The breeze that had threatened Birdie's hat now tugged at the stained lace ringing the hem of Princess's dress. "You will not! I'm faster'n I look, and you know it, Birdie Scott!"

Birdie laughed, but she picked up her pace. Princess was barefoot, so she had a good chance of winning the race now that the ground was prickly and uneven. Birdie had lost too many times to take her opponent for granted. By the time the winding scar of the creek's path came into view, she could hear Princess's breath puffing right behind her. She reached out and gripped at a tree trunk, using it to slingshot her along to the left.

Princess appeared out of nowhere at her shoulder. A grin split her face, but her eyes were set in a determined squint. Birdie's stomach dropped. She had started her sprint too late, and now she had no chance. Princess's arms were windmilling wildly, tiny high heels gripped tight in her fist. Sweat stuck strands of her dirty blond hair to her cheeks, and Birdie's pace dropped even further as she watched the girl streaking between the trees. Birdie was mesmerized, struck by the sight of her friend at her most determined. This was Princess's most dangerous weapon, the one that always did Birdie in.

"Told ya you'd never beat me!"

Princess spun and planted her fists on her hips. Her smile was so smug that it almost made Birdie mad. Almost.

Birdie crossed her arms over her chest and shrugged. She decided to stop and walk the last few steps, just to show she didn't care.

"I letcha win."

"You did not!" The smile slid off her face and her eyebrows jumped up. "You didn't, didya Birdie?"

The collar of Birdie's flannel shirt felt suddenly a lot tighter around her neck, and she had to swallow hard before she answered, "Nah, Princess. You know I didn't."

Princess smiled as bright as the June sun and threw herself at Birdie. The girl flung out her arms just in time to wrap around her friend and hold her in place. The strength of their bodies colliding forced the breath out of Birdie and some of that sweaty blond hair stuck in her mouth. She held every muscle perfectly still. The only part of her showing life was her wildly beating heart.

"You're the best ever! I knew you wouldn't let me win. Not you, Birdie!"

"Yeah…well…" Princess let go of her and scampered off to their tree. She pushed the hat a little higher up her brow with dirty fingers. "A good cowboy'd never be untrue."

Princess leaned her back against their tree and adjusted her tiara. The silver paint had chipped off in a few places and one of the little paste diamonds was missing. Birdie hooked her thumbs in the belt loops of her jeans and tried the wobbly, bow-legged swagger she'd seen in old Westerns. She looked over at Princess, but the girl's eyes were on the tree trunk rather than her.

Birdie frowned. "Whatcha doin'?"

"Just checkin' on our initials. What if we didn't carve 'em deep enough?"

Birdie picked at a pebble, prying it loose from the dirt. "Aw, they're fine. Come sit with me?"

Princess spun and grabbed two fistfuls of frilly pink dress with dirty palms. "You sure they'll stick?"

Birdie looked around her to the tree. Two days ago they had stolen Larry's pocketknife and run down here. They struggled to carve their mark into the tree they'd claimed as soon as the last of the spring storms swept down from the mountains. Princess made the outline of the heart and neither of them minded that it was a little flat on the left side or a little too round on the right. Birdie took the knife next and stabbed at the papery bark until the spiky and uneven "RS + SC" had appeared.

"They'll stick."

"Promise?"

"Promise."

Princess swung her arms from side to side, waves of pink intermittently exposing her knees. "Good."

Birdie fell back deliberately on her butt and stuck her feet out in front of her, the heels of her boots inches from the water line. Princess skipped over and plopped down next to her, leaning against Birdie's shoulder. After a long minute, Birdie decided that a good cowboy would probably wrap her arm around her best friend's shoulder, but she was afraid to do it. Princess wrapped both hands around the soft flesh and sweaty flannel of Birdie's arm, just below her armpit. If anyone else had tried that, even her mom, she would have shaken them off. Not Princess. She let Princess do anything she wanted.

Princess beamed at her when she let go. Birdie's return smile was too big, so she turned away quickly to stare off into the woods. They spent the next few minutes throwing pebbles into the current, watching each one disappear beneath the lazy flow before throwing the next. Cotton ball clouds drifted by over their heads. The forest came to life around them the longer they sat still. Bright patches of color flashed between the leaves accompanied by snatches of birdsong. Rubbery branches swayed under the weight of squirrels hopping through the canopy. The groundcover of old leaves and pine needles rustled and swayed as tiny paws made their way through, ignoring the kids by the creek. Most of the animals who lived here had seen the pair often enough to know they were no threat.

When Princess took off the tiara, the combs caught in her tangled hair. She poked at the empty socket where the fake jewel once lived. Her fingers swept over the spots of pale plastic exposed by heavy use, the silver paint long since worn away.

"Some princess I am."

Birdie finally wrapped her arm around her friend's shoulders and pulled her close. In the last few weeks Birdie had noticed her chest was swelling. She liked the way Princess's arm pressed against it when they held each other tight.

"You're the best princess there is."

"Nah. A princess needs a crown and I ain't got a nice one."

Birdie frowned down at the tiara. Sudden inspiration made her pluck the hat from her own head and press it down over Princess's little ears.

"Eww! It's all sweaty!"

"Cowboys get sweaty." She looked at the pointed toes of her boots. "You shouldn't be a princess anyhow. You should...you could be my cowgirl instead."

The hat was too big for her, and the dark ring around the brim was obvious. Still, Princess grinned wide, showing tiny square teeth with wide gaps between them. She squashed it down further on her head and her eyes disappeared. She and Birdie giggled for a long time, scaring a pair of birds from a nearby branch.

When their laughter subsided, Princess pushed the brim of the hat back up so she could look at her friend. "You sure you want me to be your cowgirl, Birdie Scott?"

"Yeah. I s'pose I do."

Princess's bony chin landed on her shoulder and huge blue eyes fixed on hers. "How come?"

"I dunno. I just do."

"'Cause I'm your best friend?"

"Yeah."

"How come I'm your best friend?"

"I dunno. I'm your best friend, ain't I?"

"Yeah."

"How come?"

Princess just shrugged.

"See. You don't know either."

"You're my best friend, Birdie."

"I know."

"You're always gonna be my best friend."

"Always is a long time."

"Yep."

"What if you move away or somethin'?"

"You'll be my best friend no matter where I live."

"You too, Princess."

"Promise?"

"Promise."

Princess leaned over quickly and used one stabbing finger to draw an X across Birdie's suede vest. It was on the opposite side from where her heart fluttered like a bird caught in a storm, but neither of them noticed the mistake.

"Cross your heart."

Birdie swallowed hard and traced the same motion on her chest.

"Cross my heart."

Princess sat back up and grabbed her knees to her chest. She wiggled her toes and little flecks of dirt and stone fell off. One of her hands went to the hat and fingered the brim. Birdie made herself look away, following the progress of a leaf from the little waterfall at the far end of their clearing through until it disappeared among the pine trees off to her right.

When she looked back, Princess was watching her. There was something in her eyes. It was a look that Birdie didn't understand. She wanted to understand. Wanted it desperately. A part of her knew that, if she were only a little older, if her shoulders had finished rounding out and the swelling in her chest expanded and she was a bit taller than she was now, she would know what it meant and she would know what to say in response. As it was, she just smiled to cover her ignorance. Princess smiled back.

Birdie suddenly decided she did know what that look meant after all. She knew what it meant and she knew what to say.

"I love you, Princess. I'll love you forever and ever…Amen."

CHAPTER ONE

The trees whipped by tall and jagged like a line of proud soldiers guarding the perimeter of the road. The emerald carpet of alfalfa and cornfields stretched behind them. Robin watched it all slide by with a detached wonder. Over the years she had forgotten what the world could look like when it wasn't palm tree-studded concrete. A stretch of rusted train track drifted closer to her side, like another driver merging gradually into the lane beside her. Only there was no other traffic. There wasn't even another lane except the one for nonexistent oncoming traffic. After a long way, the track finally settled into parallel with the road.

After another handful of miles she came upon the train. Her speed gave it the illusion of movement for a time, but as she started to pass the cars it became clear they were still. Their wheels were the same copper-brown as the tracks below them and sun-faded graffiti covered more than one car. There was no engine at the lead of the frozen vehicle. The train was just another silent sentinel, guarding this quiet section of Route 33, the same as the trees.

She turned a wide curve and the train tracks fell away, swallowed up by the forest. Ahead of her now was nothing but a straight stretch of empty blacktop. There was a house now and then off to her left, but the yards were empty and the cars still tucked away under carports or a thin layer of dew. The mountains loomed hazy and purple in the distance. She could feel them growing closer and closer with every mile that ticked away.

Suddenly, the silence hit her. It was a foreign sound and it pressed hard on her eardrums. She was alone with the whine of tires on asphalt. Her hand shot out to the radio and she fumbled to find the right button on the unfamiliar dash. The music started with a shout and she banged at the volume controls until the words came into focus.

And all those things you do
God if you only knew
I love you
I love you forever and ever
Amen

Robin spent several seconds while the guitar faded out considering whether to switch the radio back off. For perhaps the first time in her life, music did not bring her comfort, but the thought of hearing the tires again stopped her. The song ended and the DJ spoke over the last few notes. Robin ground her teeth at the rudeness of it. If there was one thing she couldn't stand, it was DJs talking over the end of songs. Especially the end of her songs.

That was "Forever and Ever" by Robin Wren Scott. If you had tickets for tonight's sold-out Robin Wren Scott show at the Richmond Coliseum you are out of luck. We got the announcement this morning that she's canceling the last two weeks of her tour. Sadly, her mother, Katherine Scott, died last night and Robin is going home to be with family.

Robin didn't realize how hard she had been gripping the steering wheel until she felt the sharp pain of pinched skin. The DJ explained about refunds and rain checks for the canceled concert, but she didn't hear him. It had always been easier for Robin to block out noise than silence. She turned another bend and saw a gas station up ahead with a shabby convenience store attached. She slowed quickly and pulled into the parking lot, just the thought of coffee making her mouth water and her eyelids droop.

That coffee, sold to her by a sleepy clerk busy watching the tiny television tucked behind the counter, was so old it could probably vote and buy cigarettes. Robin forced it down only because she hadn't slept in nearly two days and her life quite clearly depended on staying awake.

When she stopped for coffee the second time Robin took the opportunity to fill the gas tank. She was just outside the town of Madison. It was perhaps one of the most inconsequential towns in Virginia, boasting little more than a Dollar General and a mom-and-pop Italian restaurant to fill the hundred yards or so of road that constituted the city limits. She thought her mother mentioned once that she had a distant cousin who lived in Madison. It occurred to Robin now that she would never find out who that cousin was.

She stepped out of the car and gained a new appreciation for her clothing choice this morning. Robin had never been a fan of shorts. Her hips were too narrow and her legs too long to find a pair that fit both her style and her body. She wore jeans until they were threadbare and torn, then she wore them a few years more. Today's pair was still new enough for the navy dye to be nearly intact. More importantly, they were warm. Despite the season, the sun had not yet risen high enough to burn the overnight chill from the air. That was for the best really. Even here at the foot of the mountains, summer in Virginia was a far more humid heat than she was used to. By the time she reached her childhood home she would no doubt be regretting the denim.

It took her quite a while to figure out how to access the rental car's gas tank and, by the time the fuel was flowing, she was hugging herself for warmth. Her shirt was a simple, close-fitting button-up with short sleeves and a high collar. It flattered her long, lean frame and small chest, though her interfering manager had called the design "uninspired." He wanted her to dress the part of a rock star. In her opinion, she did, but more the old-school rock star of her youth than the supermodels who played now. When she found a piece of clothing she liked she bought it in every available color just to fill out her wardrobe. She owned this same shirt in blue, green, black, and gray in addition to the cherry-red she wore today.

She bought the shirt mainly because she liked the way it accentuated the muscles in her forearms, the only part of her body with any definition. She had always spent a lot of time outside, but she wasn't athletic. She had never been able to build the muscle or stamina required for it. She had, however, managed to cultivate extraordinary breath control, which helped her enjoy swimming and hiking enough to get her fill of sunshine. Since one of her few assets was an ability to tan to a Mediterranean shade, she took full advantage.

Much like the rest of her body, Robin's face tended toward the long and lean. She joked that she had a face only a mother could love. It was rectangular, with a pointed chin, high cheekbones and a straight Grecian nose. Her agent once suggested that it would make her look more mysterious if she could have someone break her nose, but she was almost certain he was joking. She had bushy eyebrows that grew back too quickly for her to bother waxing and her hair was dark to the point of appearing black. These days she kept it short with long bangs sweeping across her face to cover one eye before tucking behind her ear. That gave the added benefit of distracting from how deep set and heavily lidded her eyes were, no matter how much sleep she got. And as a lifelong musician, she rarely got enough sleep.

She was to the point of stamping her feet and walking around to keep warm when the pump stopped with a loud pop and she was able to head inside. The moment she pushed the heavy glass doors open, she knew the coffee would be good. Not flavored or frilly, just simple, dark roasted happiness in a cup. The store was out of large cups, so she filled two mediums with black coffee and headed to the register.

The man standing behind the counter was tall and round and wore a T-shirt advertising one of massive sporting goods chains that can turn a profit even in a town with a population under five hundred. His hat was decorated with a fine layer of grime and there was an inch-wide yellow stain around the brim where old sweat had taken up permanent residence. He watched her as she crossed the store, a mildly puzzled look in his eyes, but his smile was warm and genuine when she set the coffees down in front of him and fished her wallet out of her back pocket.

"Pump number two and the coffees."

He nodded and pecked at the register. "You look awful familiar, but I know you aren't from 'round here."

"No sir, I'm not from around here."

He shrugged as the tape spat from the printer and coiled beside her. "Twenty-seven fifty."

She pulled a card from her wallet and looked for a place to swipe it, but found nothing. She held it up and he smiled, revealing a central trio of suspiciously white teeth. Most of the good old boys she'd met in her life had at least a partial bridge. They were usually acquired when the owner's mouth came into contact with another good old boy's fist. This one looked a lot cheaper than the ones she was used to, but she wasn't in a rich town.

"Sorry, machine's busted. I'll have to do it the old-fashioned way."

He pulled an old slide machine from under the counter and a stack of carbon slips.

"Hang on. I think I've got cash."

She fished around in her wallet for bills while he stared at her with a pleasant grin. "You the girl that married Arthur Hennessey's boy?"

"Definitely not."

He gave her a knowing look. "Got it. Didn't wanna assume."

She shook her head and handed him a pair of bills. "Not a problem."

The drawer of the register shot out with a loud clang. He took his time counting out her change. "Been on a reality show or somethin'?"

She shook her head.

He dropped some rumpled singles and a pair of quarters into her outstretched hand. Light dawned in his eyes as he looked at her palm. "Now say! Those're callouses from playin' guitar as sure as I live and breathe."

"Yes, sir, they are."

He snapped his fingers and pointed at her. "You're that singer!"

She shoved the change into her pocket and nodded.

"That's right you are! My granddaughter's just nuts over you. Robin somethin' or other! From up Sperryville way!"

She held out her hand and he shook it with both of his. "Robin Scott. Pleased to meet you."

"Pleased to meet me? Shoot, my little Janey is gonna be over the moon her grandad met her favorite singer! Got tickets for your show in Charlottesville and everything. Been braggin' about it for weeks now." He put his hands on his hips and grinned with such delight it was impossible to believe he was old enough to have a granddaughter. "She's got all your records, mind. Not just this last one what made you so popular on the radio. Oh no, she's been a fan of yours since way back."

She picked up her coffees, stacking them on top of each other and catching the tantalizing whiff of dark roasted beans. "That's very sweet. Tell Janey I appreciate it."

"I don't suppose I could ask ya to sign somethin' for her?"

"Sure."

He rummaged behind the desk, grabbing and discarding a few things before finally yanking a sheet of paper from the printer next to the lottery ticket machine and sliding it across the counter to her. Robin grabbed a ballpoint pen from a cup on the counter. Someone, presumably Janey's grandfather, had taped an empty chewing tobacco can to the end of it to protect it from thieves. He bounced on the balls of his feet as she scratched a few lines to her fan and added her spiky signature at the end.

"Thanks much. Awful kind of ya."

She headed toward the door, throwing a wave over her shoulder and slipping back out between the pumps. She slid quickly into the car as a rusted pickup truck turned into the lot. The driver gave her a double take, so she gunned the engine and got back onto the road before the newcomer could stop her. The man behind the counter was undoubtedly on the phone already, telling all his friends about his celebrity moment. Within a few minutes, the store would be packed and Robin wanted to be as far away from that as possible.

Robin had turned from Route 29 for her long trip down Route 231 before she realized the man had said his granddaughter had tickets for her now-canceled show tomorrow night. She flipped the radio back on and gunned the gas pedal a little harder.

CHAPTER TWO

When Robin was seven years old her father disappeared for the last time, and her mom finally moved the two of them into the house she had inherited from her parents many years earlier. Robin was terrified. Her father had said they were too good for that place and that his family was going to live in a nicer house and have a better life. They didn't. Even at her age, she could see that what they were living was not a great life. So if that was better, what horrors awaited her here in this house?

Robin would never forget the set of her mother's jaw as she stood in the driveway and stared at the front door. She had fallen down the stairs again last night. Or tripped and hit her eye against the doorknob. Or ran into a wall. Robin couldn't remember which story it was this time. In any case, her mother's eye was a puffy, angry red and by nightfall it would be a deep purple-black. Her one good eye burned in a way Robin had never seen in her mother before. Something about that look took the fear from Robin's heart. She knew they'd be safe here. She knew her father wasn't coming back this time. She knew they wouldn't sleep in the car anymore. Or the break room at the factory where her mother worked. They were home now.

She looked back at the house she had heard so much about but never seen. It was tall and thin, taking on the same shape Robin was even now growing into. There was a wide, deep porch on the front that wrapped around one side and went all the way to the back of the house. In the years to come a swing would be added along with chairs and potted plants, but at the moment it was bare apart from a few dead leaves rustling around on the slats.

What really caught Robin's attention were the windows. There were dozens of them, hundreds to her dazzled eyes. They had lived in trailers and apartments and basements all her life. She'd never had a room with her own window. They were lucky if there was a single window in the entire apartment or rented room. But this house was simply covered in windows. They were dotted in the pale blue, chipped clapboard face of the structure and it was those windows, along with the new fire in her mother's eyes that won Robin over.

The house was a mess. No one had lived there in years. The furniture was covered in white sheets and there wasn't much of it. The electricity was disconnected and the cold was so complete it seemed to live in the walls. There was no running water until the power was turned on, so they made a game of using the hand pump in the backyard for the first week. They cleaned and cleaned, and cleaned some more until the hardwood floors shone golden brown and the windows sparkled like diamonds in the sun. It was hard work, but it was their hard work. They shared the triumph and they ended up with a home. A home that was theirs and no one else's. Full of their laughter and their memories. Just the two of them.

As Robin pulled in, the crunch of gravel under her tires scared a long line of crows from the electrical wires that flanked the driveway. She could see the house from the road, and she watched it grow larger in her windshield. She had to take it slowly on the half mile that stretched between the road and her mother's house. The gravel was sparse and potholes dotted the track. Her mom never could remember to gravel the drive regularly. It usually took a flat tire for her to finally get around to putting in an order.

Parked in front of the house, Robin closed the car door harder than she intended. A loud caw drew her attention back to the wires overhead. A single crow remained after the others flew off. Its inky black eye fixed on her for a long moment before moving off to inspect the strip of corn planted between the pair of houses and the road to her left. She kept watching it, wondering if it would fly off now that it had asserted its superiority, but it stayed still and watched.

She turned at the screeching of a rusted screen door, expecting to see her mother walking onto the porch with a big smile and her arms outstretched. But the door was still and silent. Her mother wasn't home. The door that opened belonged to the neighboring house.

"Welcome home, Birdie."

Robin met Larry Johnson the day she and her mom had moved in. They had walked through the old place, Robin's mouth open and staring, her mom crying silent tears. Robin went back to the car for her one little suitcase, and when she turned around, there was Larry. He was tall and broad at the shoulders with a huge smile that lit up his eyes and a jaw of carved Appalachian limestone. When he offered to help her with her suitcase, she refused and started toward the house. He followed with a noticeable limp in his right leg. With childish curiosity, Robin asked him what happened. His answer of "a youthful indiscretion" was completely indecipherable to her, but she was too proud to say so.

When her mother came out onto the porch with her arms crossed and distrust written plainly on her face, Larry came up short. He stood there like a boxer who didn't yet know that he'd been knocked out.

Larry was their closest neighbor, occupying the nearly identical house right next door. It would have been hard for him to be closer in fact. No more than a five-foot-wide strip of weedy grass separated the two houses. The second house had been bought from a Sears catalogue eighty years earlier by Robin's great-grandfather for his eldest son, Robin's great-uncle. He had intended that they would work the family farm together, but Guadalcanal changed his plans. He ended up spending all of his energies trying to get his son's body home, and the farm slowly but surely failed. By the time Robin's grandfather took over, he had no choice but to sell it off piece by piece. The house changed hands three times before it came to Larry.

He spent the rest of that afternoon helping them move in to their new home. When the sun set he asked her mother on a date. She said no, but he was back the next day with coffee and doughnuts and he helped all day again. When he asked her on a date again that evening she turned him down again. He asked her thirty-six times more before she finally agreed just to get him to quit asking. He didn't quit asking. He had asked her out on a date twice a week for the last twenty-eight years. She never said no again.

"It's good to see you, Larry." Robin wrapped her arms around his neck and held on. He smelled just like he had since she was a kid, like a mixture of wood smoke and clean cotton. The stubble on his chin rubbed against her neck as he hugged her tight. His eyes were glassy when she let go of him, but there were no tears on his cheeks. "How have you been?"

He smiled and a thousand lines etched his cheeks. He was only in his mid-fifties, but Larry had always been aged beyond his years. He hopped a little on his bad leg as he answered, "If you'da asked me that question yesterd'y I'd had a much different answer. Let's just say I'm breathin'."

"What happened?"

He looked out across the stalks of corn rustling in the breeze and squinted hard. "I can't rightly say. She went to work same as normal. Said she'd be home for our date round about five. Got a call from her boss at threeish. Your momma'd said she didn't feel well. He saw she looked a bit pale, so he told her to head on home. Went to grab her purse from her locker 'n' they found her there on the floor 'bout an hour later. She's gone by the time the ambulance got there."

Robin looked down at her feet until the urge to throw up left her.

"Had she been sick?"

"Nope. Fit as a fiddle, just same as normal." She heard a sound like sandpaper on leather and looked up to see him rubbing his cheek with the heel of his hand. "I can't account for it 't all. Musta just been her time."

Robin didn't have a response, so she hooked her thumbs in her belt loops and searched the scenery for something to look at. She found nothing that could soothe the itch in her feet or the hole in her gut.

"Folks 'round here'll be tickled pink to see you, no matter the cause. The whole town's real proud of you, Birdie girl. The radio says you're the next Mumford and Sons, whoever they are."

Robin gave him a grin and his shoulders settled a little lower.

"You know this town don't know much about music. Hell, most 'em ain't cared 'bout what's on the radio since ole Reba gave Fancy one chance not to let 'er momma down."

"I met Reba, you know."

"You didn't!"

"I did. She hosted that benefit concert for the hurricane last summer and I met her then."

"You'll be eatin' free down the diner on that un long as you're in town." He shook his head and the grin slipped a little. "Your momma woulda liked hearin' 'bout that."

This time Robin's tears did come out, but only a couple. She should have told her mom about Reba. How she was kind and looked you in the eye when she shook your hand like she actually wanted to know whose hand she was shaking. Why hadn't she told her mom those things while she still could? The nausea that had been her constant companion since Larry called last night was back with a vengeance. She leaned against the car and took a couple of slow breaths.

"Nice wheels."

She put her hands on her knees. "It's a rental."

His hand squeezed her shoulder. "Where's that wife a yours?"

Robin opened her eyes and the dirt at her feet spun a few degrees before righting itself. "Still in Richmond. She's dealing with the tour company and my manager."

"They givin' you a hard time 'bout cancelin' the shows?"

"Rick's a dickwad. He would give a hard time to his own moth…" She couldn't finish the word, so she moved on. "I'm just glad I was so close. So I could be here quickly."

"Speakin' of." The sound of the car door opening next to her made her look up. Larry grabbed her duffel bag from the backseat and slammed it shut. "We gotta go see to things at the funeral home. Appointment's in an hour. Better getcher self cleaned up."

He had maneuvered her toward the front porch without her realizing it. When they got to the bottom of the stairs, he handed her the duffel and said, "Key's under the mat like always if ya ain't got yours."

"I've got mine." She looked up to the door. Somehow the three steps up to the porch looked like Mount Everest. "You aren't coming inside?"

The look he gave the door broke her heart. "No. I'ma head on home. See ya in a bit."

Without another word he turned and limped off next door.

CHAPTER THREE

"Please accept my heartfelt condolences." The two hands that wrapped around Robin's were soft and unpleasantly warm, but living in Los Angeles for so long had trained her how to disguise the cringe. "Katherine was loved by all of us here in town. She will be missed."

"Thank you."

Larry stepped forward and filled the silence left by her inadequate reply. The man, whose name Robin could not remember at the moment, turned to him with the same simpering kindness.

"Larry. No words could express my sympathies."

"She was a special woman."

He gestured to the door behind him and Larry made toward it. Robin had to force her feet to move. The carpet was too thick and the walls were too dark. The tiny greeting room was bad enough, thick with the gaudy scent of roses, and she knew with the certainty of inexperience that entering this man's office would be one of those memories she would never be rid of. He stepped behind her and put a light hand in the center of her back. It did not exert any pressure, only the reminder that staying in the foyer would not change the reality of the moment. Robin wondered how many people he'd dragged, weeping and wailing, into his office during his career.

She walked toward the door and suddenly remembered the man's name. Jacob Peters. He had inherited the funeral home from his father, a man who had been skeletally thin, resembling a bird of prey. She had gone to school with his daughter, Kelly. She wondered what had become of her after graduation. There wasn't a single person from her school days with whom she kept in touch. No matter how many times they scribbled promises to be close forever on the cover pages of yearbooks, Robin had lost touch with them all. She didn't regret not knowing where Kelly landed, but she'd been nice and Robin hoped that she was happy somewhere. Now, however, was not the time to ask after her.

The office was a long, narrow room with a heavy block of a desk crammed on one side against the short wall. Two guest chairs were pushed close to it and the surface was perfectly empty, not even a pen or a single sheet of paper disrupting the gleaming surface. It looked disturbingly like an examination table. The far side of the room was dark, the light bleeding out into the darkness just a few steps behind the guest chairs. Robin squinted into the gloom and made out familiar shapes. Her stomach turned with the realization that the office was also a showroom for coffins.

The hand on her back kept her from retreating through the door.

"Please have a seat. May I call you Birdie?"

Her belt buckle pushed uncomfortably into her stomach when she crossed her legs.

"Yes, of course."

Leather creaked loudly as he sat. He leaned forward and steepled his fingers under his doughy neck.

"You'll both be happy to hear that this will be rather easy." He turned to Robin. "Your mother purchased a program with us several years ago." He turned to Larry. "So thoughtful of her to take that burden from you, but that's just the kind of person she was, isn't it?"

"Sure is, Jake." Larry had changed into a blue and white checked shirt and navy trousers. They looked like they'd been ironed recently and smelled like starch. "So we don't need to do anything?"

He opened a drawer and pulled out a thin folder. "I took the liberty of writing up an obituary for the paper. Your mother wrote one many years ago, but it lacked the warmth one likes in these things."

He leaned forward, holding the paper out to them. Robin didn't reach for it. She wanted nothing to do with it. Larry took it from him.

"Please look over it and make any changes you prefer. Instructions for a service were part of the program she prepared. I'm sure the Reverend will be by to visit with you today."

There was a chip in the corner of his desk closest to Robin's chair. She stared at it for so long she started to wonder what was wrong with her. The drone of male voices continued beside her, but she let them wash over without touching her. They discussed the minutiae of the funeral and Robin couldn't tear her eyes from this insignificant flaw in a stranger's desk. She occasionally felt Mr. Peters's eyes on her. He didn't seem to mind her silence, so she continued it until Larry stood.

"While I regret the circumstances it is nice to see you back home, Birdie."

He put his hand on her back again, but she made for the door without needing his encouragement. She didn't want to feel that gentle, pitying pressure again. He had not turned on the lights at the back of the room or taken them anywhere near the coffins hidden there. The relief she felt provided all the energy she needed to put one foot in front of the other.

"We were starting to wonder if we'd ever see you again. But your mother made sure to keep us all up to date on what you were up to. She was so terribly proud of you, as I'm sure you know."

His toothy grin didn't falter at her stony look, and he gave her another two-handed shake as he ushered the two of them to the front door. The stifling heat was a welcome change. The scent of nature and car exhaust was preferable to the gaudy perfume of that place. If Robin never entered the building again, it would be too soon.

"Jake Peters never was real good at talkin' to livin' people." Larry looked out over the nearby rooftops toward the outline of mountains in the distance. "His daddy was the same way. Face of a vulture and the warmth of one too."

Robin looked down the sidewalk. The rental car was parked at the end of the block, dust covering its tires and the bottom few inches of black paint. A couple of streets beyond was Main Street. Brenda's Café wasn't visible from here, but she knew it was just off to the right.

"Want to get some lunch at Brenda's?"

The smile Larry gave her had a little too much understanding, and it made her angry. "I'm not hungry," he replied. She shivered a little at the thought of going back to her mother's house. She couldn't be sure Larry missed it. "You go on ahead. I'll walk home."

"You sure? It's a long way."

He limped past her with his hands in his pockets, walking away from the car and the café alone.

"Nonsense. That's the California in ya talking. Say hi to Rusty for me."

It was a short walk to Brenda's Diner. Every walk in this town was a short one. Robin used the time to reacquaint herself with the hometown she hadn't seen in years. Sperryville, Virginia was small. In fact, it was difficult to get much smaller, both in size and in population. The town itself was little more than Main Street, dotted with a few local restaurants and shops and the occasional small home. More streets radiated off Main, but they were short and narrow, usually little more than a handful of old houses for a block or two.

As far as population, it topped out at just over three hundred. Most had lived here their whole lives, like their parents before them and, in most cases, their children after them. Like most small towns, Sperryville was nearly impossible to escape. Most of the time because the place got into your blood and you would never dream of leaving. Sometimes because fate and poverty held you in place, and you would always dream of leaving. The people were unvarying, the people you knew when you were young would be the same people you knew when you were old. Small-town folks found that sort of stability comforting. Robin found it oppressive.

In Robin's mind, Sperryville's saving grace was its location, tucked into the very foot of the Blue Ridge Mountains, right on the edge of Shenandoah National Park. It was actually the last spot of civilization, minimal as it was, before one entered the park. The trip from Sperryville to the Thornton Gap entrance to the park was a gorgeous, winding trek through lush green forests and sunny mountainsides bordered by precipitous drops of bare shale. The Blue Ridge Parkway ran along the spine of the mountains, affording incredible views of both the valleys and peaks. Black bears, white-tailed deer, and an assortment of birds and small mammals shared time with hikers and campers among the loveliest waterfalls and forests Virginia had to offer.

All of that right at the edge of town. There was only one real way into Sperryville—Route 522—and that was also the only real way into the national park. As a result, the town was a throughway and final pit stop for tourists from spring until late fall. On any given day during the height of summer or the foliage season, the town would triple its normal population. Money flowed in regularly, if not extravagantly, and the restaurants, coffee shop, and breweries did passable business.

Those same tourists were also the inspiration for Robin's fantasies of flight. They drove in from all over the country. They even hiked in from the Appalachian Trail in the summer. Dirty, happy people who had started walking in Georgia, pointing their boots toward Maine and not looking back for two thousand miles. Robin envied them, and knew one day she would be one of those transient visitors to her own hometown. And that's exactly what she became.

CHAPTER FOUR

The moment the bell over the door tinkled to announce her entrance, Robin regretted going to Brenda's. Half the town must have been in the little diner. Every head turned to her. There was a moment where they all stared at her and she stared back at them. She forced herself to smile and not run out the door.

"Well, if it ain't Birdie Scott as I live and breathe." A large woman wearing an apron and a huge smile sauntered over to her. "Here I thought LA went and swallowed up our favorite girl."

Robin let out a long breath. "Hey there, Nancy. How've you been?"

Nancy wrapped her in a hug that smelled like bacon grease and coffee. "Fat and happy, like always. Fat and happy." She pulled back from Robin and yelled over her shoulder. "Rusty! Look who just walked in our front door!"

A beanpole of a man turned away from the pile of hash browns on the cook top. He had a mullet, bushy eyebrows, and rosy cheeks. "Birdie Scott! Ain't seen you in a dog's age, girl. Welcome home."

That broke open the floodgates. Vinyl creaked as the patrons cleared their booths and stood from their barstools. They made for Robin, slowly at first, then in a rush. All patting her on the back and shaking her hand and offering their condolences. No one criticized her absence with their words, but it was there in their eyes. A silent demand for explanation. A wistful remark about how they had all missed her. And always her mother. How proud she had been of Robin. How she had told them all about every album, every concert, every contract.

When she felt like she might scream if another person touched her, Nancy shooed them all away.

"All right then. That's enough. Birdie's starvin' can't you see? Let her eat her lunch in peace now."

They melted away reluctantly. Back to their booths or their perch at the counter. Nancy put a fleshy arm around her shoulders and pulled her close. She'd been like a second mother to Robin when she was a kid. Somewhere between a friend and a moral compass when she was a teenager. And always, always kind. That kindness, as much as the food, was why she was here today. With the quiet sadness of Larry and the cold detachment of Jacob Peters, Robin yearned to know there was something of the Sperryville she remembered still here.

"Set ya up in the back booth. Make sure none of these vultures mess with ya."

Robin sat with her back to the entrance, facing the swinging door with its porthole window leading back to the pantry and bathrooms. Robin had her first kiss in that dark hallway. A furtive, sloppy encounter with a girl from Vermont hiking the Appalachian Trail. It was a great, dark place to hide in the bright light and wide window storefront of Brenda's. She should've asked to sit back there next to the cans of peas and jugs of fry oil.

"What'll it be for ya, Little Bird? Patty melt and a strawberry milkshake?"

Robin laughed. "I'll take the patty melt, but swap the shake for a coffee, would ya?"

Nancy gave her shoulder a squeeze before toddling off. Robin ventured a glance over her shoulder and was relieved to see that the other diners had gone back to their meals. She recognized a few faces, but most of their names were lost in her memory. She counted off the years since she'd been back in Sperryville, and was shocked to realize the number was thirteen.

She'd come back only twice since graduating from high school. Her mom had been hospitalized with a bad bout of pneumonia and Robin spent two days on a bus getting to a stop where Larry could bring her the rest of the way. They'd gotten into a fight within a day and Robin was on another bus back to California in less time than it had taken her to arrive. The second trip she came with her soon-to-be wife, Della. It was even more of a disaster than the first trip.

Robin couldn't shake the memory of disappointment in her mother's eyes both times she announced her early departure until Nancy came back with a greasy plate and a pot of strong coffee. Robin flipped the mug in front of her and Nancy filled it. Robin's nerves jangled just at the sight, but she took a long sip anyway. It was so hot it scalded her throat. Nancy pulled a glass bottle of ketchup from her apron and put it down on the table. She hesitated for a moment, waiting to see if Robin was interested in talking, but Robin reached for a french fry and the waitress moved off. Her cheery voice tinkled from a few tables away.

The fries were everything she remembered. Crispy, salty wedges of potato in perfect half-moons. The patty melt dripped with juice and gooey cheese. There was so much butter on the toast that it bubbled around her teeth with each bite. It was nothing like the food in LA, where every calorie would be counted a dozen times over, before and after it was consumed. Here there was no avocado or lettuce or goat cheese. No assurances the bread was wholegrain or the beef grass-fed or the onions heirloom. It was simple. She didn't have to think about it. It was perfect.

As she ate she looked around the diner. Just like the food, it hadn't changed an ounce. The walls were sparsely decorated with classic Coca-Cola signs and grimy fingerprints. The floors were tile of an indeterminate shade. There were ten booths, each with Formica tables and red vinyl seats. The jukebox in the front had an "Out of Order" sign taped to it. The sign was in Robin's handwriting. The summer between middle school and high school she had played the thing until it wore out. Rusty said he would look into getting it fixed, so she'd attached the sign. She wanted him to fix it soon because it was the only place in town were she could hear the great music she loved. Leonard Cohen, Simon and Garfunkel, Joni Mitchell, The Velvet Underground. Whether Rusty left it broken to save money, or because the residents of this country music-mad town had no interest in it being replaced was up for debate. Robin was devastated, but she was on the cusp of becoming a teenager then and everything devastated her.

Robin spent a lot of time here as a kid. In this very booth. There were a lot of long evenings here when her dad was still around. Her mom would pick her up after school and they would come here for dinner. Robin would drink her milkshake and hum along to whatever song was weaving through her mind. Probably from a cartoon in those days. Her mom would watch the door and sip at her glass of water with no ice. Nancy would talk to her in a low voice, shooting little smiles at Robin, but there was a sadness in her eyes that even a child could see. Years later, Robin figured out that they were hiding from her drunken father, but at the time she just saw strawberry milkshakes and her mom.

Brenda's had come to be synonymous with her mother. Even when Larry would sometimes tag along, they always had their special nights at Brenda's. Thursdays were dinner-at-Brenda's nights. Her mom didn't have to cook, so she was less tired and she would regale Robin with stories from work. Robin didn't understand either the jokes or the frustrations, but her mother was confiding in her, and that was the important thing. Even when she was angry or brooding, Robin would set her problems aside for Thursday dinner at Brenda's.

As much as the memories, there was the mystery of Brenda's that reminded her so strongly of her mother. The incongruity of the place. It was simple, unassuming food, but it was delicious and satisfying in a way fancy restaurants just weren't. The windows were always smudged, but there was never lipstick on the glasses. The place dared you to figure it out. Even the name—there was not and never had been a Brenda. When pressed, Rusty merely shrugged and said he liked the name and he had to call the place something. When her mother heard that she just laughed a deep, joyful belly laugh that said everything and nothing with the same sound. That was Brenda's and that was her mother.

When the telephone factory shut down, her mom got a job here waiting tables a few nights a week until a new company took over and hired all the workers back. Every major event in her life was celebrated with a patty melt in this booth. Birthdays, graduations, chorus competitions, guitar recitals. She'd been sitting in this very spot when she told her mom she was leaving for college, the sound of creaking vinyl her accompaniment as she shifted uneasily. Told her about the scholarship offer. How she'd be moving to California.

The grease congealed in her stomach. The onions and beef stuck in her throat. She pushed her plate away and stared across the table.

"How's that food treatin' ya?"

Nancy splashed more coffee into Robin's cup before she could protest. "It's good. Thanks."

The coffeepot clicked gently as Nancy set it on the table. "How're you doin', Birdie Girl?"

Robin looked at the wall beside the booth. There was a new addition after all. A yellowing chunk of newsprint stuffed into a too-small frame. The headline read "Local Girl Takes LA By Storm." It looked like it had been cut from the local paper, but there was no date. The faded photograph attached to the article was of Robin and her mother, sitting in this very booth. They both looked young and happy. Robin wore an oversized flannel shirt, her mother's bangs were teased and hairsprayed high over her forehead. She was smiling wide at the camera.

"Your momma was a special lady."

"Yes, she was."

"The way you looked at your momma then." Nancy smiled at the picture on the wall, her hand gently squeezing Robin's shoulder. "You'da thought the sun rose and set in her eyes the way you stared at her."

"It did back then."

"Not anymore?"

Robin looked away from the picture. "It's complicated."

"Take it from me, dear heart, it only gets more complicated now she's gone to Jesus."

The bell above the door chimed and Nancy looked to see who had walked in. The smell of the coffee turned Robin's stomach, and she pushed it away.

"You know what, Nancy. I think I will take that milkshake."

"Comin' right up, darlin'."

Robin looked back at the article on the wall. She read a few lines. It must have been quite old, not just based on the deterioration of the paper and the travesty of fashion, but because it mentioned her first album's new release. It was a flattering biography, much more hopeful about her career than she herself had been at the time. The author had no doubt Robin would be a star. Robin always knew the first album wouldn't be a hit, but she also knew there were good songs in her and she was anxious to get her name out there. So was the record company. Had she understood the industry then the way she did now, she doubted a second album would have followed, much less the third or the fourth that had made her a household name in towns much larger than Sperryville. She had a determination then. A wild passion for her guitar that was dulled by the passage of time.

A glass frosted with ice and smoking in the summer air slid across the table in front of her. The smell of ripe strawberries and vanilla ice cream filled her world. She turned to smile up at Nancy, but the woman standing by her table, one hand on a slim hip, wasn't Nancy. She was Robin's age. Slim and tall with a twinkle in her eye that made Robin think of Peter Pan.

She reached out with fingers still cold from carrying the milkshake and pushed the bangs back from Robin's forehead, tucking them behind her ear. "Hey there, Cowboy."

CHAPTER FIVE

Robin had never used drugs. Never been interested in an out-of-body experience. The idea made her slightly queasy. Whenever she thought about what it might be like to be stoned, this moment was exactly what she imagined. A feeling of your mind rejecting everything your eyes knew to be true. A feeling of confusion so profound it created its own reality. She knew what year it was. Knew that she was thirty-five and an outsider in her hometown. Knew that her mother was dead and her song was playing on a thousand radio stations across the world. And yet she sat here, in a booth at Brenda's, with a strawberry milkshake in front of her and Sara Carson sitting across the table.

Sara Carson with the same twinkle in her blue eyes that she had when she wore that tarnished tiara all those years ago. Sara Carson who smiled with those perfect teeth that never needed braces and that skin that was tanned to a light olive by the sun instead of an odd orange by the UV lights and pigmented sprays so popular in California. Sara Carson with her bright blond hair in a pixie cut that worked so perfectly with her heart-shaped face. Sara Carson with an expansive cleavage and a narrow waist, the same as she had when everyone else was a gangly, awkward mess of limbs and acne. Sara Carson who ran off without a word the day after their high school graduation.

It was like Robin was eighteen again. She reeled from the disorientation and sipped her milkshake for something to do.

"Sorry about your mom, Birdie."

Robin swallowed her mouthful of strawberry with difficulty. Her voice came out in a half-frozen, raspy croak. "Thanks."

Sara reached out and pulled the glass to her. She took a long sip from the straw and pushed the glass back across the table.

"When'd you get into town?"

"This morning."

"That was quick."

"I was in Richmond. On tour."

Sara smiled wide as a tomcat. "I like your song."

Robin grabbed her milkshake, swirling the contents with the straw and avoiding Sara's eye. She pretended not to feel the heat rising up her neck. Sara had left a sticky smear of lip gloss on the straw.

"Thanks."

"How's Larry holding up?"

"Okay I think." Robin took another sip. She could taste vanilla from Sara's lip gloss mixed with the strawberry. "You know Larry. He doesn't talk about his feelings much."

"Really? I've always found Larry to be surprisingly open. Not like my dad was. I never could get more than a few words out of him."

Robin could still remember exactly what Sara's dad looked like. A big man with hairy arms and boots that clunked noisily when he marched into a room.

"Well, we were only ten when he died. You talked a lot back then."

Sara threw back her head and laughed at the ceiling. It was a loud, long call. Completely uninhibited. The corner of Robin's mouth twitched up and it felt strange on her face. When she was done laughing, Sara said, "True. He probably tried to talk all the time and couldn't get a word in."

Nancy appeared beside the table, scowling at Sara. "Your lunch is ready." She dropped a Styrofoam container on the table and turned to Robin. "How's the shake, Birdie dear?"

"It's great, Nancy. Just like always. Thanks."

"Need anything else?"

"No." She reached for her wallet. "I'm all set."

Nancy put a hand on her shoulder. "You're money's no good here, sweetheart." She looked over at Sara. "I put yours on your account."

Robin pulled out her wallet out anyway after Nancy left. She wedged a couple of bills under the ketchup bottle and stood. Sara stood too, watching Robin with those sparkling eyes. Sara had always been just a few inches shorter than Robin, but the tight white cotton pants ending just above her ankles and the long, loose tank top lengthened her frame.

"Let me walk you home."

"I drove." Nancy gave Robin another smile as she moved through the door, Sara at her heels. "Thanks for the offer."

"It wasn't an offer. I'm telling you I'm going to walk you home. Let me just lock the library and we'll go."

They stopped outside a small clapboard building tucked between a pair of shops on Main Street. It had housed the Sperryville Public Library for as long as Robin could remember. In her mother's day, it had been the one-room schoolhouse, but it closed when integration finally came to town. Robin's generation had to take an hour-long bus ride to a larger public school and the old building was renovated with a grant Sara's mother worked hard to win when she was the town librarian.

Sara reappeared with a heavy ring of keys and a "Be Back Soon" sign. The Styrofoam container was nowhere to be seen. Robin wanted to protest, but the odd, drug-like unreality of the day wouldn't let her. Sara locked the door and skipped down the steps.

"I haven't seen my best friend in eighteen years, I'm not letting you drive away again without catching up."

Robin decided not to mention that she wasn't the one who'd driven off last time. "Don't you want to eat your lunch?"

"The library has a microwave." Sara walked down the sidewalk and Robin fell in step beside her. "Why did you drive? It's only half a mile to your mom's place."

"Habit I guess." The smell of grass and living things filled her nostrils as she walked. She'd forgotten how green everything was here. "You're the librarian now?"

Sara giggled and grabbed Robin's arm, holding it as they walked. It was a habit she'd picked up in middle school. Robin thought at the time that it meant Sara shared her feelings. She had been wrong.

"Yeah." Sara looked up into her eyes and Robin found herself staring. "I worked in the school library over in Luray after I got my degree. Then mom retired five years ago and moved with the Step Drag to his house on the river, and I got to come back home."

They turned off Main Street onto the side road that led out into the country behind town. "She's still with him?"

"Yes. Twenty years married last month. They threw a party. It was awful."

"And you followed in the family business?"

"Didn't your mom tell you?"

"It…never came up."

"After I got my wild years out of my system I graduated in library science. I've been working on my master's online for a while."

Sara and her mom were close when they were young. Robin assumed it was because they were alone for so many years before her mom remarried, just like Robin and her mom. The new relationship did them in though, and mother and daughter fell out in a loud and permanent way. Although Robin had always liked Larry and was thrilled when he entered her life, the same could not be said for Sara's stepdad. Maybe the difference was that her mom never married Larry. Maybe it was that Larry was a country boy and the Step Drag, as Sara always called him, was a rich jerk from Luray. Whatever it was, Sara and her mom weren't close again once he entered the picture. It never occurred to Robin they would have such similar interests in work.

When she felt the silence stretch uncomfortably long, Robin asked, "What did you do to make Nancy so mad?"

"Oh. That."

"Well, now I know it's a good story."

"I sorta dated her niece a few years back." Packed dirt crunched under their feet as they left the town behind. "It didn't end well and Nancy's never really forgiven me."

"Still setting the town on fire with gossip."

"It's what I'm best at."

"Always give the people what they want."

They turned and walked past the rows of corn that ended at Robin's house. "You seem to be doing that too, Birdie. Big rock star. Just like you always planned."

At the porch Sara let go of Robin's arm, sitting on the middle step and lounging back on her elbows with her ankles crossed in front of her. Robin leaned against the chipped paint of railing.

"I guess you could say that."

"You're not gonna give me that mopey crap about how awful it is to be rich and famous are you?"

There was a crunch of tires on gravel behind her, and Robin turned to see a car pull into the driveway. "No. It's not awful, but it is definitely not what I expected."

"Hit record. Sold-out international tour. Nominated for three Grammys. Money rolling in by the truckload. Happy marriage. I read all about it in a magazine in the line at the grocery store."

The car stopped and the door opened. Robin sat up wearily. "Don't believe everything you read in grocery store magazines."

The car wasn't familiar, but the woman who got out of it certainly was. Still, it was always tough to know what you were getting with Della. She was wearing an outfit Robin hadn't seen before, a suit with a coral pencil skirt and a sleeveless white blouse, but it was standard fare. Her heels caught in the coarse gravel and she had to grab the car door with her free hand to steady herself. Instinct to help quickened Robin's pace for a step or two, but the cold look she received slowed her again.

Robin had never been able to look at Della without seeing the woman she'd met in a Los Angeles coffee shop so many years ago. Physically, she hadn't changed much. She was tall, nearly six feet without heels. She had narrow shoulders and perfect posture, and she tended toward clothing that accentuated her height and trim figure. The trim figure was deceptive. She was a powerful woman, full of long, lean muscle and the grace of a seasoned dancer. Her long blond hair was in its usual ponytail, pulled back tightly from her forehead enough to show off the high arc of her thin eyebrows. She rarely wore much makeup, favoring dark lipstick and little else. Her skin was ivory smooth and pale with no sign of age or the sun of her native California.

She transferred her blazer and briefcase to her other arm and reached for Robin when close enough. There was concern in her eyes that Robin would swear was genuine if it weren't for the pitying, almost condescending smile. Della kissed her cheek for a heartbeat, but pulled back immediately and gave her a searching look. They didn't hug. They rarely did these days. She did not offer any words of comfort, just stood there searching Robin's face as though it were up to her to start a conversation. Robin did not.

She did let her hand rest on the small of Della's back when she heard footsteps behind her. "Sara, this is my wife, Della." Robin turned to see Sara approach with her hand outstretched. She wore a warm smile. "Della, this is Sara Carson."

Della moved away from Robin to shake Sara's hand. "Pleasure to meet you, Ms. Carson."

"Please, call me Sara." She took Della's hand, holding it rather than shaking it. "Birdie and I go way back. It'd be weird for my best friend's wife to call me Ms. anything."

"Sara it is then." Della gave Robin a hard look, but she avoided eye contact. "I thought it was only Robbie's mom that called her Birdie."

"Oh no, everyone in Sperryville calls her Birdie." Sara crossed her arms and turned her warm smile on Robin. "With a name like Robin Wren Scott, she couldn't avoid it no matter how much she wanted to. She's been trying to get rid of that nickname her whole life. She's always hated it, but it stuck and now she'll always be Birdie here."

"I don't hate it."

"Sure you do." Sara turned back to Della. "She tried everything to get rid of it back in high school. Had me call her Wren for a whole year trying to create a new image. Thought it sounded poetic. Didn't work."

"Our friends in LA call her Wren."

"Ha! You finally got your wish then. Had to move across the country, but you got to reinvent yourself."

Robin kicked at the gravel while the two women watched her. It was too hot out here. She just wanted to get inside.

Sara seemed to read her mind. "Well, I should be getting back to work." She pulled Robin to her by the shoulder, folding her in a gentle hug for a little longer than she expected. "I'm glad you're home, Birdie, even if it's for all the wrong reasons. Come see me at the library so we can catch up. I'm not letting you get away again."

As Sara moved past her and down the driveway, Della walked to the house. Robin stood and watched Sara go until she turned the corner and was lost to sight behind a row of trees.

CHAPTER SIX

"It's been a long day."

Robin sat on the couch with her knees pulled up to her chest, staring at the cushion under her feet. She heard Della's words, but they didn't sink in.

"Do you want to come to bed?"

"Not yet." Like rusty hinges, Robin's voice creaked from lack of use. "You go ahead."

Hesitation hung in the air between them, but Della eventually left without further protest. Robin continued to sit and stare for a long while after she'd gone upstairs. Her mind was blank and her body tired, but she couldn't bring herself to stand.

When her back finally ached enough to make her move, she heaved herself to her feet. The house was quiet by then, the lights upstairs having gone out long ago. There was a chill in the air that had as much to do with her mother's absence as with the cold of a summer night in the mountains.

Every time Robin looked around, she expected to see her mother come around the corner, her wide smile accentuated by bright white teeth and a prominent overbite. It was a warm smile. A comforting smile. Her whole life, Robin would do anything to earn that smile. Standing there alone in the house, Robin realized she would never see it again. The realization hit her like a punch to the gut and she nearly sat down again. She walked toward the kitchen.

It had been clean and neat and so cold in the living room. The dining room was even colder. A vase of lilacs on the dining table made the room smell the same as always, but they were starting to wilt. The floorboards creaked under her feet. They must have been refinished recently. Even in the dull, reflected light from the kitchen they glowed like fresh maple syrup.

The kitchen was barely lit by the little pendulum light over the sink. The warm glow couldn't stop the room from swimming in shadows. Robin leaned across the sink to flick the switch off and, without the reflected light, she could see through the little window. It looked out over the side fence toward Larry's.

Not for the first time, Robin wondered at the arrangement Larry had with her mom. It amazed her that two people who were so in love could live so close, but not together. She wondered if they lived apart because her mother had never invited Larry to move in, or because he had never asked to. It would be because he knew what the answer would be. He'd learned, Robin supposed, after all those early rejections not to push too hard.

She could see a dim light through his kitchen window. Robin wasn't surprised to find they were both up late tonight. Still, she didn't have any interest in going next door and Larry seemed content with his solitude as well. She paced around the island, squeezing her toes against the ceramic tiles. Her hand trailed along the countertop, knocking something off the edge with a clatter.

"Damn."

Stooping to pick it up, she heard the creak of bedsprings upstairs. Robin held still, not wanting to wake Della, but she didn't hear anything else. She swept her hands on the dark floor, looking for whatever it was she dropped. Her fingers brushed against hard plastic and she grabbed it.

Robin stood, holding a cordless phone. She hit a button at random to see if it still worked and the screen lit up. The battery was low, but it worked. Robin went to hang it back up, but stopped in her tracks. When she checked the phone, she'd pulled up the call memory and she saw her own name and phone number on the display. The call was from two days ago at six p.m. Hitting the arrow, Robin scrolled to the next call on the log. It was her name again, seven days before the first, at six o'clock. Every call on the memory was from Robin. Every one of them was a Tuesday at six o'clock. Not even a minute variation for three months.

If there was one thing that was sacred to Robin, it was Tuesday night at six o'clock. No matter where she was, no matter what she was doing, she always made time for that phone call. The first thing she did whenever she went on tour was to find out where she'd be on Tuesday night, find out what time zone it was in and figure out what time she needed to be available to call her mom. It wasn't the easiest thing, especially when she did her Australian tour last year.

It wasn't just the time difference that made things hard. In the last few years, Della had become increasingly annoyed by the calls. It started one day when they had plans to go out after. Unfortunately, Robin had just had some great news from her label and she'd talked to her mom for much longer than normal. She hung up after four hours and walked into the living room to find Della irate. They'd missed their dinner reservations and there wasn't much chance of making the movie either.

They'd worked things out after that, deciding not to make plans for Tuesday nights just in case. Things were calm for a while, but Robin could feel Della's frustration every time she got off the phone. She felt ignored. She felt lonely. A couple of hours once a week didn't seem like much to ask considering they spent so much of their lives together, but Della felt neglected and there wasn't any way around that.

It wasn't Della's fault. She simply didn't understand what it was like to be best friends with a parent. She came from a big extended family. She had siblings and distant parents. Enough people around her to dilute the focus. Robin had her mom and that was it. It had always been Birdie and Kathy Scott against the world, sometimes with their sidekick Larry. Della couldn't understand that, so Robin accepted the occasional disagreement about it all.

Robin moved through the empty rooms in the dark house, while her mind wandered over their last phone call. It was just like all the others. They talked about everything and nothing. Robin had learned a long time ago how to avoid all the taboo subjects. Topics that made her mother pause or cluck her tongue in that disapproving way. The ones that reminded her why she called instead of came home.

That was part of why Della hated those calls, of course. She didn't understand how Robin and her mother could be so close because she wasn't an only child, but she also couldn't understand because she knew how Robin's mother continued to hurt her. The things she said, that stung so badly because they were so close.

Robin had coped by turning her back on Sperryville. She stopped to look out a window at the full moon spreading silver over the dark world. This place. This town. She convinced herself a long time ago that it was this place that made her mother so cutting. That it was the small-town mindset. She attached the unkind aspect of her mother to where she was from in the same way people dismiss a historical figure's bigotry to being "a product of their time."

As she looked out over the moonlit corn swaying in a gentle breeze she knew that she had been unfair. Sperryville wasn't to blame. She didn't have to be here a day to see the way people embraced her and took pride in her. Still, it had been easier to give up her hometown than to give up her mother. She'd made that tradeoff long ago and she'd had years of love from her mom, even if it had been on the other end of a phone rather than in person. The next few days would no doubt tell her whether the tradeoff had been worth it.

As the grandfather clock chimed once and went silent Robin turned off the foyer light and mounted the stairs.

CHAPTER SEVEN

The stairs were cold on Robin's bare feet. The fourth stair from the bottom creaked when she stepped on it. It had creaked since the day she and her mother moved in. When she was a kid, she always skipped that step, but it'd been long enough that she'd forgotten. The sound cut through the dark house. The last time Robin spoke to her mom she had said she was going to ask Larry about fixing it. Now she remembered the details she couldn't think of last night. It had rained in LA the day before, and Robin told her mother about it. She hadn't really been able to explain how big a deal it was to get rain there. It rained in Sperryville all the time. For some reason, it annoyed her that her mother didn't appreciate the significance no matter how hard Robin tried to explain it.

She'd thought about inviting her mom out for a visit, but the conversation never went in that direction and she forgot to ask. It wasn't the first time she'd forgotten to ask. As Robin's feet landed hard on the living room floor, it occurred to her that it would be the last time she forgot. The thought sent a shiver through her body that had nothing to do with the mountain air.

The smell of coffee was heavy in the air. Robin headed to the kitchen and poured herself a cup. Della wasn't there, and Robin checked all of the rooms on the first floor before heading out to the front porch to find Della showered and dressed. She'd curled her hair, and it hung around her shoulders in glossy waves.

Her coffee cup was balanced on the arm of an old rocking chair. Her mother's rocking chair. Her mother had sat in it every night when the weather was good, reading an endless supply of paperback thrillers. If it was raining or snowing her mom would perch on the very edge of the couch in the living room, shooting the occasional look through the window, trying to wish away the storm that kept her inside. When she was little Robin had sat at her feet playing, only moving to the nearby porch swing in her teen years before disappearing entirely when she was old enough to go get rowdy with friends. She called the chair her mom's throne. Della's coffee had dripped, leaving a stain she hadn't noticed on the worn cushion.

"You're up early."

Della looked up at her and tried to smile. "I couldn't sleep."

"I didn't hear you get out of bed."

"You were pretty out of it." Robin moved over to the porch swing and Della's eyes followed her. "When did you come to bed?"

"Late."

As Robin sat down the thin flannel of her pajama pants caught on the wood of the swing. The chains above her creaked ominously, and she transferred her weight to the center of the seat. She'd held the wide eye bolts for Larry while he searched for a stud in the porch ceiling from which to hang the swing. She tried to remember how old she was, but her mind didn't want to expend the effort. She sipped her coffee. Della emptied her own mug and without a word went inside to refill it. Robin considered asking Della not to sit in the rocking chair when she came back, but she didn't have the energy for that inevitable fight either. She watched it sway on the twin rockers as though someone still sat in it. The sound of it rolling back and forth against the slats of the decking sounded like her mother's voice.

Della came back outside. She stopped for a moment and eyed the expanse of empty swing. She waited, and Robin knew she was waiting to be invited to share the seat. A couple of years ago, Robin wouldn't have hesitated. Five years ago, she would have insisted Della sit with her. Ten years ago, they would have sat close, Robin's hand on her thigh, and would have ended up in bed within a half hour. Today, Robin turned and stretched out her legs, filling the seat.

There was a flash of emotion on Della's face. It could have been pain or it could have been anger, but Robin turned her eyes to her coffee so she didn't have to interpret it. When she looked back, Della was sitting in the rocker, her expression clear again.

"I saw the obituary in this morning's paper." Della was watching her, but Robin studied the rows of corn. "It was lovely. Did you write it?"

"No." Robin cleared her throat and continued, "Mom pretty much wrote it. She took care of everything a few years ago apparently. Everything was all set when Larry and I got to the funeral home. Mr. Peters said she'd planned and paid for the entire service. He just touched up the notice she wrote for herself."

"That was considerate of her."

Robin squirmed. She wanted to tell Della that it wasn't. That it was selfish. That it made her feel hopeless and, worse, useless. That taking away her part in her own mother's funeral was cruel. Thoughtless. That it made her feel like an outsider. That now the whole town had read her mother's obituary, but she hadn't. That wasn't right. She wanted to yell at Della to get out of her mom's chair. Instead she quietly sipped her black coffee.

"Are you okay, Robbie?"

"I'm fine."

"Do you want some breakfast?"

"No."

"Are you sure? I can make us some eggs."

"I'm not hungry. You go ahead."

"When was the last time you ate?"

"I'm fine Della."

She hadn't intended to be sharp, but the ringing silence made her realize how loud she'd been. Della spun the cup between her delicate fingers and watched the handle's circular progress.

Robin's voice was much softer when she spoke again, "I really am fine."

"She loved you very much."

Robin squinted up at the sun, hanging halfway up the sky. It made her eyes burn. "I guess."

"I *know*. She loved you and she was a wonderful lady."

Robin swung her feet down to the porch and stood. "You two didn't spend much time together."

It came out more accusatory than Robin had intended, and she could tell Della felt it by the way her voice wavered. "No, we didn't. She didn't like me, but that doesn't matter." A good wife would have argued that her mother did, in fact, like Della, but it would come across as hollow. They both had enough evidence to the contrary. She decided to let it go.

"And I know how much you loved her," Della said, her voice soft in the still air.

"How do you know?"

"I have a little experience with what it looks like when you love someone."

Robin looked over her shoulder. Della gave her a sad smile and she wanted to scream again. If she'd been wearing shoes she would have walked off down the driveway for no other reason than to hear the crunch of gravel under her feet. Maybe she'd take a run. Head off into town. Run all the way to the little creek where she spent half her childhood, Sara by her side.

Robin looked away so Della didn't see her swelling anger. She didn't even know why or with whom she was angry. Della for her pity? Her mother for dying? Herself for not inviting her mother out to LA the last time they spoke? Probably a healthy slice of all three, but she couldn't see clearly enough just now to analyze her emotions. She could barely feel them.

The decking creaked behind her and she knew without looking that Della had stood. She would walk over to Robin.

Put an arm around her. Put her chin on Robin's shoulder. Not
hug her. They didn't hug often. But Della would come over
here and she would crowd Robin's space. She could already feel
the air close in around her. She nearly shouted at Della to stop
pushing.

"I need to get some work done." Della's voice was far away.
Robin turned to see that she hadn't crossed the deck, she was
still standing in front of the rocking chair. "Is that okay?"

Bitterness flooded into Robin. Of course she had to
work. Della always had to work. It didn't matter that it was less
than a day after Robin's mother died and she needed comfort.

"Yeah. Fine."

"I'm sorry. It's just that my deadline is so close." The screen
door squealed when Della opened it. "Are you sure it's okay?"

How very Della. To ask permission to go when she was
already halfway inside the house.

"It's fine."

"I'll be in the dining room if you need me."

Robin didn't answer and, after a moment, the screen
door clicked against the frame. She looked out at the corn until
her bitterness dissolved and the loneliness faded away. The view
had always been peaceful to her.

Larry planted the rows of sweet corn every year, using a
beat up old rototiller to loosen the soil and carefully watering
and fertilizing all spring and summer. He took the ears up to a
farmers market on the road to Shenandoah National Park. One
year he tried to show her mother how to till the soil, and she had
lost control of the diesel engine, sending it careening off across
the little two-lane road, narrowly avoiding the Cadillac driven
by the local pastor. Robin and Larry had teased her at dinner
until she threw a roll at Larry, hitting him square in the eye.
Even when his eye swelled shut, she didn't apologize. It became
a joke between the three of them. Be careful what you say or
Mom'll throw a roll at you.

Robin walked farther along the porch, rounding the
corner until she couldn't see either the rocking chair or the
corn anymore. This side was narrow and faced south, making

it uncomfortably warm and bright year round. Robin's mother took advantage of the prospect by putting her potted plants on this side during the winter, when they would get the most sun and still be protected from the worst of the weather.

In the winter months this section of the porch was full of life struggling to survive. Her mother spent hours every day babying her plants and coaxing just a little more beauty out of them. She would put on a thick sweater that had belonged to her father and come outside with a watering can of warm tap water, making sure there was enough sunlight and water for all. If snow was predicted, she covered the plants both on the porch and in the backyard with threadbare, faded bedsheets to protect them. Robin opened the doors of the old tin cabinet and saw the stack of them, neatly folded and ready to be deployed when the season turned. She wondered if Larry would remember to come over and use them when the time came.

Her mother loved all plants and flowers. Her rose bushes in the backyard were her pride and joy, but she also grew azaleas, irises, and hydrangeas in a rainbow of colors. During the summer, the backyard sang with every shade of purple, red, and pink. The only thing you wouldn't find back there were white flowers. She hated the way they browned so quickly around the edges. White flowers were like white cars, she said, bright for all of one minute before they got dingy. She wanted her flowers vibrant, not sickly.

Being summer, the porch was bare apart from the cabinet and a few brittle remnants of leaves from the previous autumn. The deck boards were brighter in a few spots, the wood around them faded and sprinkled with dirt. Her mother had always drafted her for help with some of the larger pots. Robin loved it when she was little, but complained about the task endlessly when she was older.

One year, during the height of her teenage rebellion, when she lay on her twin bed, lazily picking at her guitar, writing terrible love poetry and listening to her Sarah McLachlan cassette until the ribbon stretched and distorted, her mother came upstairs and asked Robin to help her move the plants back to their spring homes. Robin refused. Her mother ordered her. Robin had inherited her mother's stubbornness, and did not respond well to orders. She had released her considerable teenaged angst in a flurry of accusations and recriminations. Robin couldn't remember what she said, but she remembered the hurt on her mother's face.

The look made her instantly regret her words, but she found it impossible to take them back. She still sometimes thought about the look on her mother's face that day, and how she had turned without a word, gently closing the door behind her as she left Robin's bedroom. Robin restarted her tape and turned up the volume as high as it would go. When it clicked to a stop a half hour later she could hear her mom calling for help.

Robin ran outside to find her mother sprawled on the cracked concrete of the patio. She had tried to move a pot on her own and fallen down the short flight of stairs leading to the back door. The heavy pot had fallen on her ankle, breaking it in two places. Robin had no idea how long she'd been stuck there, unable to move, in pain and calling for help, but no other pots had been moved, so this must have been her first. It was likely she'd been there for quite some time, but Larry was at work and they had no other neighbors close enough to hear her cry for help. Robin was the only person who could help her, but she'd been too busy brooding upstairs. Her mother never said a word of criticism to Robin, blaming herself for being too stubborn and impatient to wait for Larry to get off work and help her, but Robin knew it was her fault.

Robin squatted there, staring at the spot for a long time. The memory coursed through her like poison. She turned when she heard the thump of footsteps nearby, expecting to see Della. Instead it was Sara, beaming at her from the shade at the front of the porch. She leaned against frame of the house, looking just as she had the day before, like a beautiful phantom stepped right out of dreamy memories.

"I decided not to let you wiggle outta coming to see me."

Robin stood, crossing her arms to cover the fact that she wasn't wearing a bra under the tank top she'd slept in. "Don't you have to work?"

Sara didn't hide the way her eyes traveled over Robin's chest, but she looked back at her face when she answered, "It's a sleepy town. Not many people come to the library until school lets out. That gives us a couple of hours to catch up. Wanna take a walk with me?"

"Sure. Just let me go change real quick."

Sara's smile widened. "Probably a good idea."

CHAPTER EIGHT

The first stop they made was at a little sandwich shop in town that sold the best hot dogs in the world. At least Robin considered them the best hot dogs in the world. Sara thought they were just okay, but loved going there because they served cream soda in the old-fashioned glass bottles. Sara had always been a sugar junkie. When they were kids, Sara's meals often consisted of candy, soda, and ice cream. She called them her own personal food pyramid. Despite the fact that the closest she ever came to a salad was green M&Ms, she was never overweight.

Robin's weakness was meat and cheese, preferably in the same bite and with more than its fair share of grease. Fortunately, her metabolism in those days matched Sara's. These days she stayed thin because of a chronic forgetfulness when it came to meals. Larry's phone call hadn't exactly helped with that either. She couldn't remember eating anything but the patty melt at Brenda's yesterday.

The minute she stepped off the porch, Robin realized she was ravenous. Maybe she should have taken Della up on the offer of breakfast, but it was too late now. She didn't want to go back to Brenda's either. The idea of sitting in a booth and waiting made her skin crawl and her heels itch. Sara immediately suggested hot dogs and Robin couldn't agree fast enough. Portable food was just the answer. She'd never needed a walk as badly as she did right now.

The shop was little more than a garden shed with a grill inside and half a dozen small picnic tables in the lawn around it. In a rare burst of creativity from the large, greasy owner and sole employee, Martin had named his venue "Bird Dogs." Ever since the health department told him the ancient brown and white pointer, Mallory, couldn't stay inside with him, he'd kept her in a kennel next to the stand. Her likeness graced the sign on the roof.

When Robin and Sara first started coming to Bird Dogs, Mallory's predecessor held sway, regaling the crowd with her mournful barking. Martin would close the stand every Saturday during hunting season to take her out. The elderly dog finally died the summer before Robin moved to LA, and by then Martin had Mallory II, just a few months old and already full of her own personality. Now she was so old she could barely stand, but she sat in her house all the same, nose poked out the door to catch the aroma of grilling meat and toasting bread.

"Well, hey there Birdie Scott." Martin grinned wide and the stubbly flesh under his chin wobbled. "Awful nice to see you back in town."

"Hey Martin. How've you been?"

"Can't complain, sweetheart." His cheeks fell and his eyes, to Robin's horror, filled with tears. "Was real sorry to hear 'bout your momma. She was a fine woman. Loved you to pieces."

Robin's appetite vanished in an instant. Her throat was dry, so she just nodded and looked over at Mallory, snoozing in the shade of her doghouse. She was from the same breeder as the first Mallory and had the same features, right down to the gray on her muzzle and the sad droop of her jowls. Robin had heard so much about her in the weekly phone calls with her mother that she almost felt like Mallory II was a friend.

Martin leaned through the glass partition, the press of his elbows bowing the plywood counter. "She used to bring you here all the time. Her and Larry. You would laugh about how it was your place, on account of the name."

Robin took a step back deciding she'd rather walk than talk, but Sara grabbed her arm and held it tight. She gave a little hop and said with exaggerated cheer, "Speaking of your hot dogs, Martin, can we get four with mustard and two cream sodas? I've got to get back to the library."

"Oh sure, Miss Sara. Sorry. You know I just can't resist runnin' my yap when Sperryville's favorite daughter comes back to town after so long!"

He waddled off to the grill, and Robin let out an uneven breath. "Thanks."

Sara shrugged and hugged Robin's arm close to her. Her hand stroked a soothing path over Robin's bicep, catching on the soft cotton of her T-shirt as it moved up and down.

"A lot of folks here are so happy to see you, they forget that you're grieving. Me too in fact." She reached up with her free hand and stroked Robin's shoulder. "How are you really doing, Birdie?"

"I'm fine."

"No, you're not."

"No." Robin's eyes prickled, but she was well-practiced at self-control and the tears stayed inside. "I'm not, but I really don't want to talk about it."

Sara watched her for a long moment, tilting her head a little to the side. Then she dropped her hand from Robin's shoulder and said in her cheery voice again, "Okay. We'll talk about something easier then. Why'd you run out on me without saying goodbye eighteen years ago?"

Robin's jaw dropped. She was about to launch an indignant response when Martin appeared at the window again, four aluminum foil-wrapped bundles in one hand and a pair of sweating glass bottles in the other.

"Here we go! On the house. Nancy told me you don't take kindly to a free lunch when it's offered, so you can just keep that trap shut. No arguments allowed."

Robin started to protest anyway, but Sara reached for the food. "That's sweet of you, Martin. Thank you!" She shoved the hot dogs into Robin's hands and reached for the napkin dispenser, pulling out a large handful. "Oh, and the new Dan Brown novel gets here next week. You're first on the waiting list, but don't drag your feet coming to get it. Mrs. Harrison knows she's second and she'll hound me to death until I let her have it."

She dropped to pat Mallory's head, then headed off down the sidewalk. It took a moment for Robin to process everything, but she eventually waved to Martin and jogged off to follow. Sara snatched a hot dog from Robin's stack and peeled back the foil. Her first bite left a smear of bright yellow mustard on her upper lip, and Robin fought the impulse to wipe it off for her.

"Is mustard the new look for summer, Princess?"

"Oh yeah, it's all the rage is Paris and Milan. Didn't you know?" Sara elbowed Robin in the ribs and then wiped at her face with a napkin. "Thanks."

Robin bit into her hot dog. It was perfect. Juicy and slightly charred, wrapped in a buttered and baked bun. It tasted like sunshine and happiness and grass under her bare feet.

"You won't thank me when you realize you smeared it all over your face."

Sara swiped at her mouth with a fistful of cheap paper and Robin threw her head back laughing. Sara stopped wiping and squinted at her.

"Birdie! Come on. It's not funny. Where is it?"

"I'm teasin', Princess. You got it the first time."

Sara kicked at her ankle. "You're so mean!"

Robin hopped on one foot, still laughing and rubbing at her ankle. "Ow! Who's mean now? Are you going to roll me around town in my wheelchair?"

"Sissy."

"Drama queen."

"Whiner."

"Bully."

It amazed Robin how quickly they could fall into their old patterns. Their old closeness. She'd never had a friendship like this, before or since. They came to a trash can chained to the sidewalk on the corner of Main Street. Sara stopped to drop in the crumpled napkins and foil wrappers of their first dogs. As they started again, she unwrapped her second and asked, "So are the Bird Dogs as good as you remember?"

"Better. Best thing I've eaten in years."

"They don't have good food in LA?"

Robin took a long swallow of her cream soda, the sickly sweetness mixed perfectly with the salt of the dog and acidic tang of the mustard.

"They have great food in LA. If you like wheat grass and avocado on everything."

"Avocado's weird. The texture is like...a stick of Crisco. Yuck."

"I love avocado. Just not on everything. You can't sell anything in LA that isn't artisanal. Or organic. Or gluten-free, non-GMO, ethically sourced, sustainably made." She finished her hot dog and balled up the foil, crushing it smaller and smaller in her palms. "There's a farmers market around the corner from our place. Not a single farmer there, but there is a bleach-blond, collagen-injected, spray-tanned woman who sells sustainably sourced potato chips. Potato chips! She's got more plastic in her than the toy section at WalMart and she's lecturing me on maintaining the cultivar of her heirloom potatoes."

Sara laughed, taking Robin's arm again and forcing her to a slower pace. "I bet they're amazing potato chips."

"They were greasy." The look Sara gave her was full of judgment, and Robin hurried to explain, "What? Della wanted to try them."

"Liar. No way she gets a body like that eating potato chips, sustainable or not."

"You were checkin' out my wife?"

"Just curious that's all. You don't have to worry." She grinned up at Robin and continued, "She's not my type."

"As I recall, the only requirement you had was female and breathing."

"Ouch! You are mean." They passed the wide glass windows of Brenda's and both waved to Nancy, who was cleaning the front booth. "I did have a type. Anyone who could get me out of this town was my type back then."

"But you came right back here to run the library."

There was silence long enough for Robin to look over at Sara, who was studying her own toes with a thoughtful expression. She said in a small voice, "Things change."

Robin felt a twinge of regret. She didn't know Sara's story, but there was clearly one there. She just didn't know if she had the courage to ask. She cleared her throat. "You're right about that."

Sara shook herself and looked back up with a reasonable attempt at a smile. "Anyway...tell me about Della."

Since Robin couldn't even fake a smile, she looked off at the familiar outline of the mountains dominating the skyline. "What do you want to know?"

"Everything. What type of woman does it take to win the heart of a rock star?"

"Della's..." She struggled, but failed to come up with a glib description. "She's an historian. More of a writer these days. She's on extended sabbatical to work on her next book. Teaching is in her genes though. Her mom is a professor of art history and her father is a professor of applied mathematics. They both teach at Cal, and they are very...I don't know... scholarly. Very UC Berkeley types. Smart hippies. They smoke hash and talk about quantum entanglement but couldn't find a bus stop if they had a gun to their heads."

"How'd you meet?"

"At a coffee shop the summer after my freshman year. She was writing her senior thesis and I was playing for tips. We got married a week before I graduated. Within a year she had her master's and a book deal and I'd signed my first record contract."

"Commitment ceremony or Vermont Civil Union?"

"Commitment ceremony. We made it official the minute they legalized in California, but we celebrate the original anniversary."

"You've been married a long time."

"Yep."

It wasn't said with the sort of happiness that invited further explanation. More like a weariness that put it off. They both let the word hang in the air. It walked beside them for a while, a companion with too much baggage and too many questions. Looking over, Robin saw that Sara seemed at ease, which made her feel the tension in her own shoulders. When she let them fall there was an ache in her neck, like she'd slept too long on her side. It was a familiar feeling. One she'd lived with for longer than she cared to admit. It made her tired. She drained her cream soda and let the bottle dangle from her fingertips.

"She seems nice."

"She is."

The silence stretched again as they reached the little bridge over the creek that marked the edge of town. Robin leaned on the wood and steel railing. A car with North Carolina plates crossed the bridge slowly and then paused at the stop sign for the nonexistent traffic, its turn signal clicking. It turned left and Robin followed it with her eyes. She knew exactly what the car's trip would look like. The route ran like a familiar piece of film through her mind.

Down the road on the right was the fire station, sitting alone on perfectly manicured grass. Then the touristy log cabin-style hotel run by a man from out west who never came into town unless he had to. The pottery and farmers market on the left, a solitary house on the riverbank and then the buildings gave way to nature. The road wound through forest along the edge of the mountain. At the top was the ranger station at the entrance to the National Park and the beauty of Skyline Drive.

She and her mom had talked for years about renting a convertible and driving along the spine of the Appalachians from start to finish, letting their hair stream out behind them and singing into the wind. Just the two of them. Wild and carefree. She tried to push the thought out of her head, but it stuck fast. Just another dream that would never come true. Another regret to pile on her shoulders and walk around with forever.

Robin stood and started walking back to town.

"Hey! Slow down!" Sara caught up and fell into step beside her. "Where's the fire?"

"I just wanted to walk."

"Sure. Okay."

They went in silence for a while. Robin knew it was only polite for her to ask about Sara, to find out how she had spent the previous seventeen years. But there were things closer to the surface than she realized when she thought about Sara in those years apart. Things that stuck in her throat and made her quiet. As much as the image of her mom smiling ear to ear in a cherry-red convertible hurt her heart, thinking about Sara hurt more. Thoughts of her moving on from the life they shared as best friends. Things that would make her acknowledge that the woman walking beside her now was not the girl Robin knew then. She didn't want that. She wanted Sara to be frozen in time. Unchanged by the inevitability of life. She hated herself for the imbalance and she wanted, more than anything else, to be alone.

She wanted to be back home in the pool house she'd converted into a studio where she could spend hours writing lyrics and letting her guitar do all the talking. Where she didn't have to think about her mother. Or the woman who used to be the girl she was in love with. Or the band who always wanted to hang out. Or the screaming fans who pried into her life. She didn't want to think about the wife who was always in the library or her office or at the gym. She didn't want to think about the Della who used to drink cheap beer and smoke menthol cigarettes. Della who let her get to second base the day they met and then wouldn't give it up for two months. Did that woman who made her nineteen-year-old head spin even exist anymore? Had she ever? Had the Sara in her head ever been the Sara of flesh and bone? Why hadn't she invited her mother to LA the last time they spoke?

The mental roller coaster rushing through her head made her motion sick. She focused on breathing to keep herself from throwing up until she could get home and sit in her dark bedroom and try to make the thoughts stop long enough to take a deep breath.

When they got to the library, Sara said, "You're going to be okay, Birdie."

It wasn't a question and Robin waved over her shoulder instead of answering. She wanted to thank Sara for the hot dogs and the walk. For talking to her about anything other than her mom. Wanted to apologize for not asking her about her own life. Assure her they'd talk again and she would be a better friend. Or at least a better whatever people who were inseparable as children became when they were no longer children and had separated. She didn't say any of it. She was afraid of what would happen if she opened her mouth. So she kept walking without saying anything.

CHAPTER NINE

Robin waved at three people before she came to the turnoff to her mother's house. Fortunately, they were all on the other side of the street and she was able to hurry on before they could cross and try talking to her. Unfortunately, she would have to cross to get back to the house. No one else was in sight, but small towns were tricky. One moment you were alone, the next moment you were surrounded.

Robin didn't want to be surrounded. She didn't want to talk. She just wanted to be still. There wasn't any stillness to be had at the house, though. Della would be there and she would want to know how Robin was doing. People would be dropping in to console them. Larry would wander over for a chat. The reverend would be stopping by. The very thought of all those people, all that staring and talking, made Robin break out into a panicked sweat.

So she didn't turn down the little road by the Methodist church. She didn't even turn down the next one that could lead her back to the house if she took a detour through the unfenced backyard of a few older residents. She kept walking down Route 522. Toward the Baptist church and old Sperryville Cemetery on the hill leading out of town.

If she'd been driving, she couldn't guarantee she'd stop there, she might drive off into rural Virginia and not come back. But she was on foot, so she pried open the rusted cemetery gate as carefully as she could and closed it behind her again. When she was younger, she made this trip often. Not as often as the trip down to the creek with Sara, but often enough that it should've been familiar. Only it wasn't familiar. It felt wrong, utterly wrong somehow that she was here. That she was weaving between the headstones on her way up and over the hill.

Her mother purchased a plot, Jacob Peters said. Was it here? It would have to be, Robin supposed. Would she come across them digging the hole today? The thought made her stop cold. She held one foot in front of her, one behind on the gentle grade of the hill. She couldn't decide if she wanted to go forward or back. Would it be better to suffocate from a crowd of well-wishers or watch a pair of old men dig a hole to shove her mother into? Indecision kept her frozen. She shifted her weight a handful of times, sometimes one way, sometimes the other, but never got far enough in the decision to take a single step.

In the end, silence won out. The fact that the cemetery itself was silent. If they had been digging, Robin would hear it. The whisper of metal blades cutting through rocky soil. The hiss of dirt flying through the air and piling up in an uneven mound. The sounds of a fresh grave. She heard nothing, so she continued. She stopped looking at the headstones, stopped seeking out familiar names etched into marble.

After the cemetery was a field. It was neatly trimmed, the grass cut low. It must belong to the cemetery or one church or another. This was prime agricultural land—if a farmer owned it, the crops would be high this late in June. Robin was happy for the low grass. She was able to run without fear of snakes or hidden gopher holes. She let loose, her legs flailing behind her in an inelegant, spontaneous sprint.

The trip to the tree line wasn't long, but Robin still sucked hard at the warm air around her. Fitness was not her thing. That was Della. Robin just didn't seem to gain weight no matter what she did. Her manager told her that lifting a few weights would lift her album sales, but she wasn't the type. Just the thought of walking back to the house exhausted her.

Two years into high school, Robin and Sara had had a falling out. It was brief and neither of them discussed it, mainly because Robin couldn't tell Sara the reason was her broken heart. Of course, after so many years of being so close, Robin found herself with few other friends. If she wasn't with Sara, she'd just spend her afternoons alone.

She'd find someplace outside, where the wind could rush through her hair and the smell of grass could lift her spirits. Someplace that wasn't the little creek in the woods. Someplace that was just hers. One day, she got off the bus from school and started walking. She walked away from her house. Away from Sara's house. In the exact opposite direction of the creek. She went through the gates of the cemetery and up over this hill. She walked to the tree line and beyond until she found that perfect spot.

A clearing in the woods right before the land sloped up into a series of foothills. A local winery had owned all these woods. Cheap land they were keeping in anticipation of a future of endless acres of grapes. At the time, however, the little clearing was nothing more than a natural break in the trees, just a patch of undisturbed underbrush, a dozen steps across at its widest spot. A tabletop of rock sat off to one side like a miniature plateau. She had lain on the rock and watched the clouds blow by.

That first trip led to another a few days later when the pressure of her teenage troubles became too much again. Then again the next day. She was a regular visitor over the next year or so. Sara was into her own thing and no one, including Robin, knew what. Even when their connection was reformed again in senior year, Robin never told Sara about this place. She never told Sara about a lot of things. This place was just hers and she had wanted to keep it that way.

The clearing looked the same as it had then, only smaller. Robin was able to direct her footsteps in the right direction without thinking. She probably could do the same with the creek and the tree, but she wasn't particularly interested in finding out. That place was her childhood. This place was where she started to grow up.

She sat on the stone, barely able to pull both knees onto the surface, and looked around at the clear sky and green trees. When she first started coming here, she wrote terrible love poetry in scores of composition books on this rock. Over time, she progressed to terrible love songs. When she started bringing her guitar, she started producing nearly decent songs.

Robin got to her feet, standing on the stone and looking around. This was where it all clicked for her. Where her future really began. On this rock. This rock that became her stage. She played her first concert here to an audience of oak trees. She pretended the stone was her stage and all those tall trunks were screaming fans. They waved in time with her music, not the wind. The feeling was like nothing she ever knew before. It was addictive. She'd been chasing it ever since.

The acoustics of the place were incredible. She found that out, not only through her practice concerts, but also when she brought Emily Brock up here one day in spring of senior year. She and Sara had finally spoken again for the first time in a year, but then she had bolted again to wherever. In Sara's absence, Robin finally noticed that Emily, a charmingly awkward acquaintance from back in the days when Robin tried playing softball for all of a few weeks, smiled a little too widely and a little too long whenever they ran into each other in town. Then Robin noticed how often they started running into each other. It didn't take much imagination to figure out that Emily arranged most of these chance meetings.

She kissed Emily on the swings in the elementary school playground one night when their group of seniors was running through the streets making trouble. Emily didn't say anything, but she didn't stop Robin either. They hung out a few times, neither of them calling them dates. One day, Robin led Emily up here, sat her down on the rock and played her a song she'd just written.

The song wasn't great. It needed a lot of work on timing and chords needed tweaking. Years later it would find its way onto Robin's first album, but what she played that afternoon was only a shadow of the final track. Either Emily wasn't a music lover or the song was okay, because the minute Robin stopped playing and looked at her, Emily grabbed her by the shirt and pulled her down on the rock. It was typical teenage sex, with all the fits and starts one would expect from a pair of girls who didn't know their own bodies that well, but it was something. Something with a girl who wanted her.

Emily became extremely clingy and then very jealous when Robin and Sara became good friends again. There were tears and more than a few fights, some of them in this very clearing, and then it was over. In the end, neither of them minded much. Emily was going to Richmond for college in a few months and Robin was going anywhere that wasn't Sperryville. They didn't part as friends, per se, but they kept it together enough to maintain the secret of their relationship.

Emily had sent Robin a letter a few months back. Robin had just been nominated for her Grammys and her name was in the news. Emily wanted to congratulate Robin and thank her for the part Robin played in her own journey. She was living in Spain now with a chef wife and a baby on the way. She wasn't sure she'd even have come out if it weren't for Robin.

It was nice to know she'd been remembered well by any of her exes. Robin dated a few women when she got to California, and slept with a few more. If a lesbian with a guitar could get a closeted high schooler in rural Virginia, she could score epically at USC. Of course, she met Della after a year there and was officially off the market. It wasn't that she was disappointed. Della was sexy as hell and different from any woman she'd ever met, before or after. At nineteen, she knew she found the one.

The thing was, Robin wasn't nineteen anymore, and Della wasn't twenty-one. Everything was just different now. When they first met, she and Della could barely stand a few hours at a time apart. Now they sometimes forgot the other was in the room. Or worse, wished she weren't. It wasn't that their love was gone, it was just tamer. Less intense. Boring.

Robin stood and dusted off the seat of her jeans. The light was changing. The angles were getting sharper. If she didn't leave now, it would be dark before she made it to the front door. She learned the timing of that trip years ago to avoid the wrath of her mother. The thought even flashed briefly that she didn't want to be late or her mom would yell.

To stop the tears Robin set her feet into motion. She didn't want to cry. Didn't want to feel. It wasn't the time. She had to hold it together now. One day soon, when she was back in California and didn't have to worry about upsetting Larry, she would let it all come out. Not today.

She followed the slowly setting sun back toward her mother's house and tried to stop thinking of it as her mother's house.

CHAPTER TEN

When Robin turned down the driveway the sun was setting huge and orange behind the house. It cut into her vision and stung her eyes but she welcomed it. It reminded her of stage lights hung at that perfect angle to block her view of the audience. The stadiums she'd been playing more and more frequently for the last year and a half were lit differently, but the concert halls and theaters she was used to were perfect. Especially the ones with footlights. Then the bright white spotlight shone on her from two angles and, if it weren't for the occasional roar of delight, she could pretend she was all alone playing her music.

Robin had always loved to play. Loved to write music. Loved to sing. She just didn't love those huge crowds. She missed the days when she had a stool and a guitar in a coffee shop. Or even the bars and festivals where she and one or two guys would play for a few dozen people. She craved the intimacy of the smaller venues. She could feel the music there. Live inside it. It felt like something alive then. Something beautiful. It was art. Now she just shouted into a crowd. The crowd loved it, but she hated it. So she let the lights blind her while she pretended she was happy.

Close to the house, she could see Larry on the porch, his bum leg stretched out in front of his straight-backed wooden chair. Della was in her mom's rocking chair again. She had her knees pulled up to her chest and she was hugging them to her, her bare toes curled around the seat. She rocked slowly, her mouth moving nonstop, and there was a very familiar look on her face. Irritation bubbled in Robin's chest. She knew that look so well. It was the look Della had every time they "needed to talk." Every time Robin had too long a conversation with a doe-eyed fan backstage. Every time she smiled too much during an interview with a female reporter. Every time she spent too much time in her studio. The fights were getting repetitive. The insecurities annoying.

What really made Robin's blood boil was the fact that Della was now pushing it all onto Larry. He just lost the love of his life and Della burdens him with her baggage. It was selfish. Wearing a sad smile she watched Robin approach, and Robin forced herself not to scowl. Larry didn't need to be dragged into their drama. She gave Della a warning look, and she stopped speaking abruptly. Larry shifted his gaze to Robin as she slowed to a stop at the bottom of the steps.

"Hey there, Bird. Been havin' a nice chat with your wife here." He reached out and patted Della's knee. The look of gratitude she gave him served to melt Robin's heart just a degree. "You have a nice walk?"

"Yeah."

"Nancy said you were walkin' with Sara Carson."

She avoided Della's eye. She hadn't said where she was going or with whom. "She stopped by and said she wanted to catch up."

"She's calmed down a fair bit from when ya'll used to spend time. Sowed her wild oats young just like her daddy. He went and settled down though. Not sure she's the type."

Robin started up the stairs, taking them one at a time. "We didn't 'spend time,' Larry. We were just friends."

"Ya'll were thick as thieves from the cradle." He turned to smile at Della. "Did you know Birdie here used to spend every waking moment runnin' all over town with Sara Carson? Got into so much trouble. Not a week'd go by without her momma and me gettin' a visit from the principal or the priest."

He laughed his high-pitched giggle that no one could resist. Della's smile almost made Robin forget her annoyance.

"She always said she was a terror growing up but I can't get any stories out of her. She mentioned one about the front window of an ice cream shop? I never got the full story though."

"Oh, that's a good one."

"Don't get him started, Dell, he won't stop."

He ignored her, cool as could be, and rocked faster with delight at the chance to gossip.

"Birdie here and Sara wanted a dipped cone. You know those ones with the vanilla ice cream dipped in chocolate so it makes a shell? But her momma was busy with her roses. Ya'll were, what, nine? Ten?"

"I don't know. Ten probably."

"So Birdie gets all upset and Sara drags her off when we aren't watchin'. They run through town, hollerin' and jumpin' all around. They get up to the place with the ice cream. Sperryville Custard and Fudge. And Sara shouts about how it ain't fair that they can't have ice cream on account of Birdie's mom being too busy. She's as riled up as a June bug by then. Ends up putting a rock through the front window. Old Jack Harper ran the place and he came outside just a yellin'."

"You two threw a rock through the window?"

"It was an accident."

"An accident my left foot. Sara was spoiled and vindictive. Maybe things went farther than she intended, but that don't make it an accident."

"Her father'd just died. She acted out a lot. It wasn't her fault."

"You always did give her more slack'n anyone else. Anyway, Birdie gets to apologizin' and cryin' and makin' a fuss. Jack wasn't the best with children. Specially girls. So Sara goes up to him and grabs his hand and tells about how Birdie didn't mean to break the window she just wanted a dipped cone and got carried away. Birdie stands all tall and tells him she's sorry about breakin' the window and she'll pay for it outta her allowance each week."

"But you didn't break the window."

Larry shifted in his chair, dragging his leg to the side with a grimace. "Damn arthritis. Gets worse every year. No, she didn't, but Birdie here was always apologizin' for things Sara done."

Robin shrugged. "Her mom grounded her if she got in trouble. She'd have to sit in the library after school instead of hanging out with me."

"So you took her punishment." Della rocked back in the chair and looked at the ceiling of the porch. "How noble of you."

If Larry hadn't been there, Robin would have bit back with something sarcastic. Since he was there, all she could do was scowl. Apparently, he didn't notice the tension, because he continued, "Well, it worked out for her that time. Jack said she was raised right for tellin' the truth and he ended up givin' 'em both dipped cones on the house."

Robin smiled at the memory. She and Sara sat on the half-wall outside the shop and licked their cones until long teardrops of melted chocolate and sticky vanilla poured down their fists. They were going to keep it a secret from Robin's mom, but Mr. Harper told her anyway. Still, it was one of the best ice cream cones she'd ever eaten.

"That maybe wasn't the best lesson for me to learn."

Larry laughed his hyena cackle again and said, "No, Bird, it sure wasn't."

"Whatever happened to Mr. Harper?"

"Died of a heart attack ten years ago."

Silence ballooned between the three of them. Funny how mentioning her mother hadn't brought the ghost onto the porch with them, but mentioning someone else long dead had. Larry's eyes shined in the dark. Robin's throat burned. Della hugged her knees closer even though the night was warm.

Just when the weight of it became unbearable and Robin thought she might scream, Della released her legs and slid them to the ground. She stood in a fluid motion and said, "It's getting late. Are you hungry? You missed a visitor earlier, Robbie. Mr. Harrison. He brought a lasagna. Larry, why don't you join us for dinner?"

"That's kind of you, dear. I think I will."

She touched his shoulder as she went to the door. "You two visit. I'll call you when it's ready."

She slipped inside and left them alone together with their thoughts. Robin didn't feel hungry at all. Her exhaustion had wiped all the hunger from her body.

Larry pulled a thick envelope from his back pocket. He looked at it for a long moment, testing the weight in his hands before he spoke, "Ernie Harrison didn't just come to deliver his wife's lasagna. Brought this too." He slapped the envelope against his open palm. "Your momma's will."

If Larry had informed her he was holding a live grenade it could not have been more unsettling to Robin than this bland announcement, but she could see that it was a forced blandness. Larry stared at the boards of the porch like they were the most important thing in the world at the moment, and Robin knew she had to work as hard as he was to accept the situation. For the first time she saw the strain it put on him to maintain his composure.

"Have you read it?"

Larry nodded.

"What does it say?"

"Explained her wishes with the funeral, but we already knew about that. Made me the executor of her estate. Don't know what that means precisely, but Ernie said he'd help me out. It won't be tough 'cause she was real clear what she wanted. Everything goes to you, Birdie. The house. That fancy car you bought her. What money she had. All of it."

Robin's face was numb. "No."

"Won't be much to worry about with the house. It's in good shape, I made sure of that. And I'm happy to keep an eye on it when you and Della ain't here."

"No."

"Car's a different story. Your momma took good care of it, but no use keepin' it 'round. I can find someone what comes through the garage'll give you a fair price for it."

"Larry, no."

He looked over at her finally, his bushy eyebrows knitted together. "What?"

"You should have the house. And the money. All of it."

"Got my own place, Birdie."

"Which is too small and you rent it." She waved an arm a little too enthusiastically over her shoulder. "This place is paid for and it's only standing because of the work you've put into it."

"I like my place, and the rent's low."

Robin slammed her fist into her knee. "Damn it Larry, that's not...You shouldn't." She walked to the railing, gripping it so hard in her anger that a spike of pain shot through her palms where the skin pinched. "I can't believe she did this to you."

"Birdie..."

"It's not right."

"It's what she wanted."

She cut him off as she turned. "So that's it? She gives you nothing? After everything you gave her! It's wrong. It's cruel. It isn't right and I won't take it."

Larry let out a long breath. He looked at her as she glared at him. She thought she might cry finally, not out of sadness but out of anger, and feeling the tears only made her madder. And still Larry sat. When he finally spoke, his voice was quiet. It reminded Robin of all the times he had disciplined her as a child. She'd never heard him raise his voice.

"Birdie, listen to me here, girl. The only thing I ever wanted from your momma was her love. I never wanted a house or money or anything else. Just her love. We shared that for the last twenty-eight years. She left that with me when she went on ahead. Left some with you too. The rest of it don't matter at all."

Crickets started their song in the tree line off to the side of the house. Robin looked toward the sound because she couldn't look at Larry anymore. He was still smiling that bittersweet grin he'd had the whole time she'd been home. The whole time she'd known him. When her mother accepted his help, but not his dates. When she let him in, but only so far. He loved her, but sometimes it felt like her mom didn't love him back quite as much. It hurt to see it. It felt like he was ripping her guts out slowly. He let the tears roll down his weathered face and kept that grin in place when she couldn't tell whether she was moving or even breathing.

The matched sconces over the door blazed into life and the screen door screeched lightly. Della was trying to push it open, but she was loaded down. Larry sprung out of his chair more nimbly than Robin thought him capable of and held the door for her.

"Thank you, Larry." She held the necks of two brown bottles in one hand and the necks of two guitars in the other. She handed the bottles to Larry. "I thought you two might want these."

"Legend Brown Ale." He twisted the tops off the two bottles. "How'd you know my favorite beer?"

Della held out one of the guitars to Robin. It was her favorite—a worn acoustic Gibson she'd named Caroline during her more whimsical youth. "It's Robbie's favorite too."

Robin pulled the guitar's rainbow strap over her shoulder. Her wedding ring thunked against the body with a pleasant, hollow musicality. She looked up at Della and felt her heart swell. Della's eyes were soft in the darkening evening. Her cheeks were so smooth and fresh. Robin wanted to reach out and cup them in her hands. Pull her into a kiss and forget the swirling madness of the last few days. Maybe even the last few months on the road.

Larry took a step forward and handed a beer to Robin. She kept her eyes on Della as the ice-cold ale slid down her throat. You couldn't get Legend in California. It was a local beer, bottled in Richmond and only sold in certain markets. Somehow Della always had it around, both in the house and on the tour bus. Robin didn't know how she managed it, but, every time she saw those brown bottles, it reminded her that there were little things Della did for her. Little things that were huge in moments like this.

Della handed the other guitar to Larry and headed back inside. He spun it with a whistle. "This is a fine instrument. Much nicer 'n the one you learned on."

Robin set her beer down on the railing and climbed up to sit next to it. When she was a little girl, Larry would sit in the straight-backed chair he was in now and play guitar for her and her mother late into the evening. She would sit on the deck and look up at him, her chin resting on her fists. There was always this light in her mother's eyes when he played. Robin was too young to recognize it as love. It had looked like happiness to her because it looked a lot like the way her mom looked at her. So Robin begged Larry to teach her to play.

He used an old guitar that had belonged to his father. He put it in her lap and she could barely reach over it, the body was so big. She couldn't quite put enough pressure on the strings to make the chords. Her fingertips were red and raw nearly every day after that, but she was able to ignore the pain when she thought of the look on her mother's face.

Larry was a patient teacher and a sly taskmaster. He taught her one song with very easy chords and then made her play it every day over and over again. She whined and complained. She was bored. She wanted to know every song he knew. When she refused to practice, he would play the song all night until it got into her blood. "Sweet Caroline" by Neil Diamond. The first song she learned. The first song she fell in love with.

When she mastered it, could play it straight through perfectly without having to think about the placement of her fingers, he taught her another. She mastered it and he taught her a new one. So on it went until she had learned every song he knew and more. His tastes were heavy to classic rock—Lynyrd Skynyrd, The Beatles, CCR, Eric Clapton, Joni Mitchell, Simon and Garfunkel—so that was what they played. It also became what Robin listened to the most, imagining herself on the porch, playing them for her mom. The thought of performing for a larger audience hadn't hit her yet—that would come later. She was content to be the cause of that happy light in her mother's eyes.

It wasn't until she heard the likes of Leonard Cohen, Janis Joplin and Bob Dylan that Robin realized the deep, whiskey timbre and slight rasp of her voice could be an asset rather than an embarrassment. The singer-songwriters who became a permanent influence on Robin first gave her the confidence to sing while she played. By the time she was in high school, she was the one playing on the porch at night. She was the one her mother turned that look on, but she was long past needing that. The guitar was in her blood. Music was her passion.

Robin found her place on the railing and took a swig of beer. Larry strummed his fingers along the strings. The smell of melting mozzarella filtered through the mesh of the screen door.

"That's a fine woman you got there, Bird."

The kindness of the last few minutes notwithstanding, these days when she thought of Della she saw reproachful looks, heard the lectures and the needling. Their marriage was good, but she couldn't pinpoint when it became so much work.

A dozen different responses were cycling through her head. Robin chose the simplest one. "Yeah."

The reply was obvious in its neutrality. Larry frowned, but left well enough alone. Larry was the sort to let people work out their own problems. It was one of Robin's favorite things about him. Instead of talking, he started to play. Robin listened for all of two notes before she recognized the song. She picked up the melody on the next bar. They played "Sweet Caroline" together as the last of the sun bled away and the moon took over the sky.

CHAPTER ELEVEN

Robin's mother had never been a clotheshorse. When her father was around and money was somehow tighter than it was later with only one paycheck coming in, she got by with five well-worn but meticulously maintained outfits. That was it, for years she had only five outfits and her work uniform. Money and her father's prickly temper kept her mother from buying anything new. When Larry came into their lives, he tried hard to spoil her. She wanted nothing to do with his lavish gifts. The closest they came to ever breaking up was about a year after they started dating.

He surprised her by picking her up from work one day and driving her an hour away to the closest mall. Robin had been in the backseat, in on the secret. She and Larry were both grinning ear to ear when he told her mother that he wasn't taking her home until he bought her every piece of clothing that fit her in every single store in that mall. She told Robin to stay in the car and took Larry a foot away, slamming the car door behind her. Robin couldn't hear what they said, but her mother's voice was as loud as she'd ever heard it even muffled by the glass and steel. The argument didn't last long. Arguments with her mother rarely did. They both looked close to tears when they got back in and drove away without stepping foot inside a single store. Robin knew to leave well enough alone, even though Larry promised to buy her one of those buttery pretzels they sold in the food court and she had really wanted it.

As the years passed, her mother's wardrobe grew slowly and she was able to fill the generous walk-in closet tucked away in the corner of the master bedroom. Nothing in there was lavish, apart from the bright floral empire waist dress Robin had bought her for her wedding to Della. It was the only thing in the closet that looked like it had rarely been worn. Everything else was just like those five outfits from her childhood, worn but still in good shape.

The clothes were now in piles on the queen-sized bed. A pile for charity. A pile for trash. A pile for Della to help her decide on. A pile for Larry to look through in case he wanted a keepsake. A pile she couldn't bring herself to throw away just yet. A pile she couldn't look at without tears.

The too-loud ring of the doorbell cut through the air. The bedroom door was half-closed, but she could still hear Della's footsteps on the hardwood floor and the creak of the screen door. People had been stopping by since dawn. The news that Robin was in town had spread quickly, but most of the town had kept a respectful distance. Now it was the day before the funeral and no one with a reasonable excuse for dropping by could resist the chance to see her. Of course, in a town as small as Sperryville, everyone had a reasonable excuse. They all knew her mother and their grief was genuine even if their motivation was not. Robin tried not to let it bother her.

After a few hours of long stares and wide smiles mixed with nonstop stories of her mother, Della suggested Robin go upstairs and start sorting through her mom's belongings. It hadn't occurred to Robin, but she jumped at the opportunity. Anything to get away from the crowds. They probably meant well, but Robin couldn't tell if they were here for her mother or to get a glimpse of a celebrity.

Hiding up here and leaving Della to deal with the throng felt wrong, but she couldn't bring herself to go back down. It was barely noon and Robin wanted the day to be over. Except this day being over meant that tomorrow would arrive, and if she couldn't handle the crowds of mourners one or two at a time, she would never be able to make it through the funeral. Each time she heard Della introduce herself to another old friend of the family her throat closed a little tighter. Every time they cooed their soft-voiced condolences the world spun just a little.

Time had been moving so strangely ever since she crossed the town line. It was ticking by too slowly one moment, nothing occupying her thoughts, nothing to do to stop the pain pouring in to fill the wide chasm of her mother's death. Other times it moved too quickly, everything happening at once, rushing over her until she felt she was drowning. No matter which time she was in, she wanted to be in the other. Mostly, she just wanted to scream for it all to stop and let her breathe. Fly back to LA and get this all behind her. Or fly back in time and never answer Larry's phone call.

With a sigh, Robin headed back into the closet. She ripped the next shirt from its hanger and took it out to the bedroom where light was better. The room was at the far end of the house and boasted tall, wide windows on two walls. She took a detour to look through the sheer curtains at the driveway. There was a blue and white pickup truck with a rusted bumper parked beside the two rental cars. It looked vaguely familiar. Robin thought it might belong to one of the good ol' boys who worked at the factory with her mom. Worked at the factory where her mom *used* to work, she corrected herself. Her mom didn't work anywhere now. Her mom was gone.

Robin turned away from the thought. The muffled chatter of final goodbyes and the click of the front door closing filtered upstairs as Robin walked over to the bed and looked at the shirt in her hand. It wasn't a shirt at all. It was a sweater with a thick cable knit and a wide neck. The blue was a rich, royal blue. It was nearly the same shade as her mother's eyes. When it was new, it was exactly the same shade. That was many years ago. The year that Robin had turned seventeen. It was a very cold fall that year. It had snowed in November. Her mom bought the sweater at a department store in Charlottesville because Robin said it looked pretty on her.

They were in Charlottesville for the regional choral solo competition. Robin had learned "Sounds of Silence." She stood alone on stage with a mic stand and her acoustic guitar. The haunting stillness of the song worked with her husky voice and her quiet aesthetic.

Her performance was exquisite. She felt every word, every note. They came straight from her soul, and she won. She knew representatives from a dozen colleges were in the audience and she thought she might have earned a scholarship. She earned ten.

They went to what was for them a fancy dinner at Ruby Tuesday to celebrate. Then they went to the mall on an impulse and her mom had picked out the sweater. She dragged Robin into the changing room, put it on and twirled in it. She was standing there in the changing room, smiling ear to ear in that blue sweater and Robin had a moment of insanity.

"Mom, I'm gay."

"What?"

The smile slid from her mother's face and Robin's stomach dropped.

"I'm gay."

"Don't joke about that, Birdie."

"I'm not joking, Mom."

"You're confused because of Sara and that girl. You don't know what you're feeling."

One day that August, Sara showed up on Main Street holding hands with a girl who had blue hair and a lip piercing. Robin was walking home from a singing lesson and nearly ran into them making out in the middle of the sidewalk. The blue-haired girl's hand was under the waistband of Sara's jean shorts at the small of her back and her tongue was so far down Sara's throat anyone else would have gagged. Sara had turned and waved at Robin before going back to her make-out session. She hadn't said a word, just waved and started kissing the girl. Kissing a girl that wasn't Robin. Robin had run home and cried for three days. In that moment she realized both that she was gay and head-over-heels in love with her best friend.

It was too late, of course, but at least she knew now. Unfortunately for Sara, the rest of the town knew too. They were upset, but for a different reason. It started with whispers and it probably would have stayed that way if that had been the only display. Sara wasn't discreet, however, and she spent the rest of the summer making out with and being groped by the blue-haired girl. With each very public display the whispers got a little louder. Each time Sara heard them she responded with an even more graphic display. When the two were spotted practically humping in front of the library the explosion came. The town turned against her in a very ugly way, her mother berated her publicly and the blue-haired girl was never seen in town again. Sara showed up at Robin's house one night sobbing.

It was the first time they'd spoken since the girl had shown up. Sara apparently hadn't noticed, but Robin had. She had found her clearing in the woods by then, but Sara never asked her where she'd been when she wasn't around. She was too busy being heartbroken and angry. Robin's pleasure over her best friend's loss surprised her, but it also confirmed her suspicions about her own sexuality. Now she couldn't keep it to herself anymore.

"I know exactly what I'm feeling. I'm attracted to girls."

"No, you're attracted to Sara." Her mom took a deep breath and squeezed her hands together until her knuckles were white. "The two of you are very close and you have been for a long time. It's perfectly natural at your age to think that what you're feeling is real, but it isn't. I think you need to make some other friends and then you'll see the two of you are just too close."

A ringing anger buzzed in Robin's ears. Apparently her mother hadn't noticed the distance between the two friends either. Or noticed how devastated Robin had been since Sara got a girlfriend. Did her mother have any idea what love looked like?

"Not real?"

"When you meet the right boy, you'll see."

"The right boy can't change who I am, Mom. I'm gay."

"Stop saying that!" Her voice echoed in the tiny space of the changing room. She took a breath, and when she spoke again it was in a rapid, dangerous whisper. "You need to be very careful, Birdie. It's very difficult to come back from something like this. People will remember all the disgusting details. When you grow out of this phase, you'll be sorry."

Now it was Robin's turn to shout. "It's not a phase! I'm not going to come back from anything!"

"Keep your voice down, we're in public."

Anger boiled inside Robin, threatening to consume her. "I'm not a child anymore…"

"Yes, you are."

Robin's fist slammed into the changing room door. The cheap wood cracked around the top hinge. Her mother's eyes flashed with fear and then turned to ice. She gasped and it ended in a strangled squeak like a mouse being stepped on.

"Don't you dare start…"

Robin didn't wait around to hear the rest of her words. She stormed out of the cubicle and out of the store. She marched through the emptying corridors past the last few shoppers and every step made her anger flare more. It tried, but didn't quite manage to burn away her shame and her hurt.

She found her way to the parking lot and their car. She leaned against the passenger's door, convincing herself that she did not feel the cold, and stared at the main entrance until her mom walked out into the night. It took her a long time to appear. A long time for those words she said to echo in Robin's mind like a skipping record. She hadn't expected her mother to throw her a coming out party, but she also hadn't expected that. Hadn't expected denials, insults, and rejection. The curl of her mother's lip when she spat out "disgusting details." She turned her back to her mother until her door unlocked with a hollow clunk.

Her mother opened the back door and placed her shopping bag neatly on the backseat. Robin saw the cuff of the blue sweater as she buckled her seat belt. She stared through the windshield. Her mother gripped the steering wheel lightly. They sat in silence for a long time. Eventually, her mother turned the key and the engine roared. The tape in the stereo started to play. It was a live version of "Sounds of Silence" that Robin had been listening to in preparation for the concert.

Take my arms that I might reach you.
But my words like silent raindrops fell

Her mother stabbed a finger into the eject button and the music ended in a screech of twisted tape. Silence filled the car again.

Her mother's voice was as cold as the night when she said, "I never expected you would disappoint me like this, Robin."

She threw the car into gear and pulled out of the parking lot. The view through the windshield blurred as tears spilled down Robin's cheeks. She cried silently all the way back to the hotel. The reflection of the royal blue sweater in the rearview mirror caught her peripheral vision the whole time.

I never expected you would disappoint me like this, Robin.

Those words echoed through Robin's mind regularly for the rest of her life. She heard them when she was sad, and they were more proof against her. She heard them when she was happy, and the sour taste of them killed her smile. She and her mother had never spoken about that night or those words again. Robin acted like her mother's admonition hadn't touched her. For her own part, she wouldn't pretend she was someone else, even for her mother's comfort. She couldn't. She had come out and she was staying out, no matter how much it disappointed her mother.

When Robin talked about girlfriends she could feel her mother's disapproval. She was guarded to the point of rudeness when she met Della, but eventually accepted her. More because she had to than anything else. The three thousand miles between them helped. She bent so far as to wish them happiness on their wedding day, and it almost felt sincere.

Her lukewarm acceptance was a constant source of anger for Robin. To remain close to her mom she had to ignore it, and she had to be close to her mom. She'd already lost one best friend, she couldn't lose another. Still, she felt that anger now, bubbling up the way it had all those years ago in that mall parking lot. It stung that her mother could calmly buy that sweater after crushing Robin's heart. Worse yet, each time her mother wore it, Robin silently relived that night. Relived the pain and the shame. Remembered the conditions of her mother's unconditional love.

Robin gripped the sweater in her hands. She wanted to tear it to pieces. Had always wanted to. She wanted to scream at her mother. Tell her how it felt to be a kid who wanted nothing more than her mother's love. A kid who was scared. A kid who was suffering in silence. She wanted to make her mother feel like she had felt that night. Betrayed. Abandoned. Alone. The words began to form in her mind. The words that would hurt most. That would describe her pain. That would make her mother feel the same pain. She prepared her speech, working to get the words just right.

She caught a glimpse of a framed picture on her mother's dresser. A portrait of her mother, Larry, and Robin right before she left for college. They took one every year in the little studio set up at the volunteer fire department as a fundraiser. Her mother looked happy. She smiled widely at the photographer. It was the last time they had a portrait all together. Robin had barely come home since. The anger in her evaporated. The speech blanked out in an instant.

She would never be able to give that speech. She would never be able to take another portrait with her mom. Never hug her again with those soft, fleshy arms and strong muscles. Because she was gone. Dead. "Gone to Jesus" as Nancy said. Gone beyond Robin's anger and hurt and love. She was standing in her mother's room, hating her on the day before her funeral. Hating her for something she could neither repair nor apologize for, even if she wanted to. Hating her when she should be loving her. Hating her and hating herself all the more for it.

"Robbie?"

Della's hand was on her shoulder, turning her around. It was the concern in her eyes that made Robin cry. She collapsed into her wife's arms, sobs rocking her body and stealing the breath from her. Tears poured out of her in waves, carrying all the emotions she had so carefully controlled over the last few days. They burst through her perfectly constructed walls and choked her. She was drowning in sadness. In fear. She tried to get out of the undertow of her feelings, tried to kick to the surface and breathe, but she couldn't. She couldn't escape it all. Not this time. She wailed as she cried, the sounds foreign and terrifying to her own ears.

"Oh, baby."

Della wrapped her in warm, strong arms. Her hand rubbed across Robin's back. Her mother used to do that, and the memory made her cry even more. The sweater was trapped between their bodies, the smell of her mom still strong in the fibers. For the first time since she was a little kid, frightened of how loud her dad's voice had become, Robin wanted to scream out for her mother.

Della rubbed a hand through Robin's hair. Robin's eyes were closed so hard against the tears that little stars popped up behind her lids. The feel of Della's touch on the warm skin of her neck was so cool. So soothing. Enough to make the breath fill her lungs again. Enough to make her feel her heart pick up its normal rhythm. Robin tossed the sweater away so she could hold Della close.

"Shh, love, it's okay. It's going to be okay."

Robin's voice was just a hair above a whisper. "I don't want her to be gone."

Della's voice wavered, "I know, baby. I know."

They cried together, holding each other so closely that their tears mixed on their cheeks. She buried her face in Della's neck, feeling the solid warmth of her. Robin wasn't alone.

With the sweater gone, all Robin could smell was Della's perfume. It was French, something they had found together in a boutique in LA while shopping for wedding clothes. Della had liked it, but they couldn't afford it at the time. Money was tight and they had other priorities, but Robin saw the longing in Della's eyes. They moved to the next store and the next, eventually finding everything they needed. It was a practical trip because it had to be.

Robin went back to that boutique the next day and spent every dime she had on the smallest bottle of the perfume. The tears in Della's eyes when she presented it as a wedding gift were worth the financial strain. The scent would always remind Robin of that day. Their wedding day. The day when Robin knew there was someone out there who loved her. Someone who thought she, Robin, was worthy of love.

She breathed deeply of it now, the crisp, clean fragrance taking all thought of her mother away. Need stirred unexpectedly in her. She held Della so closely she could feel her heartbeat. It thudded against her chest, so strong and sure. The steady rhythm of it seemed to engulf Robin. It made her feel her own pulse. Made her remember that, even though her mother was dead, Robin was very much alive. She pulled away just far enough to turn Della's face toward hers. Tears streamed down Della's cheeks and made her gray eyes glow silver. Her hair was down for the first time in as long as Robin could remember. It was shiny and silky smooth where it curled across one eyebrow. Robin reached out and ran her hand through the length of it. It slipped through her fingers like strands of gold. The greatest riches Robin possessed.

Touching her hair, staring into her eyes, so beautiful and so mysterious, Robin felt her world narrow. Della blinked slowly, her impossibly long eyelashes brushing against her pale cheek, then fluttering back into place. Robin stared until the rest of the world faded out at the edges. Until the trappings of reality went hazy and all she could see was the rose petal red of Della's lips. After an agonizing moment, they parted just a fraction. Enough to let out the breath she held. Robin's world parted along with them.

Robin pulled their mouths together. She was gentle, loving, but still it was a searching kiss. Their lips slid wetly against each other and Robin tasted the salt of their tears. She pressed forward and Della let out the smallest gasp of surprise as she parted her lips. The moment their tongues touched wiped the last sadness from Robin's mind. Her thoughts evaporated and her body took over. She slid her hands to the small of Della's back, pulling their bodies together as they kissed. She could feel Della's hesitation, but she deepened the kiss rather than letting her ask the questions hovering on her lips. Each second that passed, each brush of lips and tongue, each time their bodies fitted so closely together, convinced Robin that she needed this. Needed Della. Needed love right now.

She squeezed a hand between them and made quick work of the buttons on Della's blouse. The soft sounds changed to a groan of pleasure when Robin cupped her breast through the lace-trimmed satin. The feel of Della's skin made Robin wild. Her muscles loosening under Robin's touch was intoxicating. She moved forward, walking Della back to the bed, her hands never stopping their exploration. She pushed back the thin fabric of Della's shirt, exposing one perfectly rounded shoulder blade. Her lips released Della's and crawled across the perfect skin of her cheek to her neck. Della was very sensitive, particularly around the base of her neck. Robin kissed her exposed collarbone, nipping at it playfully as she pulled back the strap of Della's bra. Della's moan came from the depths of her chest.

"Robbie…" Della breathed her name as they moved together. "Are you sure you want…"

"I'm sure. Please, Dell. I need you."

Robin only caught a glimpse of her eyes as Della lay back on the bed, but it was enough to know they had darkened with need. Begging had always been the surest way to seduce her, and Robin was surprised to discover how sincere her desperation was in this moment. She needed Della. She needed to feel her body quake. She needed to hear her moan and shout. She needed to taste her sweat and breathe her air. She needed it so badly she feared her world would fly apart before they even touched.

Della lay diagonally on the bed, her hair spilling to the floor, where her head lay off the far side of the mattress. She was trying to right herself, turn to get the pillows beneath her, but Robin's impatience couldn't be contained. A growl curled from her lips and she dove on top of her wife. Robin swallowed Della's squeak of surprise with another deep kiss, pulling Della's legs up and around her waist. She rocked forward, pressing down into Della, who thrust up to meet her.

Della locked her ankles at the small of Robin's back, pulling her body close. All thought and hesitation evaporated, their need for each other perfectly matched. Della slid both hands under Robin's shirt, raking her nails down her back, leaving stinging lines on either side of Robin's spine. Robin's breath caught and her vision went instantaneously blank before returning, with laser thin focus, on Della beneath her.

The waistband of Della's slacks was too tight for Robin to leave it buttoned, but she was able to ignore the zipper. She plunged her hand beneath Della's underwear, and Della's hips rocked forward again to meet her. They fell into a familiar, frantic rhythm. A dance they'd performed innumerable times before, but one that never failed. They fit together like a hand in a glove. A perfect match. They had been from the very start.

Della whispered encouragement and love into her ear as Robin moved inside her. In between the endearments and the soft moans, Della nipped gently at her ear and neck. The feel of lips and teeth sent a shiver from Robin's scalp to the tips of her toes. Searing heat enveloped her. Arms wrapped around her back, holding her close. Even the bite of the zipper cutting into the top of her wrist made the moment calming and perfect. They moved together, their bodies knowing every curve of the other. The barrier of clothing between them was as nothing when they held each other like this.

In what felt like no time at all, Della's breath caught and held. Silence swelled and then burst in a flood of almost musical shouting. Robin joined in the screaming out of relief. Though she had not shared in the pleasure, something released in her that she had been holding onto tightly. She let it float away rather than examine it, determined to forget that it had ever existed. She buried her face in Della's neck as her cries softened and her body shivered. Her body relaxed by fractions, but Robin knew there would be more to come. She took a moment before starting again. Della liked to catch her breath a little before losing it again, and Robin could wait. The wait was half the fun.

Robin wanted to smell the perfume again, to let it carry her back to that day of pure bliss. She leaned in close to Della's neck and breathed in deep through her nose, but she was met with a wholly unexpected scent instead. The smell of her mother's perfume. She jerked away from Della. Her gut twisted and she tasted bile in her throat when she came to herself and looked around. They were on her mother's bed. Surrounded by the clothing she had been sorting. The smell of her mother soaked into every fiber of fabric and molecule of air. Now that Robin noticed it, it was the only thing she focused on. As though her mother was there in the room. In her own bedroom while her daughter had sex on top of her discarded possessions. Watching as Robin and Della made a mockery of the grief they should have been feeling.

"Robbie?"

Della was lying there on the bed, her shirt half off her shoulders and her pants open, among Robin's mother's clothing. She wanted to grab her by the wrist and haul her off the bed. The only thing stopping her was Della's hurt and confusion. Robin stood and backed away, straightening her shirt and looking anywhere but at the bed.

"What's wrong?"

Della sat on the edge of the bed, pulling her shirt tightly around her as though she were cold in the stuffy room.

Robin looked at the gaping maw of the closet and considered running into it and slamming the door. "Nothing...nothing's wrong."

She looked back at Della and saw the tears filling her eyes again. A new wave of nausea hit her, but this was of her own making. Rather than grief, it was guilt that made her feel so terrible. Guilt for the hurt in Della's eyes. She let her breath out in a sigh and walked slowly back to the bed. She fell to her knees at her wife's feet and pulled her into a bone-crushing hug. She could feel the pads of each one of Della's fingers gripping her shoulders and back.

"I'm sorry, Dell." She spoke into the waves of golden hair. "I'm sorry. I'm just so fucked up right now…"

"It's okay. I know. You've got a lot going on. I…I'm here for you. Okay?"

"Yeah." And then, because that didn't feel like enough, she whispered, "Thanks."

She pulled back and Della let her go. She stood and shoved her hands into her pockets, her shoulders coming up around her ears. Della looked at her with a watery smile, one or two of the tears falling down her cheeks. Robin bent to pick up the sweater. When she straightened, Della was buttoning the last button on her shirt. She stood and closed her pants. Robin blinked hard to cover the way her face contorted as the button slipped into place. There was a finality to that which left them both feeling out of place. They avoided looking at each other.

Della headed to the door, but paused with a hand on the frame. "Now everyone's gone, I was going to make some lunch." She turned to look at Robin. "Will you join me?"

Robin swallowed with difficulty. "Yeah…I'll, um, be down in a minute."

CHAPTER TWELVE

Considerably more than one minute passed before Robin headed downstairs. Confusion, guilt, and grief swirled around in her mind, holding her feet in place in the empty bedroom. She couldn't do anything more with the clothes today. All she could do was throw the blue sweater into the empty trash can by her mother's dresser. She felt better than she had any right to.

The doorbell rang just as Robin descended the top step, and she ducked back onto the second-floor landing, hoping to stay out of sight of the windows by the front door. Della hurried into the foyer and looked up.

"It's okay, I'll get rid of them as quick as I can."

Robin gave her a weak smile, and slipped back out of sight. How many times would Della save her life today? Robin slumped down the hall toward her own room just as the murmur of voices drifted upstairs from the front door. Robin sat on the bed and looked around.

The house had four bedrooms, and this was not the one Robin picked when they had first moved in. That was on the front of the house and had two of the windows she loved so much. It was a bright, sunny place to spend her childhood. When she morphed into a brooding, misunderstood teenager, she had moved to this room at the back and her mother changed Robin's old room into a sewing room. This new bedroom had only one small window, which Robin covered with dark curtains. The ceiling sloped with the pitch of the roof at the far end. She painted the walls a deep, navy blue that made her mother purse her lips but say nothing.

Robin's duffel bag slumped on the floor next to the closet, clothes spilling out and piled on top. Della had unpacked her own suitcase into the long, low dresser. She left plenty of space for Robin to put away her clothes, but she knew better than to expect she actually would. Robin had never been one to unpack. She spent too much time on the road to worry with dresser drawers or hangers. A wrinkled wardrobe never bothered her.

A set of neatly hung shelves on one wall still held the plastic trophies and faded ribbons Robin had won in choral competitions. Robin never wanted to keep them. Something about the cheesy statues on top of the hollow aluminum stands made her feel vaguely pathetic. When she was a kid, the ribbons hung from similar shelves in her mom's room, but they'd all been moved in here at some point in the last seventeen years. The shelves in her mom's room were gone, and she didn't know why.

The front door opened and shut, and soon Della's soft footsteps sounded on the stairs. Robin ran her fingers through her hair. She briefly considered pretending to take a nap, but it didn't seem right. Della appeared in the door, leaning her long arms against the frame. Robin looked up, but didn't move. Something passed in the air between them, something Robin couldn't identify exactly. It felt like pity, and the idea of it made her mad. It felt condescending.

Della made a small movement, or maybe a noise, Robin couldn't be sure which. Whatever it was, it changed the way Robin saw her. It wasn't mockery or pity, after all. There was a searching sort of test in her eyes. Like she was putting a toe into the bathtub to test the water. It occurred to Robin that Della was wondering if she wanted to continue what they'd begun in her mother's room, now that they were in a more appropriate location. The idea made her leap from the bed like it was electrified. Della started back, surprised by the sudden movement.

"Food ready?" Robin asked, shoving her fists into her back pockets and looking anywhere but at Della. "I'm hungry."

Della's lips twisted into a frown. She opened her mouth to say something, but closed it again without a word. She dropped her hand from the doorframe and turned to the stairs. "Sure. Come on down."

The last guests had brought a generic pasta salad full of mayonnaise and garden vegetables. Della made them sandwiches to go with it and big glasses of iced tea. She still wouldn't meet Robin's eye and her cheeks were pinker than normal. Robin wanted to start some sort of conversation to cover the increasingly uncomfortable silence, but she couldn't think of anything to say. There was nothing to discuss other than her mother or tomorrow's funeral, but that was not what either of them wanted to talk about. Instead, they sat on opposite sides of the large dining table, picking at their food.

The table, one of the few pieces of furniture left in the house by the grandparents Robin had never met, sat six. There were never, in all the times Robin sat at this table, six people around it. It was just the two of them at first, then Larry most nights. Sara came once or twice before she started painting the town red, but four was the limit. Her mother loved people and had tons of friends, but she wasn't much for entertaining. This was her sanctuary. Her special place to be with only Robin. They lived far enough outside town to warrant not having that many visitors, and Robin didn't mind. She wanted her mother to herself too.

Every night they would sit together at this table and eat what her mom cooked, no matter how much overtime she picked up. Her mom always sat at the head of the table, her back to the kitchen, and Robin always sat next to her on the left. It was a good-sized dining room, and their voices would echo strangely if they didn't sit right next to each other. That was just an excuse though. Robin, especially when she was young, wanted to be as close to her mom as she could get.

It was the same spot where Robin sat now. Della didn't sit at the head of the table. Maybe she could sense that Robin wouldn't like it. Or maybe she didn't think she had the right. She sat across from Robin instead. They would have been facing each other if the center of the table wasn't full to bursting with flowers. Some of them looked handpicked, wilted around the edges from spending the prime of their short lives still on the plant. Della must have picked them from the backyard. Most of the floral tributes had been accompanied by hams, lasagnas, and casseroles. Now they all served as good camouflage for the discomfort that sat between them.

"I ironed your pants for tomorrow," Della said to her plate. "Your jacket didn't wrinkle in the bag. If you tell me which shirt you want to wear I can iron that too."

"I haven't picked one yet."

"That's okay. When you do, let me know and I'll take care of it."

"Okay. Thanks."

"It might be too hot tomorrow for a three-piece suit. It looks good with just the vest if you'd rather."

"I'll decide tomorrow."

"Okay."

Robin took a bite of her sandwich and moved it around her mouth. She couldn't seem to make herself swallow. Della pushed a pasta shell with a pea wedged between its folds onto her fork, but didn't lift it. They didn't look at each other. After a while, Della took a bite. She started chewing noisily. The sound was somewhere between repulsive and infuriating. Robin was about to push herself up from the table when the doorbell rang.

Della jumped up, but the door opened before she could take a step. The shuffling drag of Larry's gait on the hardwood gave him away before he came into view. His shoulders slumped, making him look overly tired despite the early hour.

"Larry, come on in," Della said, moving around her chair to pull one out for him. "Can I get you a plate?"

"No, thanks Della. Sorry I barged in." He grinned lopsidedly. "Old habits."

"Don't be silly, you're welcome to come in any time." Della's smile was relieved, and Robin couldn't help but share in that relief. Anything to cut the strange tension between them. "How about a beer?"

"I'll have to pass on that too. Got a bit of drivin' to do just now."

"Everything okay, Larry?" Robin's stomach dropped, but then again, what more bad news could he possibly bring? "Shouldn't you be at work?"

"Should be. They sent me home on account of they think I need to get ready for tomorrow." He paled a shade and grabbed the cap off his head, scratching at his thick, graying dirty blond hair and plopped the hat back in place. "Thing is, ain't nothin' I can do to get ready for tomorrow and I don't really wanna sit around that empty house."

Della rubbed his shoulder and gave him a gentle smile. He seemed to take comfort in the gesture, but Robin thought it was just condescending. She grabbed her plate and moved toward the kitchen so she didn't have to watch.

"Still got your old rod and reel in the shed," Larry called after her. "Thought we'd see if you still know how to use it."

Robin turned and split into a wide grin. She hadn't been fishing with Larry in a long time, but every memory she had of sitting out on the banks of Jenkins's pond with him was wonderful. Those were the moments when Robin felt like she had a father.

"I'd love to."

"You don't mind, do ya Della? You're welcome to come of course, just didn't think it was exactly up your alley."

Della gave him one last rub on the shoulder, then walked around the table to take the plate out of Robin's hands. "Oh no, it's fine, Larry. You two go and have fun. I've got to make sure the house is ready for tomorrow."

"Are people coming here?" Robin looked from Della to Larry, aware of how childish the question sounded. "Why've they been coming all day today if they're coming tomorrow?"

"It's what we do when someone passes," Larry explained as Della disappeared into the kitchen with their plates. "People like to spend time."

Robin focused on Della banging around in the kitchen. She didn't want people here. She didn't want to spend time. She wanted the whole thing to be over and try to get back to her life. The longer she spent here, the more she had to think about a world without her mom in it, the harder it was for her to imagine what her new normal life would look like.

"I didn't realize."

"It's okay, Robbie." Della came back into the dining room, an old, dingy cooler in her hand. "I'll have everything ready. You two go and have fun."

She held the cooler out to Larry, who took it and peeked under the lid.

"What's this now?"

"I thought you might want those once you got to your fishing hole." She said with a grin. "And there's some snacks in there too."

Robin heard the familiar clink of glass beer bottles rattling as Larry closed the cooler again. "You sure can read this old man's mind. Ready to go, Bird?"

"Sure thing."

She pecked Della on the cheek and took the cooler from Larry, following him to his pickup, where the rods were already stowed next to a small tackle box and a pair of battered folding lawn chairs. Della waved them away from the top of the porch the same way her mother had when they went out. Robin watched her in the side mirror until the gravel dust and cornstalks hid her from view.

The sun was low in the sky when they got to the pond, and they had to trudge through some pretty tall grass. For years there was a dirt path leading right up to their favorite spot and Larry would park right at the end of it. He would crank up the radio so that they could hear it down at the bank of the pond and tune it to the local sports station. Robin loved listening to the broadcast of the Richmond Braves' baseball games in the summer. They were the AAA team, but they were pretty good in those days. While they fished, the hiss of AM radio static and the muffled crack of wooden bats mixed with the crickets and the frogs. Those were some truly wonderful summer nights.

While Robin was in middle school, a huge pine tree fell across the dirt track. Mr. Jenkins didn't bother to clear it out, so they had to park farther away. Too far for the car radio to reach their ears. Then Robin started high school and didn't have as much time to fish. Her mom told her in one of her weekly phone calls a few years back that the Braves left Richmond for somewhere in Georgia.

Still, the familiar squeal of rusted hinges when she unfolded the chair and the rustle of weathered vinyl as she sat down was the same. The rod in her hands as she tested the line release was familiar too. Her fingers remembered how to knot the line around the eye of the hook, though she had to peek over at Larry to figure out the proper height to secure her bobber.

He cracked open a beer and handed it to her before he cast out his line and leaned back into his chair with a contented sigh. She sipped it and sent her own hook soaring into the air. The arc she got wasn't quite as clean as his, and it landed a fair ways short of the ideal distance, but it wasn't bad considering. They fished for a while in silence, the sky blazing in streaks of red and orange.

"You had your first beer out here with me," Larry said, tipping his bottle up and keeping his eyes on his bobber. "If'n it really was your first beer."

"It was."

Robin giggled at the memory. She was fifteen, maybe sixteen. Some kids from school had been caught by the sheriff drinking beer and tossing the cans into the river just outside of town. They were close to the fire station and started making a racket when the alcohol went to their heads. When the sheriff rolled up on them, a few of the boys hopped into a car and took off, forgetting to turn on their lights and promptly smacking into the support post of a billboard. They made it all of a hundred yards, so they weren't going fast, but the town was in an uproar that the latest batch of Sperryville teenagers thought it was okay to drink and drive.

Robin didn't know the kids. Most of them were older than her and they were the rednecks she didn't hang out with, but her mother was just as spooked as everyone else. She fretted, but Larry was the one to take action. He brought Robin down here with his cooler and their rods as always, only that time he handed her a beer. She didn't know how to react at first, but in the same way she was always desperate to be perfect in her mother's eyes, Robin was desperate to be cool in Larry's eyes.

She took a long sip the way she'd seen him do, and promptly gagged. It was awful stuff. Bitter and foamy and smelling like the compost heap in the corner of the backyard. To his credit, Larry managed not to laugh his head off. She sipped the beer for the rest of the night, only managing to get through half of it, while he told her the story of his leg.

Larry had always been a car guy. He loved them. Loved engines. He could take them apart and put them back together in his sleep with one hand tied behind his back. He'd started work at the shop outside of town right out of high school and had a reputation for being polite and honest to everyone who came in. He was also just a kid and his other reputation was as a party boy. He drank whiskey the way other guys drank beer, and drank beer the way other guys drank water. Unlike Robin's father, Larry was a happy drunk. The life of the party and a perfect gentleman. He was the guy women at the bar went to for help when the other guys wouldn't take no for an answer.

He was also the guy who spun donuts in the parking lot until the tires fell off the car and drove his truck through muddy fields. He was lucky, he told Robin, that his accident happened in one of those fields rather than on the road. If he'd killed some innocent family he would never be able to live with himself. Instead, he hit a blind ditch, flew through the open window of his rolling pickup and spent six months learning to walk again. One leg was now a few inches shorter than the other, it ached like fury every time it rained and he set off metal detectors. As far as "don't be an idiot about alcohol" stories went, it was particularly effective.

"Your momma nearly scalped me when she found out I gave that to ya." He gave his rod a swift jerk as the bobber disappeared under the surface of the pond and it bent under the weight of his catch. "Didn't speak to me for near a week."

"Really? She never said she was mad."

"Well, she weren't mad at you, was she? All sorted itself out when you said beer was nasty."

Robin shook her head. "She told me she'd keep that a secret between us."

Larry's teeth glinted in the sunset. "Yeah, I know, but I wouldn't let her. Weren't like her to give up on a fight so easy. I had to know why."

Larry reeled in his catch, a decent-sized crappie that flopped around on the grass before he was able to get it up to his chair. He was careful about extracting the hook from its cheek and tossed it back into the pond with a loud, smacking splash. The fish had gotten the worm, so he propped the pole against the arm of his chair and reached for the container of nightcrawlers.

"She was right relieved. Your momma worried about you somethin' terrible day and night."

Robin watched Larry tear a piece of worm off and maneuver it onto the hook. The worm squirmed around between his thumb and forefinger, looking for all the world like it could see the hook coming and trying to get out of the way. Larry threaded the hook through the worm with a practiced skill, but it still wiggled, hanging there in midair. He cast out again and Robin saw that there were tears on his cheeks.

"She loved you somethin' fierce, Birdie."

Robin stared at her bobber. She didn't want to cry. Not again. It felt awful earlier, being soaked in grief. She had Della to catch her then, to hold her and make her whole again with the gift of her love, even if it had ended badly. Della wasn't here now, and Larry's fatherly affection could not match the comfort of a wife.

She swallowed hard, trying to keep her voice steady. "She loved you too, Larry. More than anything. Like a fairytale."

He laughed—a charming, wet laugh. "Sure was that. A fairytale. She was…Hell, Birdie…"

Tears flowed down his face and Robin reeled in her line for something, anything to do rather than let that emotion touch her. She must have had a bite at some point, because her worm was gone. She hadn't seen the bobber dip or felt a pull on the line, but then she was learning this all over again. She plucked her own worm from the wet soil, slipping it onto her hook with much less grace than Larry.

She let the worm dangle there in front of her in the fading light. It wriggled and danced on the hook, stuck in place but still trying to fight its way free. Robin wondered what it was like to be that worm. It didn't have many prospects. In the end, it was going to end up in the belly of a fish. The prospects for the fish were only slightly better. At least Larry never kept anything he caught.

Robin stared at the worm and wondered what it felt like to have a hook go right through your cheek. To think you were getting a fine meal, only to find yourself ripped out of your normal, somewhat comfortable life to a place where it was cold and you couldn't breathe. No matter how much you gulped at the thin air around you, your lungs were not made for this place. Not built to survive this strange hell you've been yanked into. You are destined to gasp, searching for breath while the world around you spins and blurs.

It wasn't a fish's world that was spinning and blurring, Robin suddenly realized, it was hers. She was gulping for air and finding nothing. She leaned forward in the creaking old folding chair, lowering her head between her knees and demanding her heart stop racing. It was pounding out of control, so much that she could see threads of red flashing in front of her vision as blood rushed through her body.

"Birdie? You all right there, girl?"

Larry's voice came from a long way off. She nodded her head and fought to control her panic. She knew that's what it was. A panic attack. She was panicking because she knew exactly what those fish felt like each time Larry snagged one on his hook. That was her life right now, wasn't it? Yanked into a nightmare with no oxygen. All she could hope was that the universe had a catch-and-release policy and she could soon slip quietly beneath the surface of her own pond, back to her life.

But then when she got back to her pond, would she recognize it anymore? Can life ever be the same after going through what she was going through now? Somehow she doubted it. She knew the sun in California would be just as big and round and hot, but it would be dimmer. The whole world would be dimmer because her mother's light had gone out. It would be a brand-new world without her mom. The only thing was, she didn't know what that world looked like. What it would feel like. What she would do with her Tuesday nights.

Larry dropped his empty bottle into the cooler and plucked out a fresh one. Robin dropped her rod to the ground and drained her bottle, chugging her beer until she sucked on nothing but air. Larry leaned his rod against his chair and handed her another.

"What say we just watch the sunset?" he said gently. "I think I may be done fishin' for today."

"Yeah," Robin said, pleased that her voice wasn't as weak as she felt. "Me too."

CHAPTER THIRTEEN

Robin's mother used to say that she hated funerals because churches always smelled like lilies. Every other day of the year they smelled like old books and candle wax, but when there was a funeral they smelled like lilies. Robin hadn't been to any herself, so she didn't know one way or the other. She never thought her mom's funeral would be her chance to find out.

Her mom was right. It smelled like lilies. Thick and heavy and sickly sweet. Robin hated lilies. Her mother had hated them even more. Half the arrangements piled up behind the closed coffin were absolutely dripping in them, and there were a lot of arrangements.

Robin was angry. She assumed the flowers were for her rather than her mom. No one would be able to resist sucking up to the celebrity even though the day was supposed to be about her mother. Reading the cards shoved in among the blooms, she saw that she wasn't entirely wrong. The most ostentatious and those heavy on lilies were from Los Angeles. Her agent, manager, lawyer, producer, and an executive from her label all sent massive displays that did not mention Larry and spelled her mother's name with a "C" instead of a "K", if it was included at all. The band had sent a nice one with a very kind note. The rest, however, were all from the folks in town. The folks who had lived their lives in her mother's company. The folks who remembered her and would miss her. They far outnumbered the arrangements intended to curry favor. Robin read a few of the cards, but the tears clogged her sinuses and the smell of the flowers threatened to make her sick. She needed fresh air.

She rushed out of the church to the brick steps in front to catch her breath. It had rained overnight and tamed some of the oppressive heat. A stiff breeze, kicked up from the much cooler mountains, washed through town. It tugged at the open collar of Robin's shirt and kept her from sweating too much in the trim cut of her vest. She was happy Della talked her out of wearing the full suit. It would have been much too hot, and she felt more comfortable. The door opened and closed quietly behind her and Della slipped her hand into Robin's.

"You okay?"

Robin wanted her to let go. The sticky heat of Della's palm made her feel crowded, but she knew it would hurt her to pull away. She swallowed hard against her discomfort.

"Not really."

Della moved closer. Robin could feel her breath stir the short hair at the back of her neck.

"Is there anything I can do?"

She knew what Della wanted to hear, what she was supposed to say even though she didn't feel it. She forced herself to smile.

"Just having you here helps."

Tears filled Della's eyes, and her smile made Robin feel a hundred times better and a thousand times worse. She knew she should take comfort in her wife's presence. She knew she should want to lean on her. She knew she should be able to cry and talk about her feelings. That's what people did when they grieved. But she couldn't. She couldn't feel anything. She kept waiting for the reality of it all to sink in, but it wasn't happening. She felt like she was floating through each day with nothing to ground her.

"Hey there, Cowboy." Sara appeared at her side, a sad little half smile on her face. "How're you doing?"

Robin looked at Sara, ready to give her prepared answer of "Fine. Thank you for coming." The words died in her throat. Sara was standing on the step below her, wearing a black dress that fit her like a second skin. It barely reached to mid-thigh and was cut low enough to call attention to all the highlights of Sara's perfectly proportioned frame. Despite her complete lack of experience with funerals, Robin could guess the dress was not strictly appropriate attire. It would look more in place at a cocktail party or a dark hotel bar. Robin's elevated position on the stairs could have been to blame, but she found it hard to look anywhere else but at Sara's ample cleavage.

"I'm...okay." Sara climbed the final step and pulled Robin into her arms. Robin's heart beat a little faster and she hurried on, "Thanks for coming."

Sara held her close, one hand slipping to the back of Robin's neck to keep her from pulling away. She slipped her other hand into Robin's, twining their fingers together. Robin expected Sara to let go, but she didn't and Della's grip on her other hand remained tight. It felt surprisingly pleasant to be held so close to Sara. All the uncomfortable warmth from a moment ago evaporated. Maybe it was the cool morning breeze. Maybe it was Sara.

Robin relaxed into the hug and closed her eyes. Some of the sadness that had been hovering just out of sight came closer. She was so relieved that she missed the sound of Larry's dress shoes clicking on bricks. The grip of arms around her loosened. She opened her eyes as Sara pulled back a little and gave her a radiant smile. Her old friend's face filled her field of vision. Her heart thudded in her ears.

"We gonna meet people here on the steps so we don't have to hang out in there with the flowers and the organ music?" Larry said, pulling Della into a hug that she returned with her one free arm. He looked over at Robin and nodded. "Damn fine idea, Birdie. Mornin' Sara."

Sara wrapped her arms around Larry's neck and held him tight. They spoke quietly to each other for a moment. The loss of Sara's warmth hit Robin like a physical blow. She waited impatiently for Sara to end her hug with Larry while avoiding Della's eye. Cars started pulling into the parking lot in front of them. A few faceless middle-aged men in dark suits materialized out of nowhere to direct traffic. The air soon filled with the thunk and rattle of car doors and the crunch of gravel under foot. Robin took a deep breath. The opening band was finishing their set. Time for her to go onstage.

Sara moved back to Robin's side. She had expected her friend to move on into the church. It would be Sara's style to snag a choice seat and avoid the company of the older generation, but instead she wrapped Robin's free arm in hers and stood on Robin's left. Della, on Robin's right, looked over at Sara, annoyed. She transferred her look to Robin, obviously expecting her to say something. Robin continued to avoid Della's gaze. So Sara wanted to stand with Robin and lend her support during this difficult time. What was wrong with that? It was, in fact, a friendly gesture. A thoughtful gesture. Robin looked past Della at Larry, whose face was as serene as always.

Well, that settled it. If Robin didn't mind Sara's presence and Larry didn't mind Sara's presence, what right did Della have to mind? Sara's fingers trailed up the length of Robin's arm, and the slight shiver that followed them told Robin quite clearly what right Della had to complain. Still, that wasn't Sara's intention. It was Robin who had battled feelings her entire life. Sara never felt a thing. She was always only Robin's friend. If Della couldn't handle Robin having an old friend, that wasn't Robin's or Sara's fault.

"Ready for this, Birdie?"

Robin nodded her response to Larry as the first group came up the stairs. It didn't take long for a line to form. Everyone wanted to talk. Robin struggled to remember their names. Some were complete strangers, but they all seemed to know her. They would tell Robin a story from her own childhood or a story from her mom's childhood if they were old enough. She would introduce Della and they would exclaim over her for a while. Then they would move to Larry and the crying would really begin. Larry let the tears flow freely down his cheeks. Everyone spent the longest time with Larry.

If anyone found it odd that Sara had joined the family in the greeting line, they didn't mention it. Robin supposed the whole town had grown used to the two of them being so close as kids, so it made sense to them now. Only Robin seemed uneasy. With Sara holding her arm above the elbow and Della holding her hand, it was impossible for her to greet people with a handshake. After the seventh or eighth time she clumsily reached out with her free hand and nearly pulled Sara off the step, Della was forced to let go. In between handshakes she put her hand on Della's back, but the gesture did nothing to thaw her chill.

Robin didn't miss the looks Della shot past her to Sara, but Sara apparently did. As much as Robin appreciated the support, she knew she should carefully withdraw from Sara's embrace. The problem was she didn't want to. She still felt that quiet approach of the emotion that had been missing in her life, and she didn't want to lose it.

"Birdie Scott. Such an honor to have you back in town. Please accept my sincere condolences. Katherine was one of the brightest lights ever to grace this town."

The little speech may have been pompous, but it was undoubtedly sincere. The man was bouncy, high-spirited and almost completely spherical. He wore a bushy mustache with ends that drooped down past his wobbly chin. His brightly colored suspenders stood out against the stark white of his shirt. Pit stains were already forming on his short-sleeved shirt, explaining why he carried his suit jacket over one thick arm. Robin remembered his job but not his name. His general air of cheeriness and shape had won him the role of town Santa Claus every year since before Robin was born, and he had been mayor for just as long.

"Thank you, Mayor. She was a special woman."

"Indeed she was. Indeed she was." He took her offered hand between both of his. "And her daughter is no less so. You make us very proud, Birdie. I hope you know how proud we all are of you."

"Thank you." She made sure not to allow bitterness into her voice. "But I want today to be all about Mom."

"Of course. That's why I took the liberty of forming a little militia to keep things under control." He turned his rosy cheeks to Della. "You must be the other Mrs. Scott. A great pleasure to meet you. I'm Mayor J. C. Buckthorn. Thank you for the tip."

Della nodded and shook his offered hand genteelly, rather like a politician's wife.

Robin was completely lost. "Militia? Tip?"

"A pair of uninvited guests with cameras checked into the hotel just outside of town last night." He winked at Robin. "Tabloid journalists in Sperryville. Such a shame. Martin closed down Bird Dogs for the day. He and his nephew, Jamie, have been entertaining the men in their room. They hope you will understand their absence here this afternoon. Your lovely wife spotted the intruders and asked the sheriff for his assistance keeping the media at bay. Quite a few people volunteered to be deputized, but we decided to keep it off the books."

Robin had worried the paparazzi would make their way to town, but she hadn't seen anyone out of the ordinary. She thought maybe the soulless press had developed a conscience. Apparently not. How Della spotted them she had no idea, but then she was always looking for trouble. She drove security at Robin's venues nuts asking them to keep an eye on this fan or that fan. It never amounted to anything but was proof of her universal suspicion. More surprising was the realization that the town was ready to protect her privacy and the sanctity of her mother's service. The thought made her eyes well unexpectedly and she turned away to collect herself.

Della spoke up, "That's very kind of you, Mayor. If there's anything we can do to repay you…"

"Careful there, Della." Larry smiled over at them and pumped the mayor's hand. "Jimmy'll take you up on the offer."

"Since you brought it up," Mayor Buckthorn said, coolly ignoring Larry. "You may remember that Sperryville throws a Fourth of July festival every year."

"I do remember, of course," Robin responded in as calm a voice as she could manage. "I looked forward to it every year as a kid."

"How would you like to take part this year? Nothing too extravagant. Just a song or two right before the fireworks? I know the whole town would just be happy as a pig in...Well... We would all be thrilled to see you perform. What do you say? A hometown concert for your biggest fans and a chance to make the festival a roaring success."

The forced smile slid from Robin's face. Before she could say anything, however, Sara squeezed her arm and bobbed on her toes. "Absolutely! You have to do it, Birdie! You always wanted to play at the Fourth of July festival."

Her enthusiasm was infectious. Robin's gut instinct had been to say no, but she found herself considering it.

Della cleared her throat. "It would be wonderful if we could, but we have to get back to LA before next Saturday." Robin turned to look at her, and Della's eyes were all business again. Cold and distant like steel balls. She tried to lower her voice, but it was too strong and carrying. "I really need to get to the USC library or I'll miss my deadline."

Sara leaned forward. "We have a great library here. What do you need?"

Robin squirmed at the ice in Della's voice. "My research is very specific. The sources I need are in a special collection and haven't been digitized yet. I doubt I could find anything comparable here. Maybe a university library would have something useful, but there's nothing of that sort nearby."

"You'd be surprised what we have in our little library."

Robin was tired of them talking around her like she wasn't there. The mayor watched the exchange like an excited spectator at a tennis match. Larry looked on with his usual lazy smile. Everyone was so carefree. Everyone except Della. She sounded like a Californian snob. It was just like the day her mother first met Della. They had been civil to each other, but her mother was more guarded than usual and it made Robin feel awful. Like she'd moved so far away from her hometown roots that her own mother didn't recognize her.

"I'd be honored to play, Mayor Buckthorn." She reached out a hand in the sudden silence and shook the man's pudgy mitt. "Thank you for the offer. I hope you all won't be too disappointed if I play acoustic without a band?"

He looked like a kid on Christmas. "That's wonderful! Thank you, dear! You truly are your mother's daughter. A credit to little Sperryville."

He moved on to the door of the church. He was the last one on the steps and the doughy form of Jacob Peters appeared to usher them all inside. Della looked furious, but it was too late to object. Sara squeezed Robin's arm triumphantly and followed her into the flowery air of the church.

CHAPTER FOURTEEN

Looking out into a stadium full of cheering fans was a lot easier than looking out into the solemn congregation. Robin couldn't back up into the glare of the spotlight to blind herself. She couldn't block out the faces looking back at her. She couldn't hide behind her guitar. She saw everything. Every face. Every tear. She stood at the altar of the little church, a figure alone with only the flimsy lectern in front of her to hold on to. To her left and right were massive flower displays and a big picture of her mother, blown up to well over life-sized on an old brass easel. In front of her was the polished oak coffin, the lid mercifully closed forever. She kept her eyes carefully averted from it.

Worse than the view was the hush. During a concert, even during a ballad, cheering filled the vast empty space. The energy here was all wrong. Quiet and solemn and uncomfortable. It felt like she was standing in a black hole, blinking into the darkness, silence pressing hard against her eardrums.

Robin looked down at her speech. The eulogy. She wrote in a cramped, spiky cursive that slanted heavily left. Leaning back on itself. Della was the only person she'd ever met who could decipher it. Chicken scratch, her mother had called it. The words blurred together. It didn't really matter. She had it memorized.

The paper flopped as she adjusted it. She had folded and refolded the single page so many times that it lay limply without Robin having to smooth it down. She did the same when she wrote songs. Folding up a scribbled page and carrying it around with her night and day, working through lyrics until inspiration finally struck her and she finished it. Sometimes she took out the paper to look at without actually reading the words. More of a talisman than a script.

She looked up again at the crowd. There was no judgment, but there would be pity if she didn't start soon. The problem was her throat was dry and constricted. She hated public speaking. It was a fear she knew she would never conquer. Most people didn't understand. She was a rock star. She performed in front of people all the time. No one seemed to notice that she rarely spoke between her songs. She ticked through her set list, did the obligatory encore and then waved as she left the stage. She sang. She didn't speak. She hated interviews, and appeared wooden.

Singing wasn't like talking. Singing was art. It was performance. It wasn't her. Singing was safe. She'd heard someone say once that humans are physically incapable of stuttering while singing. Singing is mechanically different from speaking. The same rules don't apply. The same fears don't apply.

"Every summer Mom and I would pack up the car and head down to the bay to see the Pony Swim at Chincoteague Island."

Now that she'd started, Robin was able to convince herself not to stop.

"We camped near the channel and watched the cowboys head out to Assateague Island and round up the ponies. We'd wake up before sunrise and stake out a good spot on the beach. When the sun was up and the tide pulled back, they would swim the ponies across. Beautiful creatures swimming in the surf. Palamino, dapple gray, and pinto. They swam with such grace and Mom loved watching them run up the shore. Once the herd was corralled on Chincoteague we'd pack up the tent and head back home. Mom was always real quiet on the drive back."

Sara smiled at her from the front row. She was at the end of the pew with Larry between her and Robin's vacant seat. Her eyes were shining with unshed tears. Something in that emotion was a comfort.

"She loved the ponies. She always wanted to see them swim, but hated to see them rounded up. We were already out of town by the time the auction started. Wild horses. That's what Mom was like. Wild. Unbreakable. But I don't have to tell anyone in this room that. Larry least of all."

There was a gentle patter of laughter. It loosened the knot in Robin's chest enough that she took her first deep breath of the day.

"She was stubborn. And strong. And passionate. She never did anything halfway. She told you exactly what she thought, even if you didn't want to hear it. *Especially* if you didn't want to hear it."

She heard another laugh from the room, but she didn't see the crowd. She saw her mother sitting in a dark car in a mall parking lot. Telling her things with her silence that Robin didn't want to hear. Communicating with her daughter in a way that was impossible to misinterpret.

"The thing about her, though, was that honesty never lost her a friend. She could say things you didn't want to hear, but you knew she did it out of love."

Robin's ears rang with the echo of her mother's laughter. It was always loud and carefree, bursting from her at the most unexpected times and never failing to make Robin smile. It was a unique laugh. One that Robin would never hear again.

"I'm a lot like my mom. The stubborn part at least."

Larry smiled at Della, who smiled back. The handkerchief in his hand was crumpled and damp. Della's was folded into a neat square under her thumbs, crisp and dry.

"It brought us together and pushed us apart in equal measure. More pushed apart these days. I regret that more than I can say."

Robin stared at the scratch of letters on white paper and held back her tears. If she let a single one fall, the rest would follow in a torrent and she wouldn't be able to stop them. Not for days.

"Mom always told me that mistakes are the best teachers. 'Birdie,' she would say. 'You're my daughter, so you'll make more than your share of mistakes in this life. The trick is learning enough from each one to keep from making it again.'"

Her mom had told her that one night after coming home from a date with Larry. She was later than usual and she was practically skipping around with happiness. She flopped down on the couch, kicked off her sandals, and lay her head back on the armrest. Still wearing the sundress with tiny blue flowers dotted all over it, she stared at the ceiling. Robin was probably ten or eleven. Too young to understand what it feels like to be in love, but old enough to know what it looks like. The words stuck with her more for how happy her mom was than the content of her advice.

"Mom was smarter than strangers gave her credit for. Every one of us knew, though. We all knew she was sharp as a tack. She was so full of life. It feels wrong referring to her in the past tense. She fills so much in all of us even now she's gone. She was a caring friend. A loving mother. A great neighbor. A hard worker. A devoted partner. More than anything else, she was a woman who loved with her whole heart."

Robin was able to look around now. The danger of losing control had passed for the moment. She was almost through. She saw a crowd full of watery smiles. Just about the whole town was here, their eyes fixed on Robin, but their minds solidly on her mother. It was a beautiful sight.

"Even when we were fighting, I knew she loved me. Even in those moments when I have doubted everything else, I never doubted her. She and Larry taught me what true love is better than any fairy tale. It's a winding road. There are blind curves and there are potholes, but, once you know the way, it'll always lead you home."

CHAPTER FIFTEEN

"A movin' target's harder to hit."

When Larry leaned over and whispered the words in Robin's ear, she realized her disquiet must be showing. He followed them up with a pat on the back that was also a gentle shove out of the room. She walked as calmly as she could toward the kitchen. It would have been rude to run, even though that's what her body screamed to do. She thought she would be alone in there, but she should have known better.

Every woman in town over the age of fifty was huddled around one appliance or another in her mother's airy kitchen. They stirred pots, pulled casseroles out of the oven, prepared trays of sandwiches. One group stirred mounds of sugar into pitchers of iced tea. They formed an assembly line by the sink, washing, drying, and reusing every plate, mug, and utensil in the house. They chatted among themselves. They laughed and visited. One woman, a tiny firecracker with a helmet of silver curls, kept shooing Della away from every task she tried to perform.

"Don't you worry about a thing, dear. We can't have you muss up that beautiful dress."

"Oh, no. You're our guests. I wouldn't dream of…"

"Don't be silly. We take care of each other here in Sperryville."

The way Della pursed her lips at the words made Robin turn on her heel, but she wasn't quick enough.

"Birdie, dear, what a lovely eulogy." A woman Robin thought may have been one of her elementary school teachers grabbed her hand before she could escape. "Your mother would have been so proud."

"Thank you."

She squeezed Robin's hand between hers. They were pink and still a little damp from washing dishes. "How are you doing?"

Everyone asked, but no answer seemed to satisfy. "Oh, you know, I'm getting by."

The woman, who Robin now remembered had taught her fourth grade, moved a step closer. "So what's Los Angeles like?"

"Umm…Sunny."

She giggled. "You're just the cutest thing, aren't you? Have you met Garth Brooks?"

Robin held in her sigh. "No, ma'am. I expect he lives in Nashville."

"What about Vince Gill?"

"Birdie?" Sara appeared at her shoulder, wrapping a warm hand around her upper arm. "There you are. Mr. Peters needs to speak with you about something."

The plump hands released her and Sara pulled her out of the room. She held tight to Robin's arm. The back hallway was narrow, and Sara's soft curves pressed against her bicep. Robin forced herself not to look down. Not to feel the tingle in her skin where Sara's body touched her and made her feel like a confused sixteen-year-old again.

The hall dead-ended at the door to the backyard. A steep staircase led down to the basement on the right. The mudroom, little more than another narrow hallway with a washer and dryer wedged in, opened to the left.

Sara dragged her into the mudroom and dropped her arm. She pulled herself up on top of the washing machine with difficulty considering the height of her heels and the tightness of her dress and wedged her black heel against the windowsill. Her dress was really too short for the maneuver, and Robin quickly looked away.

"Where's Mr. Peters?"

Sara slipped a hand under the hem of her dress, exposing even more of her long, tanned thigh. "No idea. Probably headed home. He hates funerals, you know." She stuck her tongue between her teeth. "Finally!"

She pulled a silver flask from under her skirt. It was scuffed and one corner was bent in. She unscrewed the lid and took a long pull before handing it to Robin, saying, "They make it look so easy in the movies. Flask in the garter. All lies. I've been walking funny all day."

Robin took the flask. It was warm. Robin realized, with a rush of excitement, that the warmth came from being strapped to Sara's thigh. There hadn't been a visible bulge, so it must have been pressed to her inner thigh. Since the skirt was short enough to almost qualify as a long shirt rather than a dress, it must have been awfully high on her inner thigh. She put an abrupt end to that train of thought.

Today, of all days, she did not need to be noticing Sara Carson's thigh. She did not need to notice the way her legs seemed to go on for days under that clinging black fabric. The way her flesh faded to a creamy ivory above the edge of her hem. The way Robin's own lungs seemed smaller when she looked at Sara, making her take several shallow breaths instead of one normal one. She didn't need to notice that today.

Still, since the service ended and the long procession moved from the stuffy church to the muggy, grass-scented graveyard and then finally back here to the cool sanctuary of familiar walls, some of the pressure had lessened from Robin's shoulders. The show finished, the last of the crowd noise faded away. Now all that was left was the after party. Greeting the fans backstage for the obligatory congratulations and awkward milling about.

Robin hated that part, but at least it meant the performance was nearly over. She could get back to normal.

Robin took a long pull on the flask. The pleasant sting of whiskey burned her throat. It was smooth and peaty with a mustiness that only came from a good, imported scotch. She let her breath out in a hiss.

Sara laughed. "I take it you approve?"

"You always did have good taste."

Sara took the flask back from her and brought it to her lips. "Only in liquor."

It was an obvious invitation to ask, but Robin was no more interested in hearing about Sara's romantic life now than she had been interested in seeing it all those years ago. A jealous beast was born the day she saw Sara kissing that blue-haired girl. If she poked it now, she might find it was still alive. Her life was complicated enough without that. Sara tipped the flask back and Robin saw a familiar design scratched into the bottom. Two sets of initials and a lopsided heart. Sara passed the flask back to her and she studied it instead of drinking.

"This isn't…"

"Of course it is."

"You got it so we could sneak booze into Lilith Fair."

"Junior year. At Merriweather Post Pavilion up in Maryland. Longest. Drive. Ever."

"Only because your piece of shit car kept overheating."

"Remember that gas station we stopped at outside of DC to put water in the radiator?"

"Remember it?" Robin tipped the flask back. "I still have nightmares about that place. I thought we'd be killed for sure."

"How our parents didn't figure out we were lesbians after that, I'll never know. I mean Lilith Fair?"

"Gay, right?"

"So gay."

Their laughter died away slowly. Sara hadn't had it any easier coming out to her mother than Robin. Robin had tucked away her hurt and pulled back into herself. Sara had exploded in a flare of teenage rebellion. She cut her hair. Got a nose ring. Got a tattoo. The fights between mother and daughter Carson became legend in the tiny town. Sara was branded a troublemaker. The upshot for Robin was that her journey was far easier than it could have been. By the time people found out about her, it was old news. She wasn't a freak or an oddity. She was inevitably compared to Sara and found to be less offensive in her gayness and her attitude. It didn't hurt that she was quieter, either.

Sara leaned back against the painted beadboard. "Speaking of, Mom sends her regrets for being unable to attend. She and the Step Drag are visiting his sister in Fayetteville."

"It's fine."

Sara gave her a long look. "Too many people here already?"

"Something like that." Robin looked into the depths of the flask. "I don't really know how to do this. All these people. They want to talk about Mom, but I don't. Or they want to talk about me, and I don't want that either. Today is supposed to be about her, but half the people here just want to know what LA's like."

"That's not really what they're asking."

"Yeah, it is. Do I know this famous person? Do I know that famous person?" Robin felt the anger boiling up in her neck. She was getting too loud but didn't feel like moderating her tone. "Can't they even wait until she's in the ground before they forget all about her?"

Sara's voice was quiet. She was calm and it made Robin feel like a jerk for shouting. "That's not really what they're saying, Birdie. They're saying that they don't know what to say. No one knows what to say at these things. They're here because they don't want you to feel alone."

"I still feel alone."

"You aren't."

Sara's expression didn't show pity. She didn't try to hug Robin. She didn't try to get her to talk. She was just there. Just quietly sat and asked nothing in return for her company. It was a welcome change. It was like fresh air after leaving a smoky bar.

Sara screwed the cap back on the flask and hiked her dress up to put it back in place. The ring on Robin's finger made her look away, but the whiskey in her blood let her get a good view first. She turned to look out the wide windows and took a long, shuddering breath. Despite what Della thought, Robin had not looked at another woman since they met. Della was a woman without compare. But this wasn't a woman. This was Sara Carson.

"Your mom always had the most beautiful roses."

The comment brought Robin's eyes back into focus. The backyard, visible through the mudroom window, was beautiful. The neat picket fence was lined with flourishing bushes. The colors were dazzling. Broad, waxy leaves in darkest green. Firm buds in yellow and blood red. A single, tall bush loaded with lace pink blossoms. Not a single Knockout Rose in sight. Her mother had loved the challenge of the finicky American Beauties and Julia Childs. Knockouts were cheating.

Robin hadn't set foot in the backyard since she'd arrived. Since the morning on the side porch, she'd decided not to venture out there. Her mother would just feel too close among those flowers. It wasn't until now that she realized she had avoided the back windows too. This was her first sight of the backyard in years. It hadn't changed a bit. Her mom might have just walked in the house from tending the roses.

"They look amazing. I can't imagine how they've survived in this heat."

"I've been watering them every day." Della stood in the doorway. She held out a cup of coffee and Robin took it. "I'm sorry, Sara. I would have brought you a cup, but I didn't know you were here."

Sara hopped down from the washer. "That's fine. I was heading out anyway." She leaned in and kissed Robin on the cheek. "Call me tomorrow. We can go for a hike."

"I'd like that."

Watching Sara leave, Della leaned against the doorframe. Della's simple sleeveless dress was sky blue and cut perfectly around her hips and shoulders. It fell just below her knee. Robin's eyes followed its simple, elegant lines over Della's slim hips. She felt another tingle, but this one didn't make her feel like a teenager. It made her feel very much like an adult. Della kicked off her shoes and rolled her neck. Robin wondered how she'd escaped the kitchen, but didn't ask. She just looked back out the window at the line of roses.

"I didn't realize there was much hiking around here."

"They aren't the Sierra Nevadas or anything, but the Blue Ridge Mountains have good trails."

"Oh." Robin sipped her coffee while Della talked. "Then you should go. It'll be good for you to get out of the house."

Robin's head spun from the whiskey. She hadn't asked for permission and she didn't need it. She wanted to shout about how she knew what was best for her, but it sounded childish even in her own head. Especially since she agreed.

"You don't mind?"

"Of course not. Spend time with your friend." The question hung in the air between them. Robin knew Della would ask, and, after a long moment, she did. "The two of you were close?"

"We were best friends since before I can remember."

The first memory Robin had was from a birthday party when she was four or five. Sara was there. Apart from the cake, she was the only thing that Robin could remember about the party. She didn't even know whose birthday it was.

"What happened?"

"What do you mean?"

"I've never met her. You've never talked about her. I just assumed…"

Robin finally turned away from the window and leaned against the wall next to Della. "We grew apart, I guess. She ran off the minute we graduated. I didn't get to see her before I left for school. It hurt my feelings at the time, but I understand why she did."

Della turned toward her. The light from the setting sun through the window glinted off her diamond earrings. Robin stared at her lips, the burgundy of her lipstick glowing like a glass of red wine in the sunset.

"Why did she?"

"Her mom didn't take it well when she came out."

"She's gay?"

"And wild." Robin smiled at her memories. "She threw it in everyone's face. They didn't like it and she just bailed."

"Then she came back to be the town librarian?"

"That's Sara for you." Robin sipped her coffee. It was rich and strong, but it made her stomach ache. She said, with no small degree of confusion, "I'm hungry."

"That doesn't surprise me. You haven't eaten all day."

"I had breakfast."

Della grabbed her hand and started leading her back to the kitchen, walking backward between the narrow walls. "You had a plate with eggs and toast on it, but you didn't eat them."

"Yes I did. I remember..." She thought hard. She drank a glass of orange juice. And several cups of coffee. She saw the plate, but she couldn't remember picking up her fork. Her stomach growled. "Maybe I forgot."

Della laughed and squeezed her hand. "Told you so. Come with me. Most of the old ladies have dragged their husbands out of here. We may even have the kitchen to ourselves. I'll make you a plate."

CHAPTER SIXTEEN

Lying on the couch, staring at the living room ceiling, Robin let exhaustion roll over her in waves. At some point during the day, someone had opened the curtains of the big picture window that looked out onto the front porch. The cars that had dotted the gravel drive and the front yard were gone. Robin and Della had parked their rental cars in the carport out back beside her mother's burgundy Mustang. The cold moonlight shone on nothing but bare grass and tall corn.

Robin sighed contentedly. It was nice to have everyone out of the house at last. To finally relax and put her feet up. The top three buttons of her shirt were hanging open, as was her vest, and it felt good to take a deep breath. She wiggled her toes, clad only in thin black trouser socks, stretching the muscles and ligaments that had been confined in her square-toed shoes since early that morning. Her belt was a little tight, but that was only because she'd had a decent meal for the first time in as long as she could remember.

Della had celebrated an emptying house by fixing Robin an extra-large plate of whatever dishes people had brought. She sat

Robin down at the little breakfast table, and Robin surprised herself by eating every scrap of food. She would've gone to the fridge for more, but Larry arrived with someone or other for her to talk to and she had to head back into the living room. Della brought her more food that Robin ate absentmindedly while she mingled. At some point she looked down to discover she'd cleaned that plate as well.

Apart from being full, the most surprising thing for Robin was that she wasn't sad. Sadness had been a companion of hers for so long it felt like her new normal. Now that weight was gone and she felt like herself for the first time since Richmond, or perhaps even before that. After the show in Atlanta, Robin had picked a fight with Della over something ridiculous. It hadn't seemed ridiculous at the time—it felt crucial then. Essential. Now Robin could see that she was tired and had lashed out at unfairly.

After the show, the mediocrity of which scratched at Robin, Della mentioned for what felt like the hundredth time that this tour was going to bring them very close to Sperryville. Either Della didn't notice Robin's warning signs—the stone-faced stare and the silence—or she ignored them. Della wanted them to stop by and see her mother after the tour ended in New York. Or, even better, to stop by on the trip between Charlottesville and DC. The drive would put Sperryville almost directly in their path, and they should take the opportunity to call in and say hello.

Della had barely finished speaking before Robin exploded. Della was pushing. Nagging. Picking at Robin when she had already said a million times that they were not, on any account, going to Sperryville. She didn't have time to stop in on her mom. She didn't have time to do anything but play and sleep. Della had no idea what she was asking. No idea the pressure Robin was under.

Della was not the kind of woman to take those sort of accusations lying down. She never had been. It was one of the things Robin found sexiest about her. She didn't take any of Robin's bullshit, and she'd rarely met anyone who stood up to her like that. Unfortunately, that trait mixed with Robin's stubbornness led to some of their worst fights. The one in Atlanta certainly qualified. It was all Robin's fault, she knew that now. She had been unkind. Unreasonable. She couldn't admit to herself, much less Della, the real reason she was so adamant. She knew her mother would be the same cold fish she had always been with Della, and Robin didn't have the strength for it. The way her mom would pretend Della wasn't in the room while doting over Robin. The way she would politely half smile and nod during any conversation about their life together. She would make her discomfort known but never addressed.

In the end, Della got her way. They came to Sperryville. She really should have scheduled a visit with her mom. She wouldn't have made it in time, but her mom would have known she was coming. That might have brought her some joy in the last days of her life. The thought made Robin's eyes burn, but the grief was not as sharp now. Not as raw with the worst over.

Della's voice was level as she spoke into her cell phone, but the forced calm was fraying around the edges. "I will not repeat myself, Rick. The tour is over."

Robin sat up, throwing her arm over the back of the couch to hold herself up, and watched Della pace the dining room. She still wore the dress that hugged every curve of her long body without being indecent and the tall heels that accentuated her finely sculpted calves. She pressed her phone to her ear with one hand and the pads of her fingertips to her forehead with the other. She closed her eyes and paced while she listened to the shrill squeal of Robin's manager.

Robin could hear it all the way in the living room. He had a nasal sort of whine. Robin hated the sound, but didn't have to deal with it that much. At some point, Robin couldn't figure out exactly when, Della took over dealing with Rick. Robin didn't remember asking her to do it, Della just knew she needed to. She read Robin as easily as the reference books filling their home and the tour bus. Robin pushed herself heavily to her feet and thought she ought to find some way to thank her.

Della looked tired. Watching her, Robin leaned against the archway between the living and dining rooms. The breeze from the ceiling fan ruffled her open shirt and cooled her skin. Della's shoulders were bunched around her slim neck. Her ponytail swung behind her stiffly, as if her neck refused to move with the fluidity that normally marked Della's every movement.

"Because her mother's funeral was today, Rick. That's why she won't meet the band in New York next week." Della ran her nails across the surface of the table as she turned the corner. It didn't take much imagination to realize she'd rather be running them across Rick's face. "She needs time to heal, and she won't get that at Madison Square Garden."

The buffet against the wall to the kitchen had been set up as a makeshift bar. Looking at the contents, a few ingredients stood out. Robin smiled and grabbed a few bottles, pouring them into a plastic pitcher with a handful of rapidly melting ice cubes.

"Then they can give the refunds. That's why we're insured. This tour has made everyone involved quite enough money already. We'll add extra shows on the next tour and they'll just have to understand."

The jar of olives was untouched, which was just as well. Della was very particular about how to make a proper martini.

"The festival is different. It's nothing like the tour. It's something she needs right now."

Robin winced at the conviction in Della's voice. She knew Della didn't want her to play the Fourth of July festival any more than Rick did, but there she was, defending her anyway.

"Are you really going to talk to me about the profit margin for merchandise sales on the day of my mother-in-law's funeral?"

Robin took the pitcher and a pair of martini glasses to the coffee table. The glasses looked new and were unlikely to be a usual part of her mother's limited bar stock.

"I'm glad you see it my way." Della's smile looked like she'd just sucked on a freshly cut lemon. "We'll talk when we get back to Los Angeles. Goodbye Rick."

Robin heard him shout a last few words, but Della hung up. "Asshole."

Robin laughed at Della's whispered insult and Della finally looked up at her. The smile she gave was weary, but a million times more genuine than the one she directed at Rick.

"Hey baby. How're you doing?"

Robin didn't answer. She walked forward and took the phone out of Della's hand, setting it down on the dining table. Then she took her by both hands and led her into the living room. Della followed without protesting, her steps tired but willing. Robin sat her down on couch and stretched her legs out across the cushions. She peeled off one shoe to a groan of pleasure, and then the other. Dropping them on the floor, she poured a martini into one glass.

At her first sip, Della's eyes rolled up and she let her head fall back onto a throw pillow.

"Thank God for you, Robbie."

Robin laughed and poured herself a drink. The pitcher held enough for them to have another couple each, provided the ice held out long enough to keep everything cold.

"Lift up," Robin said.

Della obliged, lifting her legs high enough for Robin to slip underneath them, then dropping them back into Robin's lap. They drank together in silence. It was a comfortable silence, full of nothing other than their exhaustion and happiness to be together after a day full of strangers.

They didn't get a lot of time alone together. Especially time for a quiet drink. On tour, there was always someone demanding Robin's time. Someone wanting her company. The band had been together a long time, and they were all friends. Friends were great when they went home after an evening together, but when they all shared the same space, no one ever seemed to let Robin and Della be alone.

The last time they had shared a quiet drink was their anniversary. She couldn't remember where they'd been at the time. Somewhere in the Southwest, Robin thought, but all the towns ran together. Della made them reservations, and it was early enough in the tour that they'd had a good time. It was a nice restaurant. Robin thought maybe she'd had fish. She remembered the way Della's hair sparkled in the candlelight. She remembered that they had a rare two days together with no shows, so they'd been able to linger over dinner and dessert and drinks.

Robin set her drink down on the end table and took one of Della's feet in her hands. She pressed both thumbs hard into the soft flesh, just above her heel and sliding up along her arch to the ball of her foot. She pressed the knuckles of her toes between thumb and forefinger in a bruising grip, hearing a few gentle pops as she massaged. Della groaned and sunk further into the cushions. Robin massaged along her toes before moving to her ankle and then up her calf.

"You don't have to do that," Della whispered, but her eyes remained closed.

"I know," Robin replied, moving to the other foot and repeating the movements. "I want to. You're exhausted."

"I'm fine."

"Uh-huh." Robin smiled as she watched the muscles of Della's body loosen ever so slightly. "Drink your martini. Is it strong enough?"

Della took a long sip. "It's perfect."

Robin refilled their glasses from the pitcher and went back to the first foot again. Della loved massages in principle, but was rarely indulged. She got antsy lying still as long as it took for a full body massage, and she couldn't seem to find a massage therapist who would use as much force as she liked. Even after this brief work, Robin could feel her hands aching from squeezing so hard.

Della had more of her martini, opening her eyes enough to look at the murky liquid. It wasn't clear like a regular martini, but a brown like the color of weak iced tea. For Della, a good martini used nearly all the brine from a bottle of olives.

"You know what this reminds me of?" Della asked, waggling the glass and her eyebrows in unison and puckering her lips.

Robin laughed hard. "Frederico."

"Fred-er-iiiico," Della said, drawing the word out suggestively.

Della burst into laughter. It was so uninhibited, so genuine that Robin caught her breath. It was just like the way Della had laughed at Frederico. Years after they'd been together, existing as a poor couple of college kids, Robin and Della finally found themselves with enough money to go on vacation. They'd never been on a real vacation together. There had been a few weekend trips, to San Francisco, San Diego, and Phoenix, but that was all.

A friend told them that Puerto Vallarta, on Mexico's Pacific Coast, was the spot to go. It was cheap, tropical, and dripping in tequila, everything Robin and Della were interested in at the time. They found a room at an all-inclusive resort. It was small, but had a hot tub right next to the bed and a view of the pristine bay. The sunset over the ocean lit up the beach like a sparkling diamond. The sand was full mica that caught the sun and twinkled like stars. They made love every night with the curtains open to let in the perfect moonlight and the sweltering tropical air.

It was paradise. A perfect, dreamlike escape. Because they hadn't been able to afford a honeymoon, this vacation felt like their love was blessed with perfection. Nothing could spoil it. Frederico, the teenage bartender in the resort's main lounge, had a go.

They spent every afternoon on the beach, Della tanning her ivory skin to olive with the smallest bikini that actually qualified as clothing. She bought it to inspire Robin, as though any inspiration were necessary, especially in those days. The unintended side effect was that, when they retired to the lounge in the evenings, it inspired Frederico. The beach was in full view of the lounge and Della was hard to miss.

Frederico flirted tirelessly with Della, no matter how little attention she paid him and no matter how clear she made it that Robin was the only person she had eyes for. At first they dropped broad hints, which he ignored with the confidence of youth. It also didn't hurt that he was a pretty boy, and there is no more self-assured creature on earth than a man who knows he's good looking. No more self-assured creature than Della, that is. Since he seemed content to ignore how often she rebuffed him, Della and Robin decided the only reasonable course of action would be to tease him mercilessly. Poor boy never caught on that they were making fun of him, but he may have continued flirting even had he known. Some people were just like that.

Robin adopted a thick, ridiculous accent. "You like it very dirty, señorita?"

Della giggled, burrowing into the cushions and sighing. "Very dirty señora is better."

Robin moved back to the second foot, massaging as Della flexed her toes.

"We should go back there." Della's eyes were full of the suggestion of clear Mexican moonlight. "It was wonderful there."

"It was wonderful."

"Remember the zip line through the rainforest?"

"I remember the terrifying mule ride up the mountain."

"They were cute."

"Mine tried to commit suicide with me on his back."

Della laughed and emptied her glass. She sat up and grabbed the pitcher, splitting what was left between them.

"You bought that stupid hat on the beach."

"My hat is sexy as hell and you know it."

"*You're* sexy as hell." Della caressed her face and lay a gentle kiss on Robin's lips. "The hat is hideous."

Della flopped back down on the cushions and brought the glass to her lips. Robin watched her long throat flex as she swallowed.

"I'm surprised Mom had all this booze in the house." Robin sipped her martini. It was a little warm, but still good. "She didn't drink much."

"She didn't. The mayor's wife hinted that we should have a well-stocked bar for today. Something about good old boys being especially thirsty. I didn't really know what that meant around here, so I pretty much cleaned out the liquor store."

"Did people drink that much? I didn't notice."

"Just the mayor's wife," Della said with a wide grin that acknowledged she'd been played. "Larry and I had to roll her out of here."

Robin laughed and suddenly wished she hadn't spent so much time in the mudroom. She probably should have been there to mingle. Kicking out a drunken Mrs. Buckthorn would have made the whole thing worth it.

"Thanks."

The words were inadequate. Robin wasn't even sure what she was thanking Della for. For taking care of Mrs. Buckthorn? For taking care of everything today and the last few days? For handling Rick today and the last few years? For being that girl in Puerto Vallarta all those years ago? For saying yes when Robin proposed? For deciding to go to that random LA coffee shop to work on her thesis even though some freshman dyke was banging on her guitar in the corner? Maybe for all of those things at once.

"You don't have to thank me. It was fun. I'm pretty sure she grabbed Larry's butt."

"That's not what I meant."

Della ran a gentle finger down Robin's forearm. "I know."

"Listen, about yesterday…"

"It's okay, Robbie. When you lose someone you love it can have…unpredictable effects."

"I don't want making love to you to be an unpredictable effect." Robin captured Della's hand and brought it to her lips, pressing them against her knuckles. "I want it to always be about us."

"It was about us." Della paused to close her eyes while Robin dropped a gentle kiss against the palm of her hand. "It was about you needing me and me being there for you. Just like I always will be."

Della sat up while she spoke, the soft flesh of her legs flexing in Robin's lap while she moved. Robin released her hand, but she kept it there, cupping her cheek. She had the softest touch Robin had ever felt. There were times Della held her like she was made of the thinnest glass. Like she needed to be cradled and protected. There were times when she did need to be.

Della leaned in slowly, the scent of her perfume closing the gap between them before her lips did. Robin twisted in her seat, turning into the kiss, welcoming it. Their angle was odd, but they always made do. Della brushed their lips together with the same gentleness she used on Robin's cheek. It was just a whisper of flesh at first, then a soft, gliding touch, then their mouths locked together. It was a gentle kiss, a kiss between two women who would kiss a hundred thousand times more before the year was out, but it made Robin's heart pound nonetheless.

Just as softly as she engaged the kiss, Della broke it. She smiled at Robin, then lay back down, grabbing Robin's hand and holding it tight. If she'd asked herself before the conversation started, Robin wouldn't have known what she wanted to hear from Della, but this kindness, this understanding, was just the thing she looked for.

"I should have explained."

"You didn't have to."

The words came out with confidence, but Robin remembered the look on Della's face. The hurt and surprise in her eyes. The way she tugged her shirt together to hide her skin. She had been devastated by Robin's reaction yesterday. Even if she had the perspective to understand now, that sort of pain cuts deep.

Robin leaned back in, letting her kiss heal where her words couldn't. This kiss was less gentle, more searching. Della wrapped her arms around Robin's neck, pulling her close. Robin felt every little movement in Della's body. The way her chest hitched when their tongues met. The way her lips shuddered each time they lost contact with Robin's.

She broke the kiss gently, pulling back far enough to look into Della's eyes. They fluttered open, her pupils wide and searching. She whispered against Della's cheek, "How could I live without you?"

Robin dipped past Della's lips to settle against her long, thin neck, leaving a trail of soft kisses. Della dropped her head back against the pillow. "You never have to find out."

The trumpeting ring of Della's cell phone cut through the night, shattering the intimate moment like a cube of ice falling onto a tile floor.

Robin deflated, slumping against Della. "It's Rick again, isn't it?"

Della slid her hands up Robin's back. "I don't care." After a moment she added, "Unless you do?"

Robin's skin tingled where Della's fingers had touched. She closed her eyes and the phone stopped ringing.

"Definitely not."

Robin pressed her lips to Della's neck again, trying to crawl back into the moment. It felt like a lifetime since she felt normal. Since she felt like a woman who could ignore the rest of the world and lose herself in her lover's arms. She could feel Della's smile in the heat that radiated through her.

Just as her lips brushed against Della's earlobe, the shrill bark of a phone ringing burst the moment again. It wasn't the same ring and it came from farther away, from Robin's phone this time rather than Della's. Robin opened her eyes and saw Della smiling at her. Their eyes locked onto each other for a split second before they both laughed. The ringing notes of their laughter harmonized beautifully, Della's a half octave higher than Robin's.

Robin pushed herself back off Della, shaking her head. Their laughter died away at the same time the ringing stopped, ending in a chirp announcing a new voice mail.

"You really should fire that guy."

"I know." Robin looked at her for a long moment. Della grinned at her, looking for all the world like that young woman in a coffee shop pretending not to watch the singer on the stool in the corner. "Thanks for dealing with him."

The solid band of her wedding ring clicked against the martini glass as she drained it. She set it back down, then swiveled on the couch and got to her feet in one long, fluid movement. She padded across the rug to Robin and leaned down, cupping her face between cool hands, pulling Robin into a kiss. Her lips tasted like olive juice and lipstick. Her tongue carried the sharp bite of gin and nuttiness of vermouth. She was gentle and confident and essentially, perfectly Della.

"You're worth it." She held out her hand to Robin with a wink. "Come on, time for bed. You're supposed to be up early for your hike."

CHAPTER SEVENTEEN

Robin's lungs burned like they were filled with acid. She could hear the breath wheezing in and out of her. When she swallowed there was a metallic taste on her tongue. Her right knee ached. The high tops of her hiking boots cut into her ankle each time her foot slammed into the loose dirt. Her backpack banged into her lower back as she ran.

The trail was so steep that, when she leaned into it, her chest was almost parallel to the ground. She whipped around a corner and nearly lost her footing on a section of loose gravel. A wall of shale soared into the sky on her right. To her left was a foot of trail then a sheer drop. Spindly trees clung to the edge, blocking the view, but Robin knew it was hundreds of feet down to the root of the mountain. A burst of laughter exploded in the air ahead of her and she tried vainly to quicken her pace.

She turned another corner and caught a glimpse of Sara dipping under the trunk of a tree that had fallen across the path. The trunk was only a couple of feet off the ground and wide enough that Robin wouldn't have been able to wrap her arms around it. Sara dropped underneath and cleared the obstacle with barely a break in her stride.

"Too slow, Cowboy!"

Robin would have laughed if she had breath to spare. She ran up the path, but stopped at the tree. The trunk was naked of bark, worn smooth by the weather but carved all around by wormholes. She looked underneath, wondering if she would have to take off her pack to fit under. The log above her shuddered.

She stood to see Sara leaning across the fallen tree. She was beaming, her teeth bright white in the morning sun filtering through the leaves. Sweaty strands of hair ringed her face. They stuck on her forehead. A fat drop of sweat fell from behind her ear, curling down the slope of her neck and soaking into the strap of her orange tank top.

"Can't catch up, Birdie? Must be that pampered LA lifestyle. Spend a few weeks here in the mountains and I'll whip you into shape."

Robin leaned heavily against the log and tried to catch her breath. "You'd love that, wouldn't you?"

"You know it." She smiled across the tree at Robin. They'd started out early, barely waiting for the sun to come up before driving the handful of miles into the mountains, but the air was already sticky with heat. "A chance to torture the famous Robin Wren Scott with pushups and sprints? Who could say no to that?"

Robin leaned over, hands on her knees though it was already easier for her to gulp air.

"Someone with a soul?"

"That eliminates me then, doesn't it?"

Robin found air to laugh, the sound bouncing off the rock wall beside her. She stood straight again and came up short. Behind Sara on the trail was an open area. A break in the tree line let in floods of bright, sharp sunlight. The glow of it formed a halo around Sara's hair from this angle. Her cheeks were pink from the run and the heat. Robin couldn't get enough of staring into her eyes. She felt like a teenager all over again, smitten with her unattainable best friend.

"All right, Hollywood. That's enough stalling. I promise not to run if you promise to keep up."

Robin ducked under the tree and squeezed through gracelessly.

"Deal."

They traversed the rest of the steep path and winding switchbacks at a much easier pace. The hike to Mary's Rock had been a favorite when they were kids mainly because the trailhead was so close to the entrance of the park. They could get there quickly and not have to spend hours in the car. The speed limit on Skyline Drive was strictly enforced at thirty-five miles an hour, a speed unattainably slow for teenagers. Better to spend less time driving and more time hiking. It didn't hurt that the views from the top were spectacular. The hike then was steep, but easy. From this side of thirty, however, it was decidedly less so. Even at this slower pace, Robin's chest and legs ached. Her lower back was sore. She was already dreading the trip back down. Hiking down a steep grade of loose dirt with a hundred foot drop inches from your boot wasn't exactly the safest prospect or the most pleasant on time-worn knees.

Robin stopped and made a business of getting the water bottle out of her pack. Sara gave her a knowing smile, but didn't say anything. Instead, she dropped her own, smaller pack and hopped on top of a slab of rock at the side of the trail. She pulled her knees up to her chest and drank from her own bottle. Robin knelt to adjust the contents of her pack. She could feel Sara's eyes on her. It made her happier than it should have.

Sara had always done that. Had always watched her. Especially if they were hiking or swimming. Any form of working out meant the intoxicating knowledge of Sara's inspection. It was that more than anything else that led the teenage Robin to hope Sara shared her feelings. Robin was devastated when she found out Sara didn't. A shadow of that devastation touched her now, even when the image of Della's face swam accusingly in front of her mind's eye.

She made a business of digging in her pack just to try moving her mind away from Della. Robin's pinballing emotions had taken another sharp turn this morning. Despite their bonding last night, Della had woken up all business, practically pushing Robin out the door. She said Robin needed fresh air and time with her old friend, but the way her eyes darted to the spare bedroom she'd set up as her office revealed her true intentions. Robin sulked as she dressed in the closest thing she had to hiking gear—a light T-shirt and cargo shorts that came to her knees. She didn't have any hiking boots, though. She was going to make do with tennis shoes, but Della suggested she check her mom's closet for some.

It was more jarring than she thought it would be to go back into her mother's bedroom. It had only been two days, but a lifetime seemed to stretch the hours between that afternoon and the chill of this dark pre-dawn. Della must have been in here, though. The piles of clothes they'd dissembled when they made love were straightened and neatly folded on the perfectly smooth quilt. Robin shuddered, but whether her disgust remained from the unthinkable fact that she'd had sex on her dead mother's clothes or from the fact that Della had nonchalantly come in after to tidy up, she didn't know. Both seemed equally repugnant.

Robin found a newish pair of hiking boots, decided it didn't bother her too much to wear them and she hurried back out without looking over at the bed. It didn't seem likely she'd ever be able to finish sorting those clothes. Maybe she could ask Larry to do it. Della wasn't in their bedroom anymore. She was sorting notes and powering up her laptop, preparing to work.

Of course Della encouraged her to hike with Sara. It would get Robin out of her hair so she could work. She was always working. When she wasn't, she was thinking about working. Researching, writing, interviewing, editing. Whether it was the Black Plague or the Papal Schism, medieval history was more important to her than Robin was. She never had time for something like this hike with Robin the day after her mother's funeral. Never. Sara did, though. Sara had been there at every step. She had a life, she had work. She lived here, after all. Still, it was nothing for Sara to close the library and take care of Robin.

Fortunately, the sound of car tires on gravel traveled into the room and Robin had bolted, shouting goodbyes over her shoulder instead of the insults she would have lobbed given another few minutes. Della was clueless to that too.

Here on the trail, Robin touched the barrel-shaped lens of her camera. She'd packed it so she could take a few shots of the view from the top. Something of home to take back to California. She wrapped the strap around her neck.

"You never change do you, Birdie? Do you have a guitar in there too?"

"Nope." She held the camera to her eye, aiming it at Sara. "Although it would explain why I'm having so much damn trouble getting up this mountain."

Sara smiled wide, tilting her chin a little to the left, posing for the camera. Robin snapped the shot. Her heart skipped in time with the shutter. She marveled again at how little Sara had changed. The years didn't seem to have the same weight on her that they had on Robin. She didn't look a day over twenty. Her skin was so bright and clear.

"It's not as easy as it used to be."

Robin took another couple of shots, trying to catch the way the sunlight made Sara's hair glow. Each snapshot she took made her want to take another.

"Whatever. You're running up the trail."

Sara leaned back and stretched her legs out in front of her. She tilted her head back and closed her eyes. Her chest pressed enticingly against the damp fabric of her tank top. She did not appear to own any shorts that reached even to mid-thigh. This pair certainly didn't. The thing that had been asleep for so long noticed the long movements and stirred. Robin zoomed in on her long neck and closed eyes and took one last picture.

"Doesn't mean I'm not feeling it. I'm just better at hiding it."

Robin tucked her camera away and zipped up her pack. She stood and started up the trail before her mind could wander. Before she could ask herself about the stirring in her chest or the reason she just took twenty pictures of someone she hadn't spoken to in almost two decades. Sara's hurried footsteps came up behind her. She fell into step beside Robin, looking wary and surprised at her abrupt departure. Robin pretended not to notice. Sara turned back to the trail and the look soon dissipated into the cooling air.

They covered the rest of the trip in comfortable silence. After the seemingly endless series of switchbacks, the Appalachian Trail veered off to the left. They followed the trail straight ahead to Mary's Rock and its incredible views of the Shenandoah Valley. The spur was short, only covering a handful of yards before it opened up to reveal the rolling backs of the mountains disappearing into the shimmering distance.

The overlook was named after the sloping pyramid of shale that rose from the top of the mountain at this spot. Who Mary was and why the rock came to be named for her depended greatly on which tall tale you chose to believe. No one knew the real origin of the name. When they were teenagers, Sara and Robin would sit up here and make up stories about the life of Mary. They considered themselves quite clever for giving her the last name Rock and crafting new folklore for her once a month or so.

Sara had been a storyteller since birth. She told rambling, obsessively intricate tales in simple, straightforward language. Her explanations of the name usually involved a girl chasing her dog/sheep/baby sister up the mountain after it escaped from the wagon train/lonely settlement/alien attack. Robin reveled in creating the terrible love poetry for which emotional teenagers worldwide were famous. Her tales leaned heavily toward star-crossed lovers or unrequited love that led beautiful women to throw themselves off the mountain because of a broken heart. Sara's stories were always action-packed. Robin's were always tragic.

"Race you to the top!"

Sara bent down and started scrambling up the face of the rock. Robin was slow to follow, and her body ached as she scuttled like a crab in Sara's wake. "You said no more running!"

"This isn't running. It's rock scrambling and you're embarrassing yourself again."

She reached the top and plunked down on a flat section of rock. Robin pulled herself up a moment later and settled into a seam in the stone next to her. They were so close their legs were touching. They sat, breathing heavily, and watched the clouds overhead. A strong wind blew, sending the puffs of white sailing across the sky. There was an aura of peace. Not a single sound marred the serenity.

Robin dug her camera out again and took a few shots. There was nothing like the green of the Shenandoah Valley. The black snake of Skyline Drive slithered through the scene and tiny roofs dotted the landscape far below them. The spine of the Blue Ridge Mountains stretched out in front of her, each peak a vertebrae in the earth. The day was clear enough to show dozens of swelling mounds. It felt like they were all a skip away and she could walk between them in a day. The thought was compelling.

The Appalachian Trail was right there, around the corner from where she sat. Two thousand miles of peace and quiet. Serenity stretching before her endlessly to north and south. No crowds chanting her name. No agents or record executives calling her nonstop. No empty house full of memories of her mother. No responsibilities or deadlines or pressures. Just Robin and her thoughts.

She could fall behind Sara on the hike back down, let her get a little distance ahead. It would be the most natural thing in the world after she lagged behind for much of the hike up. Then she could dip down the track leading off into the emptiness. Slip away. Disappear. This section of the AT had so many blind corners, she would be hidden in no time. She had enough water for the day. She could make it to the camp store at Big Meadows by nightfall if she hurried. She could buy the supplies and start an adventure all alone. What would it hurt to drop off the grid for a while?

Or maybe she could grab Sara's hand and drag her along. If she knew anyone who was up for an adventure, it was Sara Carson. She wouldn't even ask questions. She wouldn't press for details or want to know how they could make it work. She wouldn't complain that there was no suitable library or mention publishing schedules. She would follow. She would probably lead. And where was the harm in that?

Robin imagined hiking into the wilderness with Sara. Laughing and talking about old times. The sun going down. Lying in a clearing on a bed of soft grass. Counting the stars. Dragging Sara into the shelter of an overhanging rock. Confessing her desire. Pulling Sara into the kind of heated kiss you can only have with the woman you've wanted for half your life. They would make love on the trail and that beast in Robin's chest would finally roar again. Howl at the moon like a fevered werewolf just like in the old days.

"She was so special."

Robin shook herself. Sara's voice drew her out of her fantasy. She whipped around to look at Sara. Robin was shocked to see that tears glistened in her eyes.

"Your mom. She was such an amazing woman."

Robin blinked. The image of Sara, pinned against a rock wall was slow to recede. She shook her head again, recognizing belatedly the harm in her daydream about running away.

"Uh. Yeah. She was. Special."

"I know you two weren't that close recently." Sara gave her a bittersweet smile. "But I know you loved each other very much."

Robin fiddled with the dials on the camera just to have something to do with her hands.

"Birdie?" Sara's voice was hesitant. "Birdie, what happened between you two? Why haven't you been home in so long? What did she say that pushed you away?"

"Nothing."

Sara pulled at the tongue of her hiking boot. "I'm pushing. Sorry. You don't have to talk about it."

"That's not what I meant."

"Look, I get it. We hardly know each other anymore."

Robin laughed. "Would you shut up and listen to me? What she said was nothing. Actually nothing."

"You're gonna have to spell that one out for me, Bird."

"I brought Della home to meet Mom and Larry. Right before my junior year started. I was in love and I wanted my mom to meet her. I'd proposed the week before. We didn't care that it wasn't technically legal. A commitment ceremony was as good as marriage to us back then. We were happy. Kids over the moon for each other."

Robin fell silent, and Sara filled in the blanks. "She didn't like Della."

"I don't know. Maybe. Probably not." She watched a car wind its way along the road beneath them. A tiny blue ant crawling away in its tiny life far below. "Della didn't think she did. She can be…cold."

"It's tough to meet someone's parents like that. Sometimes you make a different impression than you intend."

"Yeah."

"So you told her you were getting married."

"Yeah."

"And she wasn't thrilled about it."

"She didn't say a word. Just sat there like she'd been turned to stone. Larry finally got up and came over. Gave us a hug. Said how happy he was. How proud. The whole thing. Mom just kept looking at me like I'd shot her dog."

"That's rough."

"Yeah. It wasn't like when I came out and she said…"

Robin didn't want to say the words, and Sara didn't make her. Other than Della, Sara was the only person Robin ever told. Not everything, of course. Not the part about how her mom thought it was Sara's fault, but somehow Robin figured Sara always knew about that too.

"She didn't warm to Della any more than she warmed to you being gay."

"Nope, but this time I wasn't a kid who had no choice but to go home after school every day. I went back to California and pretty much wrote her off."

"Not completely. I know you guys still talked."

"It took a while. I basically let her decide if it was more important to stick with her homophobia or her daughter."

Sara stretched her legs out, pointing the toes of her boots and rubbing her skin tantalizingly and completely accidentally against Robin's.

"And she picked you. Because she loved you."

"I guess. She finally called a few months later. Didn't apologize or anything. Didn't even mention the whole thing. Just started into the conversation like it had been four days rather than four months."

"You never said anything about how you felt?"

"Nope. Neither did she. It isn't our...wasn't our style."

"Did she come to the wedding?"

"Yeah. Even met Della's parents. Didn't like them, but she sat through two whole meals with them."

"Wow." Sara's smile was warm as the summer sun. "Quite the big step."

"We talked once a week since."

"And you enjoyed talking to her."

"They were the most important part of my week, those phone calls. I never missed them, no matter where I was in the world." Robin toyed with the cuff of her shorts. "I know it doesn't make much sense."

"Of course it makes sense. She was your mom. You loved her."

"That's true, but it still doesn't make sense."

The bitterness in her was obvious and Sara felt it.

"You haven't forgiven her, have you?"

"She never asked me for forgiveness."

Sara put her hand on Robin's knee, pulling it close. "It takes a while. Our parent's generation is different. They don't sugarcoat things. They're more tough love."

"My mom sure never sugarcoated anything."

"I think that was one of the best things about her. You always knew where you stood with her."

"Yeah, well, it's different when she's your mom."

"Trust me, it could have been worse. My mom practically forgot I existed once she met the Step Drag."

"You tried your best not to let her."

Sara threw back her head and laughed into the sky. "True. I raised as much hell as I could. She still didn't notice."

"I don't know about that. I was there for a few epic fights."

"Fighting for my mom is the same thing as the cold shoulder for yours. She didn't care, she screamed instead. Della got more from your mom than I ever got from mine. Your mom cared enough to worry that Della was gonna make you stuck-up too. My mom never cared about me half that much."

"What'd you say?"

"Hmm?"

"My mom thought Della would make me stuck-up?"

Sara looked away, following the slow course of a flock of birds overhead. "I mean...from what you said..."

"Sara. What did she say to you?"

She groaned and dropped her forehead onto her knee. "Crap." She looked over at Robin from the corner of her eye. "Can't we just pretend I didn't say that?"

"No."

"Okay. Look."

"Tell me."

She lifted her head, but she didn't look at Robin. One of the birds had peeled off from the group. It sat in midair, held aloft by an updraft from the valley below. It hung on the current of air, its wings outstretched and still. It looked like it was resting. Sara watched it while she explained.

"Your mom came into the library a few months back. Maybe last summer. I can't remember exactly. We got to talking and you came up, of course. I hadn't seen you in a long time, but I'd heard you'd gotten married. Okay, honestly I read it in a magazine. Anyway, I asked about you guys. Plans for the future. Kids or whatever."

"And?"

She let the words spill out, coming in an embarrassed rush. "And she said that she hoped you had kids one day, but that it wasn't with Della. She said Della was exactly like you'd think an uppity California type would be. She said she didn't want you to turn into that, but she thought you might be already. You'd been distant recently, I guess. She thought it was because of Della. That Della kept you away from Sperryville because she thought we were all low class here."

Each word Sara said stung Robin like lemon juice in a fresh cut. Not because they were a shock, but because they weren't. Of course that was how her mother felt. She had never said the words, but it was clear. Larry was better at hiding it than her mom was, but Robin thought she saw it in his look too. It hovered around them all the time. The discomfort of it was part of why Robin had stayed away. She never had the courage to defend Della against the veiled insults, so she simply ignored them and her mother. And now she was gone and Robin had buried a stranger.

Sara rubbed the inside of Robin's knee. The touch was gentle and reassuring, but it was also a level of intimacy she should probably stifle. People hugged her and shook her hand and patted her on the back, but no one touched her like this but Della. Thoughts of running away down the trail resurfaced in Robin's mind.

"It's not her fault. Della." Sara's hand kept rubbing her bare flesh and Robin didn't stop her. "She and your mom came from different worlds."

The press of Sara's skin against her made her mind reel. "She and I come from different worlds."

"That can be a good thing."

"And it can be a bad thing."

"Not bad. Complicated."

Robin looked over at Sara. Her eyes bore into Robin's soul. They were alight and alive. They were full of opportunity. Her face was close. She could smell Sara's shampoo and the sweat on her skin.

"I'm tired of complicated."

Sara's lips were inches away. Robin stared at them. They were coming closer. She could hear the echo of Sara's breath. The world closed in, everything else drifting away. Their lips were so close, they were sharing the same air. Sara's head tilted just a fraction.

The sky split with a flurry of barking. Robin jumped back just before their lips met. She dropped the camera and heard the crack of breaking glass. A golden retriever the size of a small bear came bounding into the gravel clearing below them. He stood near the last of the trees and barked at the bird hovering in midair. It flew off with a mighty beat of wings.

"Whoa Oscar! Whoa!"

An older man with a hiking stick and a floppy hat came around the corner. The dog turned to him and barked again, hopping a little off his front feet with the force. The man ruffled his ears as a pair of kids came running up behind him. The little boy wrapped his arms around the dog's neck as the man looked around. He spotted Robin and Sara and gave a friendly wave.

Sara returned it even though the man had turned to the view. Robin snatched up her broken camera and stuffed it back into the bag. She yanked the zipper and it caught. She yanked again. The slide was frozen in place. She swore and pulled again. Sara reached out a hand to her arm, but Robin scrambled quickly to her feet, dodging the touch just in time.

"Ready to head back down?"

CHAPTER EIGHTEEN

The car barely stopped in the driveway before Robin threw open the door. She stepped out and slung her backpack over her shoulder, closing her eyes for a long moment and taking a deep breath. She turned and bent to look in the open window. Sara was smiling, but Robin couldn't force her lips up.

"Thanks for the hike."

Sara's voice was low and smoky smooth. "It was fun. Like old times. We should do it again."

Robin swallowed, her mind buzzing pleasantly. "Yeah. Sure."

"See ya 'round, Cowboy."

Robin peeled her hand off the window frame. She waved as Sara pulled away. Her legs wobbled on her way to the porch, but she told herself it was from the grueling hike and not from the way Sara's hand felt on the skin of her inner thigh. She'd kept her distance on the hike back down and in the car. There was a lot more traffic both on the trail and the road in the afternoon than there had been in the morning. The din of voices kept her thoughts in better check. Still, she held her breath when they passed the turnoff for the AT on the way back down lest her fantasies force their way forward again.

The front door was locked. It was both completely natural and jarringly unnatural to reach for her key to open the door. In LA, the door was always locked and the security system on. A run-in with an obsessed fan a year ago had reinforced the behavior. Still, her mother never locked the front door if she knew someone was coming over. Crime was nearly nonexistent in a town where everyone knew each other, even with the influx of strangers in the summer. Turning her key in the lock felt like a knife twisting in her heart. Proof that her mother was not home.

She locked the door behind her and set her bag on the floor. The weight of the camera settled with a click on the hardwood. She hadn't checked the damage after dropping it. Hopefully it was just the lens that had broken. At least it was digital and there was no film to ruin if the body had cracked. Either way it would be an expensive fix. She may have to break down and get a new camera entirely. In all her years of nearly obsessive casual photography she had always been so careful. She had never dropped a camera, until today.

She thought of the near kiss that caused the accident, and felt her face grow hot. It shouldn't happen. It couldn't happen. She was a married woman and devoted to Della. Like any celebrity, she had dealt with the inevitable propositioning fans. Even before she was truly famous, she had plenty of offers. Something about a woman with a good voice and a guitar was irresistible to lesbians. Her bassist had played with Chris Daughtry for one tour and he claimed Chris dealt with the same thing. Groupies. Starfuckers. Industry Chicks. Whatever you call them, they were ubiquitous.

She had never taken any of them up on the offer. But this wasn't a groupie. This was Sara Carson. What would have happened if the dog hadn't appeared with its family in tow? Would she have gone through with the kiss? What would it have felt like to have her teenage fantasy come true? Her body trembled at the thought.

Guilt immediately flooded through her. She loved Della. She had since the moment they met. So she had changed in the last seventeen years. Who hadn't? Robin herself was nowhere near the person who had gone off to USC with one thin suitcase and a worn guitar. They had settled into domestic life. That's what married couples did. The fire didn't burn white-hot as it had when they met, but that was all to the good. Fires like that either burn out or burn you. She and Della were built to last. She was too old for passion anyway. Wasn't she?

Robin realized that she was still standing in the foyer, staring at the floor. It felt as though she'd been there a while. She looked around, wondering where Della was. Everything was clean and orderly. Very clean. She could still smell Pine Sol. That could only mean that Della hit a wall with her writing and had distracted herself with cleaning. Robin smiled to herself and headed upstairs. Either Della had worked through her block quickly, which she doubted by the extent of the cleaning, and was back at her computer, or she had worn herself out. She stopped on the landing and heard the pound of water on the glass door of the shower.

The hall bathroom was full of steam when Robin walked in. The mirror was fogged and there was a fine layer of damp on the countertop.

"Hello? Robbie?"

Robin stripped off her sweaty shirt and dropped it on the floor.

"Yeah. It's me."

"How was the hike?"

Robin dropped her boot on the tile floor. A clump of dirt detached from the thick tread. "Hot." The image of Sara's lips so close to hers floated through her mind. "You're blocked?"

Della let out a groan. "Yes. I can't seem to shake it."

Robin peeled off her sports bra and stepped out of her underwear.

"I've cleaned this place from top to bottom, but it isn't helping. I got so dusty and sweaty I had to shower again. I just don't have the inspiration."

Robin stepped into the stand-up shower and rolled the door back behind her. Della was directly under the spray, running her fingers through her hair. Shampoo suds slid down the length of her back. She was an amazing specimen. The curves of her body had never failed to inspire Robin. Her body was long and lean. She had danced until college, and the years of stretching and strengthening her core had stuck with her. Now she spent a few days a month in yoga classes in addition to almost obsessive cardio training.

Robin watched Della press the last of the suds from her long hair and shivered. For sixteen years it had been like this. Della's body was a never-ending source of reverence for Robin. She let her eyes trace it now and felt herself gripped again. Need took her at the oddest times. When Della turned her head and smiled while they watched TV. The way her hands moved when she washed dishes. The subtle shift of her hips when she skirted around some obstacle walking down the hall.

Robin would see it and she would have to have her. Know that her choice was to make love to her in that instant or crumble into a dry pile of ashes. At this moment, it was the way the muscles in her shoulders and back bunched at her neck as she ran fingers through her soapy hair. Robin reached out to slide her fingertips along the ridges of lean muscle. Della took a step backward, out of the torrent of water and into Robin's embrace. Robin wrapped her arms around Della's waist and pulled their bodies together. The soap and water let them slide into a perfect fit. Robin's senses swam at the feel of their wet skin touching. She slid her hands up Della's sides.

"Why don't you let me provide some inspiration?"

Her hands wrapped around the swell of Della's breasts. Della groaned. She pressed back into Robin, grinding against her and causing a flare of desire. Her hands slid to Robin's bony hips, holding them close.

"Mmm. If you insist."

Robin chuckled, and she felt the stretch of Della's face into a smile. She slid her right hand back down Della's body. She caressed the soft swell of Della's stomach, teasing that she might go lower, but taking her time about it. Della purred her approval, clawing gently at Robin's legs and hips, letting her own hands wander.

Her lips traveled the course of Della's long neck, starting just under her earlobe and dwelling in the spot where her heartbeat thumped against her soft flesh. Della gasped at the kiss on her pulse point, shivering as Robin knew she would. Della slid a hand behind her shoulder into the strands of Robin's wet hair. She gripped lightly at Robin's scalp when Robin nipped at her neck.

As Robin's hand slid lower on Della's stomach, she closed her eyes. She wanted to feel right now, not think. Della's hand shot out, rattling the glass door in its track and squeaking noisily down the fogged surface. Robin's heart beat faster, a surge of adrenaline matching the pride Della's responsiveness stirred in her. The animal instinct in her took over, clouding her mind and pushing out any encroaching thoughts. Something about the way Della responded to her touch always lit this fire in Robin. A primal response. A need, real as the need to breathe, to satisfy the woman she loved. To claim her and be claimed by her. It was more than lust and less than love and just as essential because it was fed entirely by both.

Della tried to turn in the circle of her lover's arms, but Robin held her in place. She liked the way they locked together like this. Liked the mingled intimacy and anonymity of not facing one another. Della's body immediately relaxed, allowing Robin to take the lead. Spray bounced off Della's bare shoulders and speckled Robin's face. Robin pressed her eyes harder together, willing herself not to think and increasing her efforts. Della dropped her head back onto Robin's shoulder. Her breath started to catch. Her hips pressed forward into Robin's hand.

"Robbie, baby, I'm so close."

"Do you want me to slow down?"

"Never. Oh, baby, please."

Robin sped her pace even more. Della's body started to buck under her touch. The sounds she made becoming more and more frantic. Her body went rigid for a heartbeat and Robin held her breath. She opened her eyes. The sight of her wife falling apart in her arms was enough to make Robin believe in God. Della shouted and trembled.

"The way you make me feel, Robbie." She turned, and this time Robin let her. She cupped Robin's face between her hands as though she were cradling a baby bird. "The way you've always been able to make me feel. It's so magical."

Robin looked into her eyes. Della could be distant at times, but there were these rare moments when she was so open it was terrifying. When Della was so vulnerable that Robin could feel the weight of her trust. In those moments Robin feared she would never be worthy of that trust, but nor could she stand the thought of losing it.

"It's not magic, Dell. It's love."

"I love you, too."

Della leaned forward. Their lips met and Robin sank into the kiss. Their mouths fit perfectly together. The feel of Della's tongue was as comforting as it was erotic. Robin pressed their bodies together, eager to feel that wonderful shape against her own. Della held her tight, wrapping a long arm around her waist. She slid her other hand between their bodies.

Robin almost cried with relief at her touch. She had long, delicate fingers like a pianist. They knew every curve and crevice of Robin's body, and they wasted no time exploiting that knowledge. She was gentle and insistent, turning Robin until her back pressed into the cold tile just outside the reach of the water. Della shielded Robin from the spray, held her close enough to stay warm but far enough to let their bodies connect fluidly.

Robin clung to her, burying her face in Della's neck to block out the world. Her mind often got in the way when they were intimate, and she had learned to focus on the sensations or else lose the moment. It was easier than she thought, now that she had given herself to Della. Allowed control to be taken into her skilled hands.

Della was nearly as impatient with Robin's pleasure as she had been with her own, and in any case it wouldn't have required much to bring her to the edge. It had been so long. She couldn't remember exactly how long since Della had touched her, but it was too long. Della had barely begun when the pressure inside built to the limit of endurance. She held on as long as she dared. She tried so hard to hold on, but it was a losing battle. The explosion, when it came moments later, overwhelmed her. She sobbed. Della held her close and whispered in her ear as her mind went blissfully blank.

CHAPTER NINETEEN

Robin was running, but her lungs didn't burn. She didn't feel a strain in her legs. She ran over grassy fields toward a distant wood. She knew that grass and those trees. The way to the creek and the tree. Sara should be here with her. Just as the realization struck her, she heard the girlish laughter. She ran, but she couldn't see her legs moving beneath her or her arms swinging at her sides. This was a memory, but it was strange. Altered. For one, she was too high above the grass.

The moment she recognized the discrepancy, her mind corrected it. Not a memory then. A dream. It was obvious now that she considered it. She was dreaming, but it was woven into her memory. One of her fondest memories. That day with Sara when they were kids that she wrote a song about. A song the world fell in love with. A song that changed her life.

Realizing that she was dreaming relaxed her. She settled into the memory-dream, happy at least that she could run like a child again. Indulge in a simpler life. She left the field behind, entering the woods. She wove in and out between the trees.

Sara appeared in the distance. Just ahead of her. So close that she should have seen her before. Close enough to touch. She reached out toward the girl in the dirty pink dress, but Sara was too far away. And her arms refused to move. Her legs filled with lead and she could barely bend her knees. It felt like she was sinking into the ground.

Immobilized, she watched Sara stop and turn. The Sara who faced her, however, was not the little girl from a moment ago. It was not the Sara from the memory. Now it was the shapely form from her mother's funeral. With perfect tan skin and curves for days. She smoothed the short skirt of her black cocktail dress with her hands. Robin stared at her hands. Fixated. Mesmerized.

She smiled at Robin. Even in her dream, Robin's body responded. Her heart raced at the glow in Sara's eyes. Robin redoubled her efforts to get to Sara, but it was in vain. She tried to call out. To ask Sara to help her. To call Sara over. To free her from whatever trap kept them apart. Her jaw was full of the same lead that was in her legs and arms. She was at the mercy of the dream and the frustration of it was agony. The more she noticed it, the more frustrating it became, everything amplified by her surreal world.

Whatever strange rules that govern dreams bent, and Sara started walking toward her. She moved with a liquid grace that no human other than Sara could match in real life. Her legs filled Robin's consciousness. They seemed to glide across the grass, barely disturbing the earth beneath. Watching them made Robin's mind spin. She wanted to know what they felt like to touch. How they would feel wrapped around her. Her mouth watered. Her body hummed. Heat grew in her belly and washed over her, spreading through her like the burn of good scotch. The world shimmered with heat. Her vision was hazy with it.

Sara's hand strayed to the strap of her dress where it clung to her shoulder. Robin's breath caught. Sara pulled at the fabric, coaxing it over the bump of her shoulder blade. She kept walking as the strap fell and she pulled at the second. She was nearly to Robin now, towering over her where she was stuck in the quicksand of the dream grass.

The dress fell to the ground. She stood, completely still and completely naked among the tall, leafless trees. Sara's body was perfect. Long legs and a narrow waist. The barest hint of softness to her belly and small, plump breasts. Robin groaned at the sight. Pressure built in her belly. Sara kept moving toward her. Robin was mesmerized. Time jumped. Sara was suddenly in her arms. Her naked skin pressed against Robin. Only then did Robin feel her own nakedness, when the searing heat of Sara's flesh pressed against her own with no barrier between them. The heat inside her grew unbearable.

Sara leaned forward. Her lips were as close to Robin's as they had been when they sat on top of Mary's Rock. Robin waited for the dog to bark. But there was no dog in her dream. Nothing to snap this moment into reality. Sara's lips crashed forward and they were kissing. Finally kissing. It was perfect. Everything she had dreamt of for decades. Their mouths fit together like they had been crafted for nothing else. Sara's lips were made of candy. Her tongue a strange fruit slipping into Robin's mouth.

Sara's hands were just touching her when Robin realized she was waking up. Fingertips hot as bubbles of molten metal trailing across every inch of Robin's skin. She fought to stay in the dream. Just one minute longer, maybe two, and all of Robin's fantasies would come true. She focused on the grass and the tree line and the woman in front of her. On the feel of their lips together. Even as she focused on them, they slipped away, one by one.

She felt her body again slowly, and knew she would lose the battle. She whimpered in frustration. She heard the sound echo against the walls of her bedroom. There was movement in the bed next to her. Warm skin pressed against her. It felt so similar to the body pressed against her in the dream, but also completely different. She wanted that pressure of touch, but didn't want it at the same time. Her body was on fire and the slightest touch burned. Sara pulled away from her and looked into Robin's eyes.

As their eyes met, the pressure inside her burst. The force of it rocked Robin fully into consciousness. Her arms were wrapped around Della, their bodies pressed close. Waves of pleasure washed over her, crashing through her like a series of unending earthquakes, but she fought to keep still. Della murmured and began to turn. The sound was strange. She didn't recognize Della's voice at first, expecting instead the liquid syllables of Sara's drawling, teasing tones. Robin's mouth hung open in a silent scream of release, but she managed to force her lips together before Della could see.

"Mmm. Good morning." Della blinked lazily at her, her smile wide and toothy. "Actually, make that good evening."

Robin tried to speak, but her tongue was several sizes too large for her mouth. Her arms and legs still felt heavy from the lingering dream. She managed a weak smile and hoped she just looked sleepy.

Della must have been satisfied. She rolled onto her back, stretching her long arms over her head.

"You're incredible, you know that?" She sighed and turned to Robin with a wide smile. "It's been years since you've dragged me into bed for afternoon sex. What brought this on?"

Robin swallowed thickly. "Y-you."

"You're so sweet."

"That's the rumor."

Della laughed and sat up. She swung her legs off the bed and stood, heading to the dresser for clothes. Robin rolled onto her back and tried desperately to calm her body. After the shower, she and Della had fallen asleep, satisfied and wrapped in one another's arms. At least Robin had thought she was satisfied. Then Sara had appeared in her dream and what followed...

"I'm starving!" Della slipped on a thin cotton sundress. It wasn't her normal style, bright yellow with tiny red flowers. Still, it suited her, and it did little to cover the fact that she wasn't wearing anything beneath. "Want some dinner?"

"Sure. Sounds good. I'll just...um, I might hop back in the shower."

Della leaned over the bed and kissed her. Her lips were sweet and soft.

"You didn't get much washing done earlier, did you?"

Robin laughed. "Not exactly."

"Go ahead." She walked to the door. "I'll start cooking while you clean up."

Robin lay still in bed for a long time after Della left the room. Her betrayal, even if only in a dream, left her feeling cold and empty. It wasn't as though this was the first time she'd dreamt of Sara, even this kind of dream, even after she'd fallen in love with Della. She could not and would not feel guilt for the inventiveness of her subconscious. Still, this felt more willful. More like a dream she brought on herself. Robin knew this dream had more to do with her near indiscretion this morning than she would care to admit. Part of her wanted this moment, and that was the part that brought the dream on.

Robin groaned and pressed the heels of her hands against her eyes until little stars popped into her vision. If only Sara hadn't run off when they were kids. If only she'd kissed Robin instead of the blue-haired girl. If only she'd broken Robin's heart by dating her then dumping her instead of always keeping her wanting, always keeping her wondering. If Sara had done all that then, Robin wouldn't be here now. Wouldn't be risking everything she had left just to know. To be sure.

She stared at the ceiling and tried to convince herself that the very real moments she had spent with Della had been more fulfilling than the dream of Sara. The lingering weakness in her body made it a tough sell.

Eventually, the smell of onions and peppers cooking in olive oil drew her from the sweat-soaked sheets and back into the shower.

CHAPTER TWENTY

If there was a tourist hot spot in Sperryville, it was Thornton River Grille on Main Street. The food was excellent, with perfectly charred burgers, fresh salads and a wonderful brunch menu, but it was always full of out-of-towners. Folks who came through on their motorcycles and SUVs on their way up to the National Park swarmed the place, knowing this was the last restaurant for miles in any direction. It was only a block past Brenda's, but it was more bistro than diner and it drew the fancier crowd. It also didn't hurt that the rest of the town shut down on Sundays, but the Grille stayed open.

It was full of those strangers today as Robin walked past. She dropped her chin to her chest and angled as much as possible away from the building, trying to hide her face. She was recognizable in town, sure, but the locals were more polite than strangers. The weekend warriors stuffing fries and pancakes in their faces at the Grille were less likely to respect her privacy. Not to mention the paparazzi Martin had waylaid two days ago. If they were still lurking, Robin didn't want to run into them.

She hurried down to Water Street, breathing a sigh of relief when she turned the corner without anyone shouting her name.

Water Street got its name from the creek that ran parallel to it. Technically, it was a river, Thornton River, but when it passed through town it didn't exactly live up to those lofty standards. She walked on the creek side of the little road. It wasn't quite wide enough to be a two-lane road, and the guardrail between her and the creek was her only protection if one of the tourists in a massive SUV came down here too fast. The little bridge that crossed the creek right before the power station was definitely only one lane and the blind curve that led up to it always made Robin run. A little flash of excitement in an otherwise dull day in an otherwise dull town.

Another couple hundred feet and Robin turned onto a potholed gravel road. Cars bounced along beside her as she walked down the little slope to Copper Fox Distillery. The gravel road opened up to a gravel parking lot shared by half a dozen local stores, restaurants, and artisans, Copper Fox among them.

Sperryville had always been a haven for artists and craftspeople who drew inspiration and customers from the nearby mountains. This little enclave of happy mountain hippies also held a butcher selling locally raised meat, and a natural store selling locally sourced and produced lotions, honey, and soaps. The triangle of those places along with the distillery, on a warm, still day like today created the sort of varied aromas that felt more natural than any farmers market in California.

Robin followed the smell of roasting grain and syrupy alcohol. Copper Fox was essentially just a big warehouse space with a tin roof. She'd heard about it often enough from Larry, always a champion of small local businesses, especially ones that made alcohol, but this was her first visit. The place looked exactly as Larry described. When she got to the porch, Robin found the massive rolling barn doors locked with a sign asking visitors to wait for the next tour in a few minutes. She leaned against one of the covered porch's pillars and crossed her ankles.

She tried to ignore the couple waiting with her. They were sitting on the carved wooden bench by the door, the woman's legs in her boyfriend's lap, their mouths glued together. They took no notice of the world around them, presumably so new in their love or lust. Based on the angry look the guy shot her way during a quick oxygen break, the pair didn't appreciate her presence.

Robin moved further off down the porch. Firewood was stacked haphazardly on the end and the summer heat here was augmented by a nearby fire. Robin couldn't see the flames, but she could feel them. She smiled to herself. Somewhere inside a wood fire roared, turning ordinary grain into whiskey. She knew the process from a tour of a distillery she and Della had taken when they were in Scotland for the Edinburgh Festival last year. The smoke of the fire would seep into the mash, broadening the range of flavors and aromas. The grain would boil in mountain spring water and ferment, then boil again and distil into copper tanks. The alcohol would go into old wine barrels and it would sit in a cool, dark room for years. When it came out of those barrels, it would be whiskey.

"Welcome to Copper Fox!"

The barn door rumbled open, letting out a billow of delicious liquor smells and a short, bearded man with deep-set eyes and a wide, elvish grin. He wore faded blue jeans and a dusty red flannel shirt. His hiking boots had seen more than a few seasons and his hands were big, weathered mitts. He had the look of old Appalachia. A mountain man.

He shot a weary glance at the couple, then turned to Robin and his whole aspect changed. "Birdie! Fuckin' ay, Birdie Scott!"

Jamie had always been exuberant. He charged across the porch, his boots slapping against the brushed concrete and wrapped his arms around Robin's waist. He crushed her in a hug, lifting her feet off the porch and shaking her.

"Hey Jamie!" She hugged him back just as hard until he set her down with a thud. "Good to see ya man."

"You got some time to hang out?"

"Sure. That's why I dragged myself all the way down here."

"It's like a quarter mile you lazy rock star."

"I know. I'm surprised I survived the trip."

He let out a booming bark of a laugh and smacked her hard on the shoulder. Robin only wobbled a little and it felt good to smile.

"Let me set the new tour up and then we'll chat, yeah?"

A surprising number of people had found their way to the porch by the time Jamie opened the door. With the authoritative voice Robin remembered so well, he gathered everyone into a group and gave a brief rundown of the distillery and the options for tours and tastings. Robin hung back and took the opportunity to look over her old friend.

She hadn't seen him since she left for college seventeen years ago. He was a gifted bass guitarist, and they had often played together around town or school events. Sophomore year they made plans to go to college together, start a band and make it big. Jamie's family had money in a small-town way, enough to get them an apartment and make college a reality for him despite his mediocre grades. Robin nurtured those plans, refined them over the next couple of years.

Unfortunately, Jamie spent that time nurturing a crush on Anna Spencer. Anna finally agreed to go to Homecoming with him senior year and they started dating. Dating was a strong word. They started screwing nonstop in every available location. Anna was bound for University of Virginia with all the other blond, preppy cheerleaders, and suddenly UVA replaced California in Jamie's future plans. He swapped his bass for a drafting pencil and Robin had to find her own way to make it across the country.

That abandonment was the best thing that ever happened to Robin. It taught her self-reliance. To make her own plans and make her own way. She came up in the ranks playing in coffee shops and dive bars, and those gigs taught her more about how to make good music than the last five years on the road had. She assumed the change of plans was the best thing to happen to Jamie, too, but since he was working at a distillery instead of an architectural firm, she now had her doubts. Still, he looked happy.

Jamie ushered the crowd inside, and Robin hung out in a dim corner of the entryway, hovering around a deep, comfortable-looking armchair and a threadbare outdoor couch. Now that she was inside, the smell of fermentation was thick in the air, almost too thick. Like rotten syrup and wood smoke. The rug was threadbare. She paced it, feeling like she was still on bare concrete.

Across the room was a little shop selling booze and the sort of cheap touristy things one finds in stores that really only have two or three products to sell, but need to round out their inventory. Soap and keychains and the like. A bored-looking older man stood behind the register, doing everything he could not to roll his eyes at the woman buying a hand towel emblazoned with the swirling drawing of a fox that was their logo.

The rest of the space, a massive chunk of the warehouse holding the entire operation, was wide-open, bare floor. At the far end, directly opposite the main door, was a comically small bar loaded with tasting glasses. A few doors led off in multiple directions, but the echoing, high-ceilinged room was mostly empty. No one stood behind the bar.

A new guy, about their age and only slightly less exuberant, came and took the handful of guests off Jamie's hands. Jamie came over to Robin, his huge grin back in place.

"What do you say we grab something to drink and find a quiet place to chat?"

"Lead the way."

He pulled her along with him, nearly skipping toward the bar.

"What's your poison?"

"Women."

He laughed again, this time not so loudly, and Robin wondered if he was, strictly speaking, allowed to be taking a bottle of booze and disappearing with an old friend in the middle of the day. It seemed like something a teenager would do, not a man in his thirties who was certainly on the clock.

He stood straight, a bottle in hand. It was half-full of an amber liquid that glinted hazel in the light. "You like rye? I can get the single malt if you want, but the rye is bangin'."

She noted the way his eyes darted toward the tour group at the far end of the room. They should probably make a quick exit.

"Whatever you like."

He snagged a pair of tasting glasses, just small highballs with the same artistic fox logo, and jerked his head toward a door at the back end of the room. Robin thought they were headed outside, but the door actually led to a narrow hall bordered on the left by the corrugated siding of the building and on the right by tightly packed shelves of wooden barrels. Most of the barrels had a few dark, wet streaks running lazily down their sides. The smell here was less of fermentation and more of that rich, musky scent of good whiskey.

They went up a metal staircase to a landing stacked high with barrels. Winding through a maze Robin could never hope to retrace alone, they made their way to an open space at the front corner of the building. It was cool among the barrels despite the season. Jamie threw himself into one of two old metal chairs and popped the cork on the whiskey. Robin sat in the other chair and they clinked glasses before taking a sip.

"Is that apple?"

Jamie sat back and sighed. "Applewood. We put applewood chips in the aging barrels to infuse into the rye."

"That's delicious, man."

Jamie tipped his glass to the ceiling, emptying it and savoring the flavor.

"It is, isn't it? I love this shit. Ready for another?"

Robin hurried to empty her glass. "Sure. You know I can hold my liquor."

"You always could." They clinked glasses again, but Jamie mellowed and lowered his. "Sorry about your mom, Birdie."

The applewood and the smoke turned sour on her tongue. Swallowing was difficult, but she managed.

"Thanks."

"Saw her at Brenda's a month ago. She hadn't aged a day."

Robin didn't know what to say, so she focused on the glass between her fingertips.

"Sorry I couldn't make it to the funeral. I was helping Martin out. Did you hear about that?"

"The paparazzi?" He nodded and she sipped more rye, pleased to note that the flavor was back to normal. "Yeah. Thanks man."

"Anything for you, Birdie."

"What was the deal with that? The mayor kind of glossed over the details."

"Just a couple of snooping assholes dropping into town. They went to the Grille and started asking a lot of questions. Your wife was in there."

"Della was at the Grille?"

"In the market."

Robin nodded, thinking of the little store attached to the Thornton River Grille. It was hardly more than a camping store, carrying the bare necessities, but there weren't a lot of other options if you didn't know the place and didn't have a lot of time to drive all over hell and gone.

"She saw them and figured out who they were. Apparently the sheriff was in the Grille eating one of his lunches. He usually has two or three, depending on how many breakfasts he had. He'd stopped by your house or something, so Della recognized him and went to have a word with him. So he kept an eye on them and Martin gave me a shout. We went over with a bottle of this." He waggled the rye bottle while pouring them both another glass. "Spent the night telling them some tall tales."

"Shit, Jamie, what am I gonna read about myself in the tabloids?"

"Not a damn thing." His teeth gleamed like the fox on the bottle. "All the tales were about Martin. The photographers would have loved to kick us out, I'm sure, but they wanted the free booze."

"I'm afraid to ask."

"They had a little too much to drink and fell asleep."

"Did you drug them?"

"Of course not!" His eyes carried a twinkle that made Robin want to call her lawyer. "When they fell asleep we left."

"That's it?"

"Well, we took all of their clothes and their cameras."

"You stole their stuff?"

"Nope. Put them in the trunk of their car." He paused to empty his glass again. "Put the keys in there with 'em."

Robin formed a mental image of the pair. Most of the paparazzi she'd met tended to be somewhere between jerks and downright assholes, unshaven and disdainful of anyone who didn't live in LA. Picturing them, waking up naked in the middle of the day in a small-town hotel with no clothes, no camera gear, and no car keys would have made her cringe if it were any other breed. Their imagined indignity and anger made her giggle a little too much.

"You need more whiskey," Jamie said, holding out the bottle.

"No, I definitely don't," she said, holding out her glass while he refilled it.

"Speaking of my little adventure," Jamie said with a whistle. "That wife of yours."

"You met her?"

"She stopped by yesterday to thank me." He waggled his eyebrows. "If I didn't love ya so much I would have insisted she thank me properly."

Robin's ears burned hot and her mind went blank for a moment. The whiskey was definitely getting into her head. There was a bite to her voice that she didn't like to hear there.

"Watch yourself, tiny man."

Her words must have come out more angry than joking, because he sobered quickly. "Don't get your panties in a twist, that girl of yours has about as much interest in me as she does a black bear."

"I'm not twisty. Fuck off." He looked at her over the rim of his glass with knowing eyes. She rolled hers. "What?"

"Just wonderin'."

"Spit it out or I'm leaving."

"Everything okay with you and her?"

Images flashed through Robin's mind. A fight in the back of her tour bus. Days of cold shoulder when Robin smiled too long at a fan. A drunken giggle from Della while they lay tangled in the sheets of some hotel or another. Sara Carson's smile in Brenda's the day she got back to town. Sara snagging the flask from under her dress, showing off altogether too much thigh. Sara's lips millimeters from hers yesterday. Making love to Della in the shower. Her dream about Sara. Della's smile when she leaned over to kiss Robin.

"Everything's fine."

Jamie barked out a laugh. "Uh-oh."

"What?"

"First," he said, leaning forward, his elbows on his knees. "That answer took way too much time. Second, Nancy told me you've been spending a lot of time with Sara Carson. Third." He stopped and looked down into his glass, his voice low. "I know that pause and that answer. 'Fine'. Nothing in marriage should be fine."

Robin let the silence linger. He touched the bare ring finger on his left hand. It was still slightly pale near the knuckle the way Robin's was from years of wearing a wedding band.

"Anna?"

"Yep."

"She left?"

He sat back and stared at the ceiling far above them, his eyes were suspiciously wet. "Took the kids to Atlanta."

"Kids?"

"I don't see them much these days. She found a great job she couldn't turn down. There's a guy too, but I don't care to know any more about him than he treats my kids good."

"I'm sorry."

"It wasn't her fault. She just wanted more from life than I could give." He paused, his glass halfway to his mouth. "Did I just quote a Tracy Chapman song?"

"I wasn't going to mention it."

He laughed and it almost sounded genuine. "Fuck me. My life is a Tracy Chapman song. Anna got pregnant our junior year. My grades were shit and I had a job at Starr Hill Brewery in town. Adam was born and somebody had to take care of him, so I quit school and that's what I did."

He pulled the wallet from his back pocket and showed her a picture of three kids. A teenage boy with bangs covering most of his eyes, a girl of maybe seven or eight with a tooth missing in the front and another girl a little younger with a matching pair of braids. They all had Jamie's wide grin and button nose.

"They're cute."

He sighed and shoved his wallet back into his pocket without looking at the picture. "I loved the brewery. Even more than playing bass."

"I didn't know that was possible."

"Not for you. Never will be." He smiled and shook his head. "Me…oh yeah."

"So you moved here?"

"Nope. We stayed in Charlottesville. Anna said I needed a real job, so I got one selling insurance."

"You?"

"It wasn't that bad. Got to be home with the kids every night."

"Bullshit," Robin said, setting her glass down on the crate. "You hated it."

"Yeah, I was miserable, but we had Ellen by then and I made good money."

"What changed?"

"Me." He refilled his glass and brooded over it for a minute. "I just realized I was sick of it. Told Anna I couldn't do it anymore. I needed a job that didn't make me feel dead inside."

"If I remember Anna, she wouldn't take that well."

"No, she did not." He drained his glass and pointed a finger at Robin. His eyes were glassy, and he had that look of a drunk man imparting what he thought was important knowledge. "Never let someone change you, no matter how much you love them. No matter how much they love you. Just be you and either let them figure it out, or let them move to Atlanta with Todd the Banker."

"I'll keep that in mind."

Robin laughed, but she couldn't help but think of the person she was the last time they got drunk together and the person she was now. The person her mother thought was becoming too stuck up for her to want grandkids from. The person who bought heirloom potato chips at farmers markets. The person who had to have everything just right. Maybe Della had changed her, but it was so gradual she hadn't noticed.

A loud, authoritative voice boomed out below them and Jamie jumped. He put a finger to his lips to indicate they should be quiet. The tour had entered the barrel room. They were hidden from view up here, but talking would give them away. Jamie snatched up the bottle and the two glasses, then waved for Robin to follow him.

The way he stumbled on the stairs made Robin wonder if he was really fit to go back to work, but he was a big boy. He'd muddle through. She just didn't realize he'd had so much more to drink than she had. Once they were back in the main room, he stowed the now almost-empty bottle behind the bar, gave a thumbs-up to the old man in the shop by the door and smiled at Robin.

"Thanks for stopping by to see me, Birdie. I sure as hell have missed you. Sorry about your mom."

She pulled him into a big hug. He smelled like cologne and booze, but then he smelled that way when they were kids too. It made her ache for the old days. When things were simpler. When her mother was alive and took care of her. When she didn't have to constantly wonder whether she was doing something to upset Della. When she wanted Sara but she was sure Sara didn't want her back, so the danger was minimal. Those days were simpler.

"Sorry for all the shit you're going through, Jamie."

He waved his hand dismissively. "I miss my kids, but they'd want their dad to be happy. I can't look after them if I don't look after me."

"But you are happy?"

Footsteps were coming up behind them fast.

"Absolutely." When she went to turn away, he grabbed her arm. He was definitely drunk, because he gripped her arm a little too hard. "Listen, Birdie. I wouldn't trade a minute of it. Not a single minute."

"Yeah."

"No, seriously." People started coming into the room, so he spoke with more urgency. Maybe he thought he needed to repeat himself because of the booze, but Robin wasn't even buzzed anymore. "Love is love, ya know? You've got to go for it. Even if it doesn't last. Even if it ends, you gotta try. If it's real, it's worth it."

CHAPTER TWENTY-ONE

The hinges of the library door squealed their disapproval at being disturbed. The door was heavy, solid wood painted white. At least it had been white. Now it was a dingy, dusty sort of white. Della would call it eggshell or ivory. Robin pushed the door closed behind her and tried to wipe thoughts of Della from her mind. It was hard though. The library, any library, was her domain. She was a researcher, a scholar at heart, and going to the library meant going to her happy place. Della always came home happy from the library. This one, though, this library would always be Sara's domain. Robin didn't like to think about what that meant.

Robin hadn't been inside the place since she was young. She'd done her best to show solidarity with Sara, and that meant shunning her librarian mother when Sara did. The moment she had remarried Robin cut her off completely. After all, that's what Sara did. Emotionally at least. She marveled again that Sara had chosen the same career path.

She took a few hesitant steps into the cluttered space. The building had soaring ceilings and few windows. It was cool and dark after the walk from Copper Fox in the height of the summer afternoon. The towering shelves blocked any natural light. They started right at the entrance, a pair of monolithic gatekeepers flanking the entrance and stretching off to both right and left. A narrow aisle directly in front of her seemed the best path. Continuing on, she saw that all the aisles were narrow. Sara's mother would have considered how to maximize every inch in favor of more books, so the layout did not surprise her. The former librarian also had a famous dislike of fluorescent lights, which explained the warm but dim incandescents fighting the gloom.

Old floorboards creaked underfoot. The smell of old paper and leather hung heavy in the air, like swollen rainclouds. It reminded her of long hours studying in their school library with Sara. They stayed there and took the sports bus home so as to avoid their parents for as long as possible. There was never much studying. There was usually a lot of giggling and joking around. Most of the time enough to get them kicked out by the long-suffering school librarian.

"You lost, Cowboy?"

Leaning against a cart in the aisle to Robin's left was Sara. She wore a low scoop-neck shirt that revealed the strap of a black bra and a heavily patterned skirt that reached her knees. A pair of sandals sat on the cart beside the books to be reshelved. Her feet were bare on the glossy hardwood, her toenails painted a deep red.

"Thought I might stop by and see the great librarian in her natural habitat."

"Figures." She pushed the cart toward Robin. "Of course you wouldn't be here for a book. Can you even read?"

"Just music."

"Then I'll have to use you for manual labor only. Push this cart for me, would ya?"

Sara didn't wait for Robin's answer, just left the cart and continued deeper into the stacks. Robin grabbed the handle and hurried to keep up.

"I'm not good for much else."

Sara reached the last shelf. She spun on her heels, her skirt flaring around her in a dizzying kaleidoscope.

"I don't know. You have quite the group of fangirls online. They seem to think you're perfect at everything." She batted her eyelashes dramatically and held the back of her hand to her forehead in imitation of a swoon. "Oh, Robin Scott is the ideal woman! Her voice is like smoke on the wind! Her songs are poetry! Oh, and the way she plays that guitar! I'd do anything for her to put those hands on me!"

Robin rolled her eyes, but her cheeks burned nonetheless. "Give me a break. They aren't that bad."

"Oh no?" Sara giggled and pulled her phone out of her pocket. "Let's check Twitter, shall we? See what the 'Scotties' have to say today."

To her eternal embarrassment, Robin actually did have a group of diehard fans online who called themselves "Scotties." They held up posters at her concerts asking her to marry them. They made YouTube videos about her. They sent her gifts and long, rambling letters. One particularly ardent fan, who had flown from Phoenix to see her play at Aloha Stadium in Honolulu, had sent her a gold-plated ukulele. She sent a fifteen-page letter with it expressing her love in two languages and describing in excruciating detail how they were soul mates. The girl explained that, even though she was only seventeen, she knew their love could overcome their age difference.

"Here's a good one." Sara cleared her throat and read in a high-pitched, Valley-girl voice, "Robin Scott is the perfect woman. Strong n sensitive. Brilliant n brave. Those dreamy eyes! Listened 2 Forever and Ever on repeat 4 48 hrs! Hashtag Scottie4ever."

"Stop it!"

Sara skipped away from her when she lunged for the phone. She pranced toward the circulation desk past tables lined with computer monitors.

"Robin Scott is a goddess onstage! I'll be your forever and ever! Hashtag Scottie4ever!"

"I remember a time when that was called a pound sign and wasn't used to humiliate me daily."

Sara dropped into the tall chair behind the circulation desk and propped her feet on the top, wiggling her toes.

"That's because you are old and boring."

"You're older than me!"

"Only by a month and I am very hip." She swiped across the screen of her phone, studying the site with a lazy smile. "Listening to Forever and Ever for the millionth time. Her voice drips sex. Hashtag Scottie4ever. Drips sex? You should see a doctor about that, Birdie."

Robin parked the cart beside the desk, banging it against the counter just enough to make her point.

"Look whose got jokes."

"Her soul is even more divine than her face! Hashtag Scottie4ever. Jeez, you write one sappy love song and now you're 'divine.'"

Robin leaned against the counter, warming to the banter. It was the kind of interaction that had been her air and sunlight as a teenager. It felt like being warm again after a long winter. Like coming home.

"Hey now! I have written several sappy love songs, thank you very much."

"Each sappier than the last."

"People pay big money to see me play."

"People pay big money to watch race cars drive in a circle too."

"Touché."

"Just keepin' your feet on the ground."

"You're a saint."

"Yep." She swiped again. "Oh! Here we go. I'd leave my gf in a heartbeat for Robin Scott. Hottest thing on the planet. So sad about her mom. RIP Momma Scott."

The warmth in the room vanished in an instant. The tears flooded down Robin's cheeks before she knew they were coming. Suddenly, she couldn't breathe. White lights popped in front of her eyes, and she bent over the cart to keep from passing out.

"Shit! I'm so sorry. I should have read the whole thing before I started." Sara was beside her in a flash. She put a hand on Robin's shoulder. "Birdie? Are you okay? I'm such an idiot."

Robin tried to catch her breath, but she sobbed harder than ever. She heard a strangled moan of pain and realized it came from her own throat. The tears were coming too fast. She was choking on them. Drowning in them. Sara squeezed her shoulder, and she focused on the pressure of her hand to stay in control. It worked only well enough to slow the tears, not stop them. She couldn't even understand what happened. She had been fine. Had held herself together since the afternoon she found her mother's sweater.

Sara squeezed her shoulder again, and Robin flung herself into her friend's arms. Sara pulled her close unquestioningly and held her. She cried into Sara's neck, drawing all the comfort she could find. She squeezed her eyes shut firmly, but the tears kept falling. Sara stroked the back of her neck with one hand, the small of her back with the other, murmuring into her ear. She didn't use words Robin could discern, just made comforting sounds that were far more helpful. Robin melted into her embrace. With her eyes closed and all her other sense clogged with tears, Robin almost believed it was her mother holding her while she cried.

The front door squealed, making Sara jump. "Shit." She looked around as footsteps approached. "Birdie, go back to the research corner. The table back there behind Reference. It's tucked away. I'll get rid of whoever this is as quick as I can. Okay?"

Robin stumbled down the aisle Sara had indicated. Her crying, if not under control, was at least quieter now. The time alone would be good. A minute to collect herself. She came to a clear spot in a corner behind a shelf of massive reference books. The table there looked like it had either been a large dining room table or a small conference table at some point.

Now it sat, solid and alone, in the farthest, quietest corner of the Sperryville Public Library.

Robin slumped into the nearest chair. She scrubbed her bare forearm across her face, smearing tears over damp skin. She experimented with a deep breath, and found that she could handle the oxygen. Her chest ached. It was impossibly tight. She felt tired. As if all of her energy had leaked out with her torrent of tears. When she leaned forward, elbows on her knees, she could smell Sara's perfume on her shirt. The muffled sounds of voices filtered through the stacks while she took deep, calming breaths laced with the scent of Sara's embrace.

She stared at the floor without seeing it. All she could see was her mother's face. Smiling at her from across the booth at Brenda's. Singing along while Robin and Larry played their classic rock songs. Even the moments of annoyance and anger were images that she knew she had to cherish. She would never see her mother again. The truth of it settled on her shoulders and threatened to drag her back underwater. Grief swelled in her and her shoulders tensed, preparing for the blow.

Soft fingers glided up the exposed skin of her neck and into her hair. The intimate touch on her scalp peeled the sadness off her. Her heart throbbed.

"I'm so sorry, Birdie." Sara's voice was quiet and close. Kneeling on the floor beside Robin, her fingers still dancing through the short hair on the back of Robin's head. "I thought you were doing better. We've talked about your mom before."

Robin's voice was foreign to her own ears, muddled by her choked sinuses and waterlogged throat. "I thought I was, too. I guess not."

"Grief's a funny thing. We think we're over it, and then it sneaks up out of nowhere."

Robin looked over at Sara. "Do you still cry about your dad?"

Sara looked away, at the ceiling over Robin's right shoulder. "All the time. It's okay, though. It helps me remember him. Remember how much I love him."

"Things just got so weird with my mom. I wish I hadn't ignored it. I wish...I wish I'd fixed it."

"You didn't have to. She was your mom. She'd love you no matter what. The people who truly love us don't stop just because of distance."

Sara's thumb rubbed along the top of her ear, and the air thickened around them. An image of Sara's lips came to Robin. She couldn't decide whether it was from the hike yesterday afternoon or the dream later. She sat back in her chair, putting a safe distance between her face and Sara's. Between herself and the memory.

"Thanks. Sorry. I feel like an idiot."

Sara slid onto the tabletop, her feet just dangling off the ground. She was so close her leg brushed against Robin's jeans with each movement.

"Don't. It's early days yet. You have every right to grieve."

Tears threatened again, and Robin nodded because she didn't trust her voice to respond.

Sara nudged her knee. "You wanna talk about it?"

"Nope," Robin said, scrubbing at her face with both palms. "Anything but."

"Got it. Easier subject. How about we talk about yesterday?"

The heat from her blush at least burned away the last of the tears. "Yesterday?"

Sara laughed. "It got a little intense there on top of The Rock. I owe you an apology."

"Um."

"It's no secret that I screwed up back in the day. I had this great thing, but I got an extra helping of teenaged angst and lost my shot. You should know that I regret that. A lot."

"Sara."

"Shut up for a second, Cowboy." She nudged Robin's knee again and looked at her toes. She scrunched her shoulders up and could not have looked more embarrassed if she tried. "None of that matters. You're married and happy and I'm just gonna have to live with the fact that I missed the boat. I shouldn't have...I'm sorry."

Robin's ears were buzzing. Sara had never, not once, shown any interest, and now this. The confession sent Robin reeling again, this time in a wildly different direction. True, she had come here today partly to talk about what happened. Or to not talk about it to the point that the air was clear. This was not going anything like she had planned, however. She had practiced her own apology. Her own explanation. One that sounded remarkably similar to what Sara had just said. She thought she had initiated the almost kiss. Sara taking ownership of it felt wonderful and terrifying at the same time. If they had both wanted it to happen, well, that changed everything.

She was quiet for too long. Sara scooted forward, preparing to get off the table. "I don't deserve forgiveness. I know. I'm sorry. I'll go."

Robin put a hand out and it landed on Sara's knee. Sara froze, waiting for Robin to speak. Unfortunately, the feel of Sara's skin under her hand rocketed a whole new series of explosions. Her mind whirled and her pulse soared. Try as she might, she couldn't keep from thinking of her dream. How Sara had felt to touch.

She shook her head to clear it. "Don't go." She haphazardly pieced together more words as her brain raced to catch up with her mouth. "I owe you an apology too. I shouldn't have flirted either. Things just happened. Things that shouldn't have happened. Or maybe should have happened decades ago. The point is…"

After a long silence, Sara asked, "The point is?"

"The point is…don't go." She smiled, and it felt good to say these things. "We can figure out a way to be friends again. Right?"

"I hope so."

This was the time when Robin should have moved her hand, but she didn't. She knew it was wrong, but the glint in Sara's eye had always made her brave and foolish in equal measure.

"Good."

"Good."

They looked at each other for a long time. Long enough for Robin to recognize danger and look away.

"Maybe we shouldn't climb any more mountains any time soon, though. I'm not in as good a shape as I thought I was."

Sara leaned back on her outstretched arms, her shoulders finally relaxing.

"You sure made it down the mountain in a hurry. I'm… um…sorry about your camera. Is it broken?"

"Yeah. Lens is shattered."

"Bummer. It looked pricey."

"That's okay. I can get it fixed."

"Get it fixed? Really? That doesn't sound like you."

"What do you mean?"

"Nothing."

Robin smiled despite herself. "Come on, Princess. Spill it."

"It's just that you've never been the type to fix something when you can just get something new."

Robin's instinct was to deny what felt like an accusation. "That's not true. I had the same crappy old guitar from the day I learned to play until my first album released."

Sara swung her leg lazily, rubbing her calf against Robin's jeans. Robin could feel the muscles of Sara's thigh flex and straighten under her hand that still lingered despite the obvious fact that she should remove it.

"That's just because you couldn't afford a better one. Remember how we used to go to Charlottesville and you would stare through the window of the music store. You drooled over that shiny Fender while I was drooling over the girls."

Robin didn't remember, but that didn't mean it hadn't happened. "Yeah, I guess."

Sara sat forward and teased, "You ran off to LA to get a shiny new life too. That worked out for you."

The hardships of the last few months on the road with Della and the band spun through her mind. She'd always dreamed of the life of a star, but her dreams never looked like what they were now. A heartless repetitive performance every night. Meaningless chatter with people she didn't know and didn't like. Having to please everyone by being someone she wasn't. It wasn't a life to be envied. Sara wouldn't understand that though, so she shrugged. "Yeah, I guess."

"You seem to have forgotten over the years that I'm always right." She accompanied the joke with a playful nudge of Robin's leg. "Go get yourself a new camera. You deserve it. You're going through a tough time—don't forget to take care of yourself."

It was eerily similar to the advice Jamie gave her a little while ago. He also said she shouldn't miss the chance for love. Robin shook the thought away, but it left a bitter aftertaste.

"Oh yeah. Poor Robin Scott. Blockbuster album. Sold-out international tour. Three Grammy nominations. Life's tough. Someone should start a charity for me."

"Yeah, well, all of that is also a lot of pressure. A lot of expectations. My guess is you haven't taken a deep breath in months. The walls are closing in. So I say again, take care of yourself."

Robin squeezed Sara's knee lightly when the tears threatened again. She was just able to hold them at bay.

"It's funny how we haven't seen each other in years and you know that about me, but my own wife can't seem to figure it out. She thinks I'm happy as long as I have a guitar in my hands."

The smile left Sara's face. "Sometimes we're too close to see everything. She's had a lot going on herself, I imagine."

It was wrong to criticize Della, especially in front of a woman she came much too close to kissing just yesterday, and she knew it. She felt like she was on a very familiar road, but that the rules of driving it had changed. It was confusing, but it was more exciting than anything else in Robin's life. A life that alternated between stale and sad just now. Still, it was safer for her to change the subject.

"Maybe I should get a new camera. The tour heads to Europe in August. Lots to photograph."

"I hear Paris is beautiful this time of year."

Robin imagined taking Sara with her on tour. Waking up late and stumbling into a café on the Champs-Elysees for espresso and buttery, flaky croissants you can't get anywhere in the States. Going out after the show to that little bar in Montmarte. Della was thrilled they were going. She wanted to visit the Bibliothèque Historique de la Ville de Paris. Leave it to Della to research her book in the City of Love.

"It is. I won't get to see much of it, though. Have to sing for my supper you know."

"Yeah, I suppose you do."

The mood had turned again. Trying to keep things light, Robin said, "Well, I know Sara Carson well enough to know you'd definitely get a new camera. Nothing but the newest and the best for you, Princess."

"Oh no. I'd get it fixed." She looked straight into Robin's soul. "I've learned from my mistakes, too, Birdie. These days, when I find something good, I don't let it go."

Robin looked back at her. They both knew she wasn't talking about the camera, but hadn't they just decided that nothing was going to happen between them? Hadn't Sara apologized and promised to back off? Was that what Robin wanted her to do? It was. It had been a few minutes ago, at least. Now, with those big, beautiful eyes looking at her the way Robin always wanted them to, she wasn't so sure.

"I'm sorry to interrupt."

Della's voice from behind startled Robin. She snatched her hand back from Sara's knee as she turned. She hoped it looked natural, like she only did it to get her body moved, not because she was caught doing something wrong. The look on Della's face was hard to read. She had perfected a cold neutral in the last few years, and it was in place at the moment. Robin looked guilty as sin, but, thankfully, Della's eyes were on Sara.

"Hi Della!" Sara slipped off the table and walked over, folding her in a hug that was barely returned. "We didn't hear you come in."

"I just followed the sound of voices." Robin sprung out of her chair and hurried to Della's side. Della turned away from her when she would normally have put an arm around her. Too late, Robin remembered they didn't hug much these days. "You mentioned that you might have some of the sources I need?"

"Absolutely! What subject area are you looking for?"

Robin put a hand on Della's shoulder, but she ignored her. "My book's about the Plague and its effect on Paris and Parisian society."

"We were just talking about Paris! You are heading there soon, right?" When Della only nodded in reply, Sara started back toward the circulation desk. "Well, we have a lot about the time period. My mother's a history buff, so our history section's better stocked than you might expect."

Della followed Sara without looking back. Robin couldn't decide if she was mad or just in research mode. The two versions of her weren't that far apart. She stuffed her hands in her pockets and stared at the hardwood floor. It had been a very strange day already, and it wasn't even lunchtime.

The choice between joining her wife and oldest friend at the circulation desk or simply ducking out of the library unnoticed was a lot harder than it should have been. She really didn't think she could find her way through the maze of shelves to the front door without passing the desk. Then there was the inevitable confusion and annoyance from both women she'd have to deal with. Sara would probably take it in her stride. She would mock Robin when they saw each other at the Fourth of July Festival tomorrow, but she was starting to enjoy being teased again.

Della, on the other hand, would freeze her out for days. She wouldn't bring up the slight, she would only punish Robin for it. Robin wouldn't mention it either, so the two would stew in their corners until it was forgotten. Della had a long memory, though, and Robin didn't have the energy to go through that dance right now. All things considered, it would be immeasurably easier to just deal with the problem by following them.

Her one rebellion was to walk as slowly as she could manage. If Della was going to start a pissing match with Sara, Robin wanted to miss as much of it as possible, and Della was definitely going to start a pissing match. She could tell by her tone that this was going to be unpleasant. She had adopted her scholar's voice. The tone she used when dealing with people she thought weren't as smart as she was. People like the librarian of a rural, Appalachian public library. Similar to the cold, detached one she used when she was talking to her parents, trying to live up to their astronomical expectations.

There was a time when Della hated her parents and the life they tried to force on her. Della and Robin would visit them often when they were in school since they lived so close. Della would bite her tongue throughout the pre-dinner cocktails, meal, and after-dinner Scotch. Then she would make their excuses and she would spend the entire drive home ranting about their elitism and their privilege.

They would stop for a cheap bottle of wine in a paper sack and drive to the Hills. They'd sit in their car, drinking straight from the bottle and talk while the stars twinkled around them. There was so much passion in those talks. So much passion in Della. She would rant about the selfishness of knowledge for knowledge's sake, about how she wanted to learn so that she could share it with the world. So that she could help people who had her same thirst for knowledge but not her resources. She hated her parents' decadence and how little they invested in their students. She would never become that. Robin would talk about the days when she could use her voice to bring people together. To heal the wounds of society and see that our differences were nothing compared to our capacity to love. They would make love there in the car with dreams of their shared future still in their hearts.

Those happy days ended a long time ago. They hadn't been to the Hills in years. They visited Della's parents less, so maybe she forgot the way they used to irritate her. Robin hadn't forgotten, though, and she despised how Della now sometimes acted just like them. These days Della slipped into the tailored suit of the life they led almost as a matter of form.

"I suppose that will do." Della bent over the counter, scanning a list of titles on Sara's screen. "It wouldn't be my first choice, but the author is well-respected enough."

Sara's smile was forced. "I knew we'd have something that could help."

Della scribbled the title and location down on a scrap of paper. "I'll admit I didn't expect much."

"You'd be surprised what our little town has to offer."

"Oh, believe me," Della said, looking up with a smile that clearly showed her fangs. "I am well acquainted with the best that Sperryville has to offer."

Robin hustled past the desk, saying her goodbyes while walking backward toward the door.

"You two look like you're in for the long haul here. I'll get out of your way."

She was met with two pairs of very hostile eyes, but it was Della who responded, "See you at home later, dear. Don't forget, we're going to bed early tonight. You have a show tomorrow."

"Right."

"Bye Birdie."

She barely heard Sara's goodbye over the noise of the door. With a sigh of relief she slipped out into the hot sunlight. Her eyes watered at the shift from dark to light, and she felt the beginning of a headache in her temples. The quicker she got away from the bickering women, the better chance she had to avoid a full-blown migraine.

After waiting for a car with Oregon plates to pass, Robin crossed the street. She wanted to get out of the direct sun, and the awnings on this side of Main Street would offer her some protection. It was impossible to forget the condescension in Della's voice. The pained looked of pride on Sara's when she spoke about her library. About her town. What had Della meant when she said that she knew the best Sperryville had to offer? Her voice was positively ringing with sarcasm. Robin had thought Della was referring to her, but the tone was more insult than boast. Robin couldn't help but think about what her mother had thought of Della. That she was making Robin uppity.

"Hey there, Birdie!"

Larry poked his head out of the front door of Brenda's, leaning heavily on the frame to support his bad leg.

"Hey, Larry. No work today?"

"Garage closed for the holiday a day early." He waved her over with his free hand. "Come on, join me for lunch."

A spike of pain shot through her temple, but the open door let out a wave of aromas—fresh coffee and old fry oil—that made her stomach growl. She couldn't remember eating any breakfast. Then the rye with Jamie and the confusion with Sara, it was enough to make anyone hungry.

"Yeah. I think I will."

He pushed the door wider to let her past him.

"Good girl. Nancy, look who I dragged back in."

Nancy waddled up, a wide smile on her face and a pot of coffee in her hand. She flipped the cup on the table in front of Robin and filled it without waiting to be asked.

"Good to see you again, sweetheart. Your speech was lovely. Your momma woulda been proud."

Another stab of pain made Robin blink hard. "Thanks."

"Want the usual?"

"Please. Thank you, Nancy."

"Comin' right up. Need anything, Larry?"

"More coffee wouldn't kill me. Since you got it and all."

While she refilled his cup, Nancy said, "I was worried I wouldn't see ya in here again, Birdie. Thought our greasy food might've done a number on your California stomach."

Larry laughed under his breath, but Robin felt her hackles rise.

"I'm not a California girl, Nancy. You must be thinkin' of my wife."

Nancy laughed and headed off to the kitchen, but Larry caught the venom in her voice and gave her a hard look.

"You feelin' all right?"

Robin took an ill-advised gulp of her steaming coffee. After grimacing through the burn in her throat she replied, "Fine."

"You sure 'bout that?"

"I've got a headache is all."

"Hmm." He studied her until she finally met his gaze. "Thought it must be somethin'. On account of it ain't like you to talk about Della like that."

She quavered under his gaze, just as she had as a child. Larry never raised his hand to anyone. His quiet disapproval was more powerful than a physical blow.

"All I said was she's from California."

It had been a sulky teenager who answered him, and he continued to speak to her like she was one. "You and I both know you said more'n that. What's more is Della knows too. She and I had a bit of a chat the other night..."

"Della's getting very good at talking about me to everyone except me."

"You sure she ain't tried? You're not always real open to talk if you don't want to." Robin couldn't deny he had a point, but he didn't wait for her to argue anyway. "She reckons you've got a lot goin' on in your life that you ain't lettin' anybody else in on, even her. She's worried 'bout ya."

"There's nothing to worry about."

"No?"

"No."

He waited again, this time keeping her gaze a long time before going on, "Saw you come from the library just now."

"Yeah."

"How's Sara doin'?"

Nancy slid a plate in front of Robin. The fries were piled high and golden brown. Her mouth watered, but she knew Larry wanted to say more. Nancy got in first, a frown pulling down the soft skin around her eyes and mouth. "Not that Sara Carson? You aren't spending time with her again, are ya?"

"She's my best friend, Nancy."

"She was, child, but there's been a lotta years passed since you knew her proper. Take it from me, that's not a road you wanna go down again."

The headache blossomed across her forehead like one of her mother's roses exploding from the tight confines of bud into full bloom. She let the pain and her hunger get the better of her.

"I shall endeavor to take your recommendation under advisement."

Robin shoved a pair of fries into her mouth and tried to chew loudly enough to cover the sound of Nancy turning on her heel and storming off. It didn't work. The next two didn't work either. Shame soured her gut and she swallowed with difficulty. Larry was staring at her, his face cold as polished steel.

She sighed and threw up her hands. "What? Give me a break here, Larry. She's my friend and Nancy has never liked her! So she wasn't the best behaved teenager. It's ridiculous of this town to hold a grudge so long."

"That's a bed Sara Carson made for herself. And she's never been real particular about how she folded the sheets. Wasn't over particular 'bout how she rumpled 'em in the first place neither. You ain't like that. That's not the kind of person your momma raised."

"What did Sara do that was so wrong? She was a gay kid who wasn't quiet about it. She didn't hide who she was and she didn't make anyone around here comfortable with their bigotry. They all hated her because she showed them how intolerant they all were. Even Mom."

Larry put his cup down and looked into it. He pushed his half-empty plate to the side. "The things your momma said to you…They were wrong and they were unkind. If you knew how much she regretted that…"

"Funny. I never heard an apology."

"You weren't around for her to apologize to."

"That's not fair and you know it. Why would I stay? When that's what she thought of me? How am I supposed to forget that?"

"Would that've helped?" Larry's voice was quiet, but not stern. "If she'd said she was sorry? Would ya be able to forget what she said?"

"No."

"I knew your momma better'n anyone. Even you. She was stubborn. Pig-headed. Didn't like to admit she was wrong. She wasn't perfect, Birdie. You can hate her for that for the rest of your life or you can love her anyhow. Up to you."

There were tears in Robin's eyes, but she didn't want to cry again. It was probably the crying that gave her the headache in the first place. Crying in the library with Sara comforting her in a way that made her heart ache. Could she love her mother despite it all? Despite the cruelty when she came out and despite her assessment of Della. The fact that she would walk into the library and tell Sara how she felt about Della, but wouldn't tell Robin stung more than she wanted to admit. Her mother may have been the only person in this town who trusted her best friend.

"Did Mom like Della?"

He reached out and patted her hand where it lay on the table. "It doesn't matter a lick. What matters is what you feel about her."

"You just used a whole lot of words to say 'no.'"

"I didn't say no 'cause I didn't mean no. I meant that it doesn't matter what she thought of Della any more than it mattered what she thought of you comin' out." He pulled his plate back in front of him and took a massive bite of chicken salad on rye. "If you want a more specific answer, it's I don't know. She never told me and I never asked. We neither of us got much time with Della."

"Don't start with…"

"I'm not criticizin', girl, I'm just explainin'. It's as much our fault as ya'll's." Robin finally started on her patty melt, and the pain in her head started to dissipate as he spoke. "She ain't much like us, it's true, but she's a fine woman."

"No. She isn't much like us." Not like Sara was. She was small-town real from head to toe. Not like Della. What had they said yesterday? Della was complicated. She was work. You couldn't know her after one day like you could Sara. It was exciting and sexy to a nineteen-year-old with nothing but dreams in her head. For an exhausted thirty-five-year-old musician, well, small-town real was a hell of a lot more appealing.

Larry put his sandwich down and wiped his chapped palms with a paper napkin.

"Listen, Birdie. I know they do things different in LA than they do here. Ya'll play things fast and loose out there. Don't hold the same things sacred we do in small towns. Whether that's right or wrong ain't up to me. What I'm sayin'…well, your friends and your family. That's a thin line here. Sometimes that's a good thing, sometimes it's a bad thing."

"Okay," Robin said, unsure what to make of his words.

"I was real young when I fell in love with your momma. Most folks I knew thought I was a damn fool for bein' so sure 'bout her. But sometimes the things we feel when we're too young to know any better. Well, those're the truest things we ever feel."

There was a twinkle in Larry's eye. He winked and went back to his sandwich.

"Larry...Did you just give me advice?"

"Hell no. You know what I think about givin' people advice."

Robin adopted a fairly terrible version of Larry's drawl. "Only folks what need advice is folks who's too stupid to figure out their own mess. You don't wanna getcher self tangled up in stupid people's mess."

Larry laughed and waggled his finger in Robin's face. "Stick that burger in your mouth 'fore more stupid falls out and you get tangled up in it."

She did exactly that, shoving far too much bread, onion, beef, and cheese into her cheeks. She chomped on it with a stupid grin on her face. She knew if there was one person in her life who would understand how she felt about Sara, it would be Larry.

"Hey, Larry? Thanks."

"Any time, kid."

CHAPTER TWENTY-TWO

Della didn't give her the satisfaction of an explosion. Not right away at least.

When Robin returned from lunch at the diner, Della was already back from the library. Clearly taking the long way home had been a mistake. Robin closed the door behind her and, by the time she turned around, Della was standing in the foyer. She gave Robin one long, level look before disappearing upstairs without a word.

For a few hours, Robin thought she'd gotten away without a fight. Maybe Della hadn't seen as much as she'd thought. Robin kicked around the house all evening, bored and restless in equal measure. She tried not to think about her mom. She tried not to think about Sara. She tried not to think about Della. She failed at each. The three women swirled around in her mind like goldfish circling in a bowl. The perpetual motion of her thoughts was enough to drive her mad.

After what felt like an eternity she grabbed a beer and her guitar and headed to the porch. Music was the only thing that stood a chance of clearing her mind and settling her nerves.

"Why are we still here, Robbie?"

Della's voice was cold and flat as frozen steel. Robin turned, her hand still on the doorknob. Della stood halfway down the staircase, her face as stiff as her voice had been. She looked so hard at Robin she might as well have been looking through her.

"The concert tomorrow."

Della's eyes narrowed to slits. "And after?"

The words Robin knew she should say stuck in her throat. They came out in an unconvincing croak. "We go home."

"Then why haven't you packed?"

"There's been a lot going on."

"So many people to see?"

The words came across Della's lips like venom dipped in honey. The sarcasm flared Robin's anger. "Yes actually. I suppose that happens when your mother dies."

Della flinched but didn't back down. "I'm sure Larry can…"

"Larry can what, Della? Grieve for me?" She released the door and strode back into the room. "I'm sorry you can't get to the USC library. I'm sorry that I have obligations to my family and my hometown. I'm doing the best I can here, baby."

"And what do you think I'm doing?" Della's voice quivered with the same rage Robin was barely holding back herself. "I'm trying to help you."

"I don't need your help, Della. I need…" Her eyes danced all around the room but they didn't land on anything of help. "I don't know what I need. I'm trying to figure that out. Can't you give me time to figure that out?"

"You spend the whole day out. You don't tell me where you're going. You smell like booze in the middle of the day. You won't tell me what you're feeling. What am I supposed to do with that?"

"I can't figure it out myself."

"Fucking try!"

Della's shout echoed off all the windows. The grandfather clock behind her and a vase between them rang with it. Robin's anger was only matched by her shock at Della's outburst. She stood feet away, shoulders and chest heaving with each breath and her teeth bared. She looked wild, unhinged.

"That isn't fair."

"Life's not fair. We have to keep living it."

"Where is this coming from?" Robin wanted to cry. She wanted to sit down and cry and have her mother wrap her arms around her and tell her everything would be okay. She was so tired and now this from Della was too much.

"There is nothing for you here, Robbie. Nothing."

"This is my home."

"No it isn't. LA is our home." Della turned on her heel, stomping up the stairs. She shouted over her shoulder, "And don't you fucking forget it."

CHAPTER TWENTY-THREE

Robin thought playing in front of her hometown would be easy. That the preshow jitters she battled through wouldn't be a problem when the entire audience was people she knew. She was so terribly mistaken. She changed clothes five times throughout the day. That was even more of a feat since she had only brought a small bag with a handful of outfits. She paced the house endlessly as the hours ticked by. She was uncomfortable, like her skin was one size too small. It was worse by far than when she had a show for strangers. On those days she distracted herself by hanging out with the band, but they weren't here to keep her company today.

She left far earlier than she needed to, just to get her legs moving and her mind still. She walked downtown with her guitar, Caroline, slung over her shoulder. She clung with both hands to the strap across her chest. The sun was just thinking about going down, but the heat of the day lingered. Sweat formed on her lower back and scalp before she was out of the driveway.

The town was alive as Robin hadn't seen it in years. She almost wondered if she'd stepped off the porch into some other place. A thriving metropolis or a busy transit town in the evening. A young couple swinging a toddler between them strolled down the sidewalk on the other side of the street. The little boy giggled as his parents held him tight and his feet kicked toward the wide blue sky. He clutched a red, white and blue pinwheel in the hand his father held. It rattled in the breeze in time with his laughter. Robin watched them for a block or more, smiling in that way that everyone does when they see a carefree child. Equal parts envy and joy.

The festival stage was set up in the little park a few streets back from Main at the end of town. There was a simple playground off to one side and a pavilion to the other. The park had been supplemented with a bounce castle for the day, and the pavilion with a dozen or so folding chairs. The young and old thus segregated to their corners, the rest mingled in the lawn between. Families spread out blankets and lounged on the grass. There was a long line at Martin's hot dog cart, and an even longer one at the sno-cone station run by the recreational soccer league. The church had a bake sale table, and the Ruritans were handing out balloons and doing face painting. There was nothing more serene and wholesome than this moment.

Robin stood alone under an old willow tree and watched it all sliding past. She hadn't seen anything like it in years. Things like this didn't happen in LA. Hell, they might not happen anywhere else in the world for all Robin knew. This was Sperryville. This was small-town Virginia. A festival that had gone on for so long no one could remember when it started, where kids played together and adults caught up on all the gossip they already knew. If a thief came through town right now, he could go door-to-door without a single person in the way. The whole town was here. Its beating heart in the laughter of children and the murmur of joyful conversation. People who knew their neighbors. Knew them too well most of the time, but loved them just the same.

"Birdie! Birdie! Birdie!" Mayor Buckthorn shuffled up to her. His little feet moved so quickly under his massive body, Robin couldn't help but smile. "I'm so happy you made it! Look at this turnout, would you? The best we've had since ninety-six! Do you remember that year? What an event!"

Robin held out her hand and the mayor shook it rather too enthusiastically. "Nice to see you again, Mayor. Was that the year we had the petting zoo?"

His face turned a shade lighter. "Goodness no! The Petting Zoo Incident was ninety-three. Never again, I tell you. Never again! A goat got loose from the pen and ate the bunting around the pavilion. When the marching band came through it spooked him and he threw it all up. Red and blue goat vomit all over the place. Then he bolted for the road and was nearly mowed down by the town fire truck. Disaster."

Robin was laughing so hard she couldn't stand straight, the memory of it coming back like an old reel-to-reel movie. She and Sara had climbed the storage shed behind town hall at the edge of the park. They were waiting for the sun to go down so they could sneak off to their spot by the creek and light the sparklers Sara had stolen from a fireworks stand in Luray. The stage would block their escape for part of the trip, but they needed darkness to cover their sprint through the open field behind it. They waited out the time on top of the shed to avoid Sara's mom and stepdad, and so they had the best seats in the house. The goat, after unloading the partially digested bunting at the feet of the band, scampered right past them. The trombonists at the front of the column of marchers didn't see the danger over their instruments. The first one slipped and fell into the mess, his fellows following him down like a line of bowling pins. The musicians behind them tripped over their limbs and discarded instruments, and so on until there was a pile of goat-vomit-soaked teens sprawled in the grass.

Her laughter did not ingratiate Robin to the mayor. His mood was less bubbly when he said, "Well, I suppose if you weren't the organizer of the event, it would be funny."

"I'm sorry, Mayor." Robin struggled to control herself. "It's just...you have to remember I was thirteen at the time."

"Yes. Of course." He still wasn't pleased, but he continued, "In any event, *this year* should be perfect. Not a cloud in the sky. Not a goat in sight."

"You've done a wonderful job," she said, his mood improving visibly. "It's picture perfect."

"Thank you. Yes. Well, the stage is over here." He gestured with a short arm and she followed him through the crowd. "We have the sound system all set up." He walked her behind the stage, where a tall curtain blocked the view on three sides. One of the old metal folding chairs from the church was set up there. There was a little table next to it with a couple of bottles of water. "Not the dressing room you have at Madison Square Garden, I dare say, but..."

"It's great, Mayor. Thank you."

He bobbed on his tiny feet for a moment. "I'll let you relax before the show then."

"I appreciate it."

It was clear he wasn't eager to go. Instead he looked around. "Where is that charming wife of yours? She didn't come along?"

"I'm afraid not." She certainly wasn't going to tell the truth. That they had a fight last night and they were both still too hurt and angry to talk about it. She decided to give him the same excuse Della mumbled to her before she left. "She's busy with work at the moment. Deadlines."

"Of course. Of course." He looked around again. "Too bad she'll miss the show."

"Maybe she'll be able to hear it from the house."

"Maybe so. Maybe so." He couldn't find any other excuse to stay, and so he finally turned to go. Robin was so relieved at the chance to be alone she nearly pushed him past the curtains herself. "I'll be announcing you just after sunset. We'll turn the lights on before you go out. Don't want to blind our star! Then you play for your hour. Then the fireworks right after you're done! I'll give you a little wave from the side of the stage to let you know when it's time for the last song. How does that sound?"

"That's great." She sat down in the chair, placing her guitar beside her. "Thank you again."

He was gracious about the dismissal. In the end he probably only wanted to be backstage long enough to make it clear they'd had a conversation. Now that people had seen how long he was gone, he could reappear triumphant.

"Have a great show, Birdie!"

She leaned back in the chair, Caroline against her knee. It seemed appropriate to play her old guitar tonight. She hoped the familiarity would make her more comfortable. Like having a friend onstage with her. So far, it was no help with her nerves, but she knew she'd be fine the minute she hit the stage. She always was.

Robin cracked open a bottle of water and swallowed half of it in one gulp. She'd left the house so quickly, she hadn't had a chance to do a check-in with her body as usual. Make sure how she was feeling. See what she needed to do for herself in order to put on the best show for her fans. Only now did she realize she was tense. Maybe a moment to herself would fix it.

Thinking about her hurried exit didn't help dispel the tension. After their fight, Robin ended up on the front porch with a beer and her guitar. She'd been working on a new song before the terrible news came in and she needed to get back to it. One beer turned into three. Della didn't come back downstairs and Robin went to bed drunk and alone around midnight. When Della finally came to bed, Robin woke up enough to try talking, but Della turned away from her and lay still.

It was a wonderful description of their marriage of late. Robin would make some tiny mistake and Della would react as though the world was ending. It was exhausting. It was cold. Then Robin came here to Sperryville, not expecting much, and she found herself wrapped in Sara's unembarrassed warmth from the moment she arrived. It was such a change. Such a welcome change when Robin needed it so much. Like the first warm day of spring.

Robin drained the water bottle and screwed the top back on. She sighed and spun the empty bottle in her fingers. Whatever Della's faults, Robin knew she was crossing a line with Sara. It seemed far more egregious after Sara's confession yesterday. A one-sided crush was one thing. After all, Robin was married, not dead, and this was Sara Carson. Still, she knew where this was heading if she wasn't careful.

Careful. Like Robin always was. Always. Ever since she could remember. She did the safe thing instead of the thing she craved. When would she get the chance to do what she wanted instead? Hadn't she been careful enough?

Robin threw the empty bottle. Not toward a trash can, which hadn't been provided, but out into the field where the litter wouldn't be found for ages. It wasn't her style, she didn't litter. She was conscientious. Polite. Unobtrusive. Passive. Still, the flare of whatever madness had started living in her head told her not to care. Screw these people and screw this place.

Unless you were quiet and meek and fit in, this town was a den of homophobia. This place didn't embrace her until she was famous. This place that kept a bright, shining light like Sara Carson locked in a dusty library with dirty looks when she should be on a pedestal. Traveling the world. When she should be in Paris.

"Ready to go, Birdie?"

She jumped at the mayor's voice, pulling herself out of her reverie. She shot her eyes guiltily to her plastic bottle in the tall grass. He hurried past her onto the stage and she slumped over to pick up the trash, setting the empty bottle neatly back next to the full one before slipping through the curtains into the glare of lights and the roar of the crowd.

CHAPTER TWENTY-FOUR

Robin chose a set list that was very different from her normal concert fare. It was heavy on classic rock, the singer-songwriters that she grew up on. She did it as a nod to Larry and the people of her hometown. They were in the South, in the country, in the mountains. These were country music people through and through. Most of them wouldn't listen to her music if she hadn't grown up around them. Most of them probably still didn't listen to her music. But they would know Bruce Springsteen and James Taylor. Everyone did. She couldn't get them right in their wheelhouse, but she could get close and still be herself. Like any good musician, she played to her crowd.

And the crowd loved it. Most of them were apprehensive at first, shuffling in place and casting nervous looks at her. She opened with John Denver, and their smiles lit up the night. Genuine happiness spread through the crowd. She had them and she knew it. She continued in that vein for a few more songs. Joan Baez. Paul Simon. Even some Cat Stevens just for fun. Then she snuck in one of her own songs and the teenagers stopped rolling their eyes. She spotted Larry in the pavilion with the older crowd. He was tapping his good foot in time with the music. Robin could spot the signs of the itch to pick up a guitar. She should have invited him to join her onstage for a song or two, but it was too late now.

It was a good show. One of her better ones for a while now. It didn't hurt that it was much shorter than her stadium shows and far less stage-managed. On tour she had basically the same set list every night. The usual menu of nearly every song from her new album, a few from her old ones, and a single cover. Her manager was adamant about that. Only one cover, and it had to be something "the kids wanna hear." That was a remarkably short list, especially for a classic rock nerd like Robin. She defied him early on at a stop in Seattle. She'd played a pair of Nirvana covers to great applause. It was Seattle, after all. Rick had gone ballistic. Della had calmed him down in the end by taking his side. That had caused a very tense night for the band, with Robin and Della fighting in the back of the bus while they all tried to sleep. It was even more tense when they arrived in Portland a few hours later and Robin bolted for the nearest bar. She gave in, of course, but not without a fight.

Robin had always been a performer at heart. She craved the energy of live shows. Needed the feedback to boost her confidence and funnel her creativity. It was so easy to hide in a crowd. To disappear in the spotlight. The applause reminded her what it was to make music. Her entire Grammy-nominated newest album was written on her last tour, late at night after shows. She was the opening act and she wrote new material while the headliner played. It was an amazing time.

But this tour had been stale. It started so well, but the last few months had felt like a flop. She was exhausted, and the crowd wasn't pumping her up. They were too polite, too cerebral. They clapped and screamed, but only at the scripted moments. Only when the guitar riffs were done or the lights flashed in their eyes. It was too contrived. Too manufactured. She hated it.

Tonight she was playing what she wanted to play, and it felt right. It felt good. It felt like home. She nearly came to stop just as she started the second verse of "Tangled Up in Blue." That was what was missing in her life. Her heart and soul was in this place. In the trees and the grass and the mountains. She'd been wrong to shut Sperryville out of her life.

She'd lost sight of that out in California all these years. She'd let other people tell her what and how to play. She'd let them tell her how to be a musician. How to be herself. It wasn't the show that was stale. It was her. Because she'd let the people around her make her into a cardboard cutout of herself. She wanted to be that girl with a guitar in the clearing again. Maybe this was where she would find herself after all this time.

She was basically sleepwalking through "Born in the USA" as the sun fully disappeared. Her thoughts were swirling around like the moths around the halogen lights.

As she finished to a huge swell of applause, she caught the signal from Mayor Buckthorn off to the side of the stage. Looking back out into the night, she saw Sara. She was leaning against the same knotted old tree Robin had stood by earlier. She was radiant. Glowing like the setting sun in a sea of bright white. Robin couldn't tear her eyes away. She wore a thin cotton dress, pink as that old lace costume, her small feet bare on the lush grass. Sara had never looked so beautiful as in this moment. Not when they saw each other again a few days ago after being apart for so long. Not when they were on top of Mary's Rock. Not when they were kids. She looked like a future Robin had never dreamed possible. All those dreams she'd had about their future together, and it never looked like this. Like it was possible.

The crowd stirred and Robin looked away at last. Her voice came back to her.

"Thank you. You guys have been great. Normally I'd close with The Boss on the Fourth of July, but there's this song I wrote."

She paused for the roar of applause. Amazing how a couple hundred people could make a noise like that. Enough to fill the half-dead stadiums she'd been playing for the last six months.

"Yeah, people do seem to like it. It's kind of a love story to this place. To Sperryville."

It was mostly true. The song was a love story and this was where it was set. Sara pushed away from the tree and started to walk toward the crowd. Robin watched her float with that liquid grace across the ground.

"So I thought I'd play it before the fireworks. This is 'Forever and Ever Amen.'"

Her fingers tingled as she played the opening chords, just as the day the song came together, music and lyrics. The day it clicked into place and she knew it would be a hit. One of her best. One of the best. It hadn't happened since. Not until tonight.

Through the summer grass we came
To the shore of the creek where we hid to be free
I carved your name

She watched Sara reach the edge of the crowd. Everyone else was still and silent. The breeze stopped blowing. The flies stopped buzzing. Sara was the only thing in the world moving. Her eyes were locked on Robin. Just like they had been that day when Sara was worried if their initials in a tree trunk and their friendship would last forever. When Sara looked at her that certain way and Robin was desperate to understand what it meant.

From my heart onto the sycamore tree
Took my knife and did the same
You said we'd never be apart
Gave your soul to me

Sara turned a shoulder and squeezed past a young guy at the back. He moved aside for her. She pressed through the crowd and they separated without a glance. Her eyes were on Robin. She had given her soul to Robin. Set it free and let Robin catch it. Let her be caught by it. She was ensnared. Trapped. Tangled into Sara and she would never be free. But that was all that Sara gave her. She never gave Robin her love or her body. Never so much as a single kiss. It was an omission that had tortured Robin later. When she was old enough to really understand desire and she ached with it every single night until she left this town.

Those nights were so long
Full of that Leonard Cohen song
Dreaming of you
And all those things you do
God if you only knew
I love you
I love you forever and ever
Amen

She had dreamt of Sara as far back as she could remember. Dreamt of her every night in those days. They were frustrating, punishing nights of fitful sleep. She was usually chasing Sara, like she had in her dream the other day, but she could never catch her. Could never find that way for them to link. She was always a step away. An aching, torturous few inches farther than Robin's fingers could reach. In those days she knew Sara was out of reach. What would happen if she reached out now? Every fiber of her being yearned to find out, but it was that same yearning that had burned her before.

We were just kids having fun
No idea we were playing with fire
Too young to know the heart's a loaded gun

Sara slipped past another line of people. Her shoulders swayed as she walked. It wasn't hard to imagine the way her hips swayed, though they were hidden by the crowd. Moving like a wisp of cloud, she snaked through the sea of faceless bodies.

Robin sang, but couldn't hear her own words. Her fingers flew across the strings. Her mind was full of the girl she loved then and the desperation to have her was back. The way it was then. The way, she finally admitted to herself, it still was. The white-hot blaze of her passion for Sara wasn't a fire that could ever be extinguished. Sara was her first love, but she'd never said a word and Sara thought they were just friends. Because Robin was too scared to tell her the truth about how she felt.

How could we understand our desire?
That was the day it could have begun
Had I been braver
Or reached a little higher

Her moment with Sara had come and gone along with her youth. She had chosen a different life. But what if she hadn't? What if she had come home that summer instead of staying to play crappy gigs in LA? What if she hadn't met Della? What if she hadn't moved so fast? Why had she? She knew the answer. Sara had broken her heart. Had found someone else. And someone else after that. Had never looked twice at Robin. When she was a teenager she buried her pain. Maybe marrying Della was her way of burying it as an adult. Maybe her stubbornness and her silence had doomed her to a lifetime of empty, sad nights dreaming of the one who got away.

She made a career out of loving Sara. Of being rejected by her. A decade at least that she yearned for the unattainable woman who was so close yet completely unreachable. She hadn't loved Sara forever, though, no matter what her song said. She had found Della and the dreams had stopped. A woman she thought she would spend forever with. A woman who was the antithesis of Sara Carson. A woman who was measured and balanced. A woman who was utterly predictable and just as unreachable. Because that's the sort of woman Robin fell in love with. Unreachable women.

No, that wasn't right. Della hadn't always been unreachable. She had been so open once. So warm and gentle. When had that changed? Robin couldn't quite remember, and she nearly lost the thread of her music. She had to rush to pick up the next verse.

But too many days went by
The forest's been cut down
And that old creek's run dry
The jewels have fallen from your crown
You're happy and I want to cry
Watching you with her
All over town

Sara was close to the front of the crowd now. Her step hadn't faltered. She was coming to Robin now. Even after all of those years away, they had fallen right back together like no time had passed. Didn't that mean something? Shouldn't that mean something?

Robin's heart thudded and she couldn't get enough oxygen. She was taking her breathing breaks like always, but her brain was buzzing all the same. Her world narrowed. Sara reached the front of the crowd and stopped. She was in full view, inches away. Robin could reach out and touch her. She wanted nothing more, but she was rooted to the spot. This wasn't a dream, but she was filled with the lead in her limbs like she had been in the past. It took all of her might to play the song out. To sing the last few lines.

Still a princess in the castle of my heart
Still a princess in the castle of my heart
Still the princess of the castle of my heart
Forever and ever
Amen

The crowd was clapping, but it was a long way off. The last note finished in the back of her throat. The strings of her guitar fell silent. Her eyes were still locked on Sara. She smiled and Robin went deaf. Sara started walking again. Out of the crowd and off into the night. Robin's eyes followed her dark form slipping into the shadows. Part of her expected Sara to start running, but she didn't. She walked into the darkness of the grass field and beyond. Robin watched her go until the night swallowed her silhouette. She didn't need to see anymore. She knew where Sara was going.

The sound of the crowd came back. The clapping and the cheering. A pudgy arm wrapped around her shoulder. The mayor spoke into the microphone in front of her. Robin looked at him but did not listen. Her eyes flicked past him to the pavilion off to the left. She spotted Larry again. His expression was stone and steel, his smile long gone. She turned away from it.

Robin waved to the crowd and slipped out from the circle of the mayor's arm. She walked to the curtain at the back, fighting to catch her breath. There was a road map in front of her. She slipped through the curtain and down the few stairs to the makeshift dressing room. The road was forked. She could take the one that stopped at the old metal folding chair in front of her and nothing would change, either for better or worse. She would continue her life with Della. It was a good life. Certain and solid. Or she could take the one that led off into the sticky heat of the night and find out if Sara really was the princess of her heart. Spontaneous and ridiculous, something few people in her life would approve of, something that would make her heart start beating again. The way it used to. The way it did when her days were full of Sara Carson.

She slung the strap of the guitar across her chest, the instrument pressed against her back. The neck of her guitar brushed against her hip and she adjusted it further back.

She marched off into the field.

CHAPTER TWENTY-FIVE

Just as Robin made it to the tree line the first fireworks exploded in a shower of red. They added to the light of the full moon to make the woods as bright as afternoon. She didn't need the light. She could have found her way to the creek and to the tree if she were blind.

Twigs and dried leaves snapped under her feet. Each step brought with it the scent of fresh pine needles and loamy, moss-covered earth. Every so often the distant pop of fireworks filtered through the treetops, their many-colored lights flashing like one of the scripted flares at her concerts. The only other sound was Robin's breathing. It echoed in her ears, deafening her. She walked slowly, but still her breathing was labored. She reached out to touch a tree trunk as she passed. The bark was dry and rough. It hadn't rained for a long time. The forest was a tinderbox, waiting for a spark to bring it roaring to an end.

When the trees thinned out, Robin knew she was almost there. She expected to be nervous. She had waited her whole life for this moment. Now that it was here, though, now that she was taking those final steps, her doubts vanished. Her footsteps were sure. The silvery light of the moon covered the world, washing the scene in a magical, ice-white glow.

She saw the glimmer of Sara's hair first. The moonlight made it shine pale as bone. It spread over her shoulder. Sara leaned against a tree, angled away from Robin toward the trickle of the creek. It wasn't *a* tree, though. It was *the* tree. Their tree.

"I knew you'd come." Sara didn't turn to Robin when she spoke. She stared at the water and the trees beyond. "I've been waiting."

Robin made it to the tree and stopped. She wanted Sara to turn to her. To take Robin in her arms and end the torment she'd suffered for so many years. "I came as soon as the show was over."

Sara finally turned to her. There were tears in her eyes, but a smile on her face. "I've been waiting longer than that, Birdie." She reached out and took Robin's hand. "I've been waiting since that day we ran down here together. When you were dressed as a cowboy and I was dressed as a princess and we did this."

She touched the initials carved in the tree, sliding a fingertip through the worn path of her heart. It was a practiced move. She didn't have to look. She'd done it a thousand thousand times before. She knew the way it curved. Knew all of its imperfections.

Robin stood in front of Sara. She put one booted foot on either side of Sara's bare ones and reached out. She lost her nerve in that final moment before skin met skin. She reached for the tree instead, her fingers delicately touching the carved wood. The cut pieces were brittle, but the scars had healed over the years. They'd been weathered by the wind and the rain. The snow and the sun. Now they were as much a part of the tree as the bark and the leaves and the roots beneath their feet.

Sara's voice was softer now that Robin was so close. "The day you asked me to be your cowgirl. The day you told me you loved me. Forever and ever amen. I've been waiting since that day for you to realize you meant it. That you mean it now. I've been waiting right here for you, Birdie."

Tears blurred Robin's vision. She couldn't see Sara's face, so she reached out to touch it instead. She ran her fingers over Sara's cheek, so soft and so perfectly smooth. She took a step closer. "I did mean it. I should have told you then, but I was just a kid."

Robin leaned forward. Her thigh brushed against the loose cotton of Sara's skirt. "Then when I knew how I felt…"

"I wasn't there." Sara turned her face away from Robin's hand. "I was an idiot and I went looking elsewhere to find what was right in front of me."

"It wasn't your fault. I was too slow. Too stupid to tell you how I felt." She moved forward again. Their bodies met. They fit together like two halves of a whole. Like they were meant to be together. "It broke me to see you with someone else."

"It should have been you. My first date. My first time. My first kiss." Sara ran her hand over Robin's shoulder to the back of her neck. She pulled their faces together. Their lips nearly met. "I should have shown up at your door with a dozen roses the minute I figured out I was gay."

Sara closed the gap between them. She tilted her head. Closed her eyes. Robin's lids started to shut. Their lips hovered, inches from each other.

Robin pulled back sharply, her eyes flying open. "Roses."

Sara lurched forward. The unexpected movement pulled her off balance and she fell hard against Robin's chest.

"What's wrong?"

"My mom's roses."

They were lush and beautiful, but not thanks to Robin. Della told her when she'd found Robin in the mudroom how she'd been watering them, but she'd forgotten. She'd forgotten a lot of things in the last few days while she spent so much time with Sara. She'd forgotten the way Della held her in that hotel room in Richmond. After Larry called and the phone dropped out of Robin's suddenly numb hand. The way Della had handled everything with Rick and the band and the rental car company.

She'd forgotten the softness of Della's voice when Robin told her she didn't want her mother to be gone. The way she'd kissed the pain away that day. But more than that. The way she had kissed her with joy a hundred thousand times over the years. She had been there when Robin was at her best and at her worst. No matter what, she had loved Robin. And, in this moment at last, Robin felt again the intensity with which she loved Della back.

Sara frowned. "What?"

Robin took Sara by the shoulders, trying to help her find her balance. When Robin would have let go, Sara held on, keeping Robin in the circle of her arms. It was tempting to stay. Sara's body radiated warmth and her skin and dress were soft as clean cotton to Robin's calloused hands. She pulled herself gently out of Sara's grip.

"Della's been watering them. I didn't notice. I didn't pay attention."

Confusion spread across Sara's face. "You're thinking about that now?"

Robin let go of her shoulders and stepped further back. Fireworks exploded in quick succession in the distance.

"This is a mistake. I have to go."

Sara pushed off of the tree. Flashes of green and red broke through the foliage and lit her face.

"Because of the fucking roses?"

"Because of Della."

She moved sideways, circling the tree and retracing her steps. Robin had no business being here. This creek, this tree, this woman wanting to kiss her. This was all her past. At home, Della waited for her to return from her show. Waited in the house she cleaned even though it belonged to a woman who never showed her kindness. Waited with a smile and a kiss and a touch she kept only for Robin. Waited with a heart full to bursting with love for Robin. Love they shared. Love that made them both whole. Unlike Sara, Della had always loved Robin. From the moment they met.

Robin stopped suddenly, unable to leave this moment until she had one question answered. "Why didn't you? Why didn't you show up at my house, Sara? Why wasn't I ever an option for you?"

When she turned to face Robin, anger had fully replaced the confusion on Sara's face. It contorted those perfect features into something ugly. "Because you weren't patient."

"I wasn't patient?" Now it was Robin's turn to be angry. Why she hadn't felt this way from the start she could not imagine. "What? I should have waited until you fucked your way through the whole state? After everyone else, you'd remember me. Is that it?"

"I was a teenager!"

"And I was in love with you!" There was a last burst of fireworks, and then the sky went silent. "I was such an idiot then. I won't make that mistake again."

In that moment, the truth of everything finally bloomed in Robin's mind. It was like she'd let her thoughts wander while driving, she blinked and found herself on a totally new stretch of road with no memory of how she got there. Ever since Sara showed up at Brenda's the first day she arrived in town, Robin had been asleep at the wheel. She'd let her grief and Sara's powerful personality take over. She'd blamed Della for helping her in a difficult time. She was mad at her wife for wanting to take care of her. Why? What had made her so bitter and cold?

"Jesus! What does it fucking take with you, Birdie?" Sara moved toward Robin, her shoulders hunched and coiled tight. "I played this fucking perfectly. I was nice, then teasing, then slutty, then mean, then vulnerable, then sweet. It was a goddamn piece of art. All that fucking work wasted!"

"Work?" Robin clung to the strap of her guitar to keep the world from spinning. "Played it perfectly?"

"Of course! Don't act like you're shocked. You aren't that stupid. I know how to seduce you."

"This whole thing has been a game?" She said it as a question, but it felt more like a revelation. "An act."

"God, you're still so fucking naïve. Tell me, Birdie, what angle did she use to get you, huh? What's her game?"

"Della doesn't play games. *That's* how she got me."

"Bullshit. Everyone plays games." Sara bent over and picked up her sandals, sliding her feet into them. Her smile was unlike anything Robin had ever seen before. Like a snake dripping venom from its fangs. "She's a player. We can spot each other."

Robin had never been more sure of anything in her whole life. "You're wrong."

"You really do love her, don't you?"

"Yes, I do."

If she really thought about it, there weren't that many arguments with Della. Sure, there had been a few, how could there not be with so much stress in their lives, but none of them were anything to worry about. Even the occasional jealousy was something they laughed about later. A teasing remark during a moment of intimacy that brought an inevitable blush to Della's cheek. The same blush Robin had all those years ago about Frederico. When had she started amplifying Della's criticisms and discounting all of her many kindnesses? Why had she? The myriad of times Della was gentle and loving had somehow lost their weight recently. When she loved Robin like no one else ever had. Not her mother and never, ever Sara Carson.

"You're an idiot, Birdie. You always were. Lovesick and blind."

Robin yearned to be out of this place. Out of these stifling trees. She needed Della right now. Needed to hold her and smell the clean, powdery scent of her flesh. Needed to hear her voice. She needed Della so badly she nearly dropped to her knees.

"Nothing you say will change how I feel."

Sara's face was a mask of mocking pity. "Too bad for you. If you'd just waited like a good little girl, you could have had all this." Sara swept a hand down her body.

Robin's revulsion was clear in her cold voice. "I'm good. Thanks."

"You don't have a clue what you're missing." Sara glided forward. All seduction in her movements had vanished. She looked desperate now. Empty. Like the women who trolled the streets at night in LA. "I could do things to you that cold bitch couldn't even imagine."

Robin's vision went blank. Pain shot through her jaw as she clenched her teeth and she grabbed Sara's arm so hard her knuckles ached. "Don't you dare talk about Della that way. Don't even think about her. You don't have the right to know her. She's a thousand times the woman you will ever be. She's the love of my life."

Far from frightened by the anger in Robin, Sara grabbed her shirt with her free hand, pulling her close. "Bullshit! *I'm* the love of your life!"

Robin's vision cleared in a snap. She couldn't figure out why it should be so surprising, watching Sara transform into this selfish being. This was the person everyone else saw when they looked at her. The person everyone but Robin had seen from the beginning. The person who hated her own mother for finding happiness. The one who threw rocks through windows to get free ice cream and blamed it on her best friend. The one that a good woman like Nancy could hate. It was all so clear now. It should have been this clear before. Maybe it would have been if she wasn't so selfish in her own right. She released Sara.

"You don't have a clue."

"I don't have a clue?" Sara let go of Robin's shirt with flick of her wrist. "Oh, that's rich. Tell me, if you love her so much, why are you here with me?"

"I…"

"Five more minutes and you'd have been on your knees, begging to fuck me."

"Never."

Sara laughed, but there was no joy in it. "Then why are you here?"

All the air went out of Robin. She felt three feet tall. "Because I'm an asshole." Shame coursed through her like poison. She didn't want to be inside her own skin. "She deserves better from me."

"That's what you get when you take something that belongs to someone else."

"Belongs to someone else?"

Sara's eyes were wild. "Me! You belong to me! Why couldn't you just be fucking patient? You screwed everything up!" She ran at Robin, her finger waving in accusation. "You were supposed to take me away from this place! You were my ticket out!"

"I'm your nothing. I never was."

Robin turned to go. She took two more steps but couldn't contain her anger another moment. This is what she did all those years ago, slipped away without a word. Without telling Sara how she felt. She never had closure, and she never let all of her heart move on. It was why she hurt, now and always. It was how she forgot about the way Sara hurt everyone in her path. It was the distance between her and Della. It was her sleepless nights, and she would not do it again.

Robin whirled around. "I was so in love with you! It killed me! Day in and day out to be ignored by you. I gave you everything but I was nothing to you. Just another knight to serve in your court, Princess. Faceless. Nameless. Another possession. Another person to manipulate. You know how Della won me? By saving me. Saving me from waiting patiently for you. She saved me from you. By showing me what love really is. And how do I repay her? I write a love song about a girl who never existed."

Robin's shame was a river of regret. It hurt to think and to breathe. Knowing how close she came to ruining the best thing that this terrible life had ever given her. She turned to go. This time she knew she would not turn back. She would not stop. She would let the wave sweep her away from the tree and forget it forever.

Sara screamed after her, "I'm warning you, Birdie Scott! You walk away now and you'll never have another shot with me!"

Robin kept walking. Her stride did not break and she did not utter a word. By the time she reached the tree line and stepped out into the field, the night had swallowed the mingled curses and tears Sara threw at her back. Her love was her armor against them, and it was whole again. If she could have flown back to Della right now, she still wouldn't get there fast enough.

CHAPTER TWENTY-SIX

Della was crying. Robin could tell the minute she set foot on the coarse gravel of the driveway. Even through the darkness and the heat in the air, the set of her shoulders was clear. She was sitting on the middle porch step. Smoke rose around her bent head and swirled like a ghost in the glow of the porch light. Della bought her last pack of cigarettes just before their five-year wedding anniversary. She and Robin quit smoking together when Robin's breath control became sporadic and Della took up yoga.

For a long time, cigarettes had been something they'd shared. In the early days, they would wake up to coffee and cigarettes, go to bed after beer and cigarettes but barely touch them in the hours between. They would smoke and laugh while the sun rose and set. It was an excuse to spend time together. To break off from any crowd they were a part of just for a moment alone outside. To talk. To steal a kiss away from prying eyes. To dream about their shared future. They would lie together in bed, an ashtray between them and the sheets crumpled at their feet. They would spend hours looking into each other's eyes and dreaming. Smoking now wasn't a habit, it was a warning sign. What happened to those kids full of hope and nicotine?

Della looked up. Her eyes were red and her cheeks were wet. Worse was the look in her eyes. For all that Della kept her feelings to herself, Robin had always loved seeing the emotion in her eyes. It was like a secret code only she could unlock. It was in her eyes. Anger. Joy. Sadness. Confusion. She knew them all. This was a look she had never seen before, and she nearly cried out in pain. It was emptiness. The vast emptiness of someone who felt truly lost, and Robin knew she was the cause.

Robin stopped at the bottom of the stairs. She pulled the guitar strap from around her neck, reached over the railing and leaned the guitar against it. The line of smoke from Della's cigarette had grown thin. She watched Robin lean her back against the deck. Neither of them spoke. They just looked at each other. Della's tears diminished as the smoke from her cigarette finally died.

Della dropped the butt into the dregs of her coffee and set the mug down on the stair beside her. She twined her fingers together and stared at them. Her knuckles were mottled pink and white. It took an eternity for her speak. Robin's hope died a little more with each second that passed.

When Della finally spoke, her voice was raw. It was the most beautiful sound Robin had ever heard. "Was she good?"

Robin's heart shattered around her feet. She could barely hear her own voice when she answered, "I wouldn't know."

Whether it was hope or indignation that gave her voice life wasn't clear, but Della sounded more like herself when she asked, "Are you saying that you didn't sleep with her?"

Robin sat, but it felt a lot more like sliding to her knees.

"No, I didn't sleep with her."

"Robbie, I was there."

She let that sink in for a moment. For a terrible moment. Robin thought back to her performance. The way she played directly to Sara. The way they watched each other. She saw it from outside herself, from Della's point of view, and imagined what that might look like. What it might feel like. She hated Sara for the image and she hated herself a thousand times more.

"You were busy. You couldn't come with me. I didn't think..."

"No. It was pretty obvious that you didn't." The tears started again. Della's hands shook as she lit another cigarette. "When have I ever missed one of your shows, Robbie? When have I ever been too busy?"

"Never."

"Never." She inhaled deeply, taking in smoke like it was all that could keep her alive. "Now I'll ask again. Are you saying that you didn't sleep with her?"

"I didn't sleep with her."

"I find that hard to believe somehow."

Robin reached for the pack of cigarettes and pulled one out. She rolled it between her fingers. She remembered the feel of it. The bulge of tobacco under the thin shell of brittle paper. The way it crinkled when she moved it, the way it smelled when she put it between her lips. Della didn't hand her the lighter. She put it on the stair between them and withdrew her hand so quickly Robin was left in no doubt that she was avoiding any chance at contact. The smoke burned in her lungs, but the tears welling in her eyes were not from the pain. They were shame. She'd used the mechanical movements of smoking to keep from answering right away, but she had used up that time.

"I know what that must have looked like. How you must feel."

"I don't think you have the slightest idea how I feel."

Somehow, throughout everything that happened over the past several days, the thought never entered Robin's mind that she might lose Della. That her actions may push Della away for good. That she might lose the woman who saved her and brought her to life. Not just by marrying her, but by matching her love so fiercely every day. A chasm opened under Robin's feet. Fear poured over her like a wave from an angry ocean. One that wanted to drown her. To laugh while it watched her die.

She dropped her cigarette onto the gravel and flung herself forward. Her knees landed hard on the wooden planks at Della's feet. She reached out blindly for Della, not caring where her hands might land, only knowing that her sole chance for survival was to cling to this love that made her whole. Made her happy. Made her Robin. She nearly burned herself on Della's cigarette, but her hands landed on Della's knees. She gripped the denim and bones so hard her hands ached.

"I make no claim to being a good person. I never have." Now that she had started, it was easier to find the words she felt. "I've hurt just about every person I've ever been close to. But, baby, I would never, ever do that to you."

"I want to believe that, but you talk about her..." Della looked away, out into the night where everything was so much clearer. "You talk about her like she's the one who got away. Like she's the love of your life."

"She's not. She never was. I was an idiot to let you think any different."

Della tapped ash from her cigarette. It fluttered to the ground near her bare feet. She kept her head turned away from Robin, but didn't insist she back off. Robin tried to be hopeful because of that at least. "Don't pretend she means nothing to you. I'm not a fool."

"I know you aren't. I didn't say she means nothing to me." Robin sighed. To explain her feelings would take a tact she wasn't sure she possessed. "It's complicated. How I feel about her. But it got a lot less complicated tonight. Some things I should have seen a long time ago finally make sense."

"If you think you're convincing me that you didn't cheat, you're doing a very bad job."

Robin ran her hands through her hair. Her instinct told her to walk away. To weather the storm alone and wait for Della to get over it. She probably would. She might just love Robin enough to accept not knowing. Some part of Robin understood that Della's love might just make her strong enough or weak enough to accept Robin even as a cheater. Walking away now, though, would mean that emptiness would never leave Della's eyes. Robin owed her more than that. Della deserved the love Robin felt.

"If I tell you everything that happened, will it convince you?"

"If you tell me, you have to tell me everything. Can you do that?"

Robin could. She did. Every last detail. She didn't shy away from the worst of it. The things Sara said about Della, the things she said about Robin, and, worst of all, how close she came to cheating. How close she came to kissing another woman for the first time in sixteen years. She was completely honest because if she left out a single word, a single thought, Della would know and she would never be able to recover. It wasn't easy. Della's tears came back with a vengeance. Robin's soul ached a little more with every drop. On their wedding night, while they lay tangled in each other's arms in the dark, Robin promised she would never make Della cry. It was the promise of a child. A naïve woman who knew little of real life, but it was a promise she never thought she'd break.

They both smoked their way through most of the pack of cigarettes, the coffee mug slowly filling with discarded butts as Robin emptied herself of her shame. When she finished, the night rung with silence. Della wouldn't look at her. Robin reached out and took Della's hand. She knew there was a chance she'd pull away, but she'd risked so much worse in the last few minutes. When Della slid her fingers between Robin's and squeezed, Robin nearly screamed with joy.

Della still stared at the night sky when she finally spoke. "I thought it was just a story. Just a song. I didn't know it was real. A real place."

"It is just a song, Dell." The skeptical look on her wife's face made her continue. "I was a dumb kid who was in love with her best friend before I knew what love even was. Before I met you. Before I found out what it truly means to love and be loved."

"Before you found a replacement for the person who broke your heart. A reaction." Della dropped her head to her knees. Her voice was muffled by the fabric of her jeans. "I never knew I was a rebound."

"No." Robin moved closer, clinging to Della's hand. "No, you weren't a rebound from her. You weren't a reaction to her. You weren't a reaction at all."

"Your mother thought I was." Della sat straight again, wiping long fingers across her cheeks to dry them. "I understand that now. She thought you were using me to fix your broken heart."

"My mother didn't know my heart. I didn't let her. And I didn't know hers. She didn't open up to me. She didn't open up to anyone. All of those long talks through the years, they were empty. Neither of us really talked."

It occurred to Robin, even as she spoke, that her mother never really did let other people in. She let Larry in, of course, but that was it, and that was only so far. He never moved in to her house. Not in twenty-seven years. Even after Robin left. She should have realized that earlier. Should have understood that she would never have told Sara what she thought of Della. Especially when she didn't tell Larry. Just another part of the game. Just another way for Sara to hurt her in order to draw her in.

"Even if she had, it wouldn't matter. What my mother thought of me or you or anything doesn't matter at all. I've never trusted anyone with my heart. Anyone but you. I let you in. Just you. Do you know why?"

Della shook her head. "No."

Robin smiled. It wasn't bitter or sad. It wasn't a reaction. It was a genuine smile. It was the sort of smile that comes from having the truest love there was. If she hadn't been so busy trying to shoehorn Sara into her life, Robin would have known that Larry was talking about her love for Della in the diner. He was perceptive, Larry, and he knew real love when he saw it.

"You should. I've told you often enough. Maybe sometimes it was a reflex thing to say, but that doesn't mean it wasn't true. It's because I love you, Dell. Real love. Not like in a song. True love."

Della finally looked over at her. The emptiness wasn't quite gone, but hope joined it in those sparkling eyes. Robin's heart hammered loudly. She felt like the nineteen-year-old kid in a coffee shop, playing a Sheryl Crow song and watching an angel sitting in a corner pretending not to watch her. For the first time all night, she truly let herself hope that she might still get her happily ever after. Might still get Della.

"Robbie?"

"Just to be clear, it's you." Robin reached out and ran a hand along Della's cheek. "It was always you. It will always be you. I didn't settle for you. You aren't some consolation prize. You are my world. My everything. You're the love of my life. You. And I have never been more sure that I am inadequate to your love than I am right now. I don't deserve you. I never have. Maybe I never will. But, if you let me, I'd like to spend the rest of my life earning your love."

Della dropped her hand and for one, heart-stopping moment Robin thought she was going to turn away. To stand up and walk out of Robin's life for good. Instead, Della wrapped both arms around Robin's neck and pulled their bodies together. Their lips met as they had so many times before, but in an entirely new way. Della's kisses were desperate, hungry, and yet achingly gentle. There was no one who could kiss Robin like that. There was no one who had lips like these.

Robin kissed back with all the fear and doubt and shame that had lived in her for so long. Yet the more she poured them into her love for Della, the more they faded away. Just as she always had, Della took all the bad away and replaced it with good. Replaced it with love. Here, in the circle of Della's arms, was the safest, happiest place in the world. When she thought of how close she had come to giving it all up, Robin shuddered. Della pulled her tighter, and the thoughts melted away.

Long after they stopped kissing, they held each other. Neither was ready to let go. Robin's knees dug into the edge of the stair. Della's leg was twisted awkwardly beneath her. Neither moved an inch. They looked into each other's eyes, silver gray into deepest blue, and the pain faded away into nothing. Time faded into nothing.

The cricket song was loud in the night when Della finally pulled out of the embrace and stood. She held out her hand and Robin took it, standing to keep their bodies as close as possible. Della voice was low and still had that note of rawness, "Come inside?"

Robin reached for the coffee cup, but Della squeezed her hand. She smiled through the tears that still stained her face but did not touch its beauty.

"Leave it. We'll clean up in the morning."

Della led her by the hand to the front door. As she opened it, the sound of a guitar came through the night. Robin looked over to see Larry's porch light on. He sat in the rocking chair on the edge of his porch with an old guitar propped in his lap. He looked at Robin. He smiled and nodded. She nodded back. He turned back to his guitar and the opening notes of "Bird on a Wire" filtered through the night air. That old Leonard Cohen song. Haunting and cold and sad. That's how it felt before. Now if felt wide open. Like a blank, white page waiting to be filled.

Robin let Della lead her into the house and close the door behind them.

Bella Books, Inc.

Women. Books. Even Better Together.

P.O. Box 10543
Tallahassee, FL 32302

Phone: 800-729-4992
www.bellabooks.com